RHATALOO

A TAKAMO UNIVERSE NOVEL

KERRY NIETZ

Rhataloo

ISBN: 978-1-64709-000-5

Author: Kerry Nietz

Editor: R. Ritnour
Cover Design: Dimitry Borodin

A Takamo Universe book

Special thanks to all those who have given their support and encouragement over the years and remembering those we have lost, Dale Hayes, Sr., and Bill Hayes.

The members of the original Takamo development team were Randall Ritnour, Bill Bunselmeyer, Alan Edeker, and Bill Hayes.

CHAPTER 1

We were led through a series of gilded arches to a massive chamber with a domed, onyx ceiling. In the ceiling's center was a crystal skylight through which the pinks of Rhotaris Seven's evening nebula streamed in. It was the most opulence I'd seen in my retched forty years of life. Enough to widen the eyes of even the most jaded first officer. Make my creased tail smooth.

Yet, the only thing that drew my attention was Captain Wendel's hands. The way he rubbed them together as we walked. Over and under and over again. As if he'd gotten something—a laminating grease from one of the ship's engines, perhaps—on the black fur there that he couldn't quite rub off. Over and under, back and forth.

I wanted to ask him about it. Wanted him to stop it outright. But I was afraid to address anything directly. Didn't want to embarrass him with two government officials so close in range.

Our escorts remained a few steps ahead of us. They were

both does—female mutos. One had tan fur, the other red and they were business-only. Didn't smile when I bowed a greeting at the landing platform. And my hand flourish brought only a sniff from one and a straightening of spectacles from the other.

They led us to a commerce building. A palace for those in the Emperor's numbers racket like I assumed they were. And by "racket," I didn't mean smalltime gambling such is found on one of the backwaters like Candis or Sesterine. This was the big numbers game. Accounting the Imperial industries over five systems.

It explained their intensity, I guess.

I still would've liked a smile. Could've used a smile for all the hand-wringing.

I forced my eyes to the ceiling and gave an appreciative whistle. That earned me annoyed glares from the does and a tail flick from the captain. "Shut that," he hissed.

I bobbed my head. "Sorry," I said. "I just—" I indicated the ceiling, the arches, the wall reliefs of every dead monarch. "All this...wasn't what I was expecting."

"It's exactly what I was expecting," he said.

"Like a cathedral on Baedeker." I tipped my nose at the does, their tails now rigidly curved toward their backs. "Who knew the stone-counters worked in such a shrine?" I shook my head as we moved through another archway, this one featuring a diamond-shaped etching. The kind of stuff I'd imagined only at the Emperor's palace. "I mean, look at this."

The captain hissed and pointed ahead to a pair of heavy, double doors.

Our escorts stopped at those same doors. The red, spectacled one rapped lightly on the rightmost door, then with her companion, drifted past us. Back the way we'd come.

"Is that it?" I said. "They knock and leave?" The doors looked like they could take a direct assault from a blaster. Pure gold, sure, but solid, I'd guess, and festooned with ornate spikes.

"The auditor will be with you shortly," the spectacled doe said, before sniffing and adjusting her eyewear.

"I hope so," I said. "We're busy. We have charters to get back to. Paying customers—"

The captain hissed again.

I wanted to say he should see a medic. Excessive hissing was a precursor to Bakal's Syndrome and a host of other maladies that highly transient mutos like us were prone to. But I held my tongue. His hands were still in motion.

Our escorts left us with nary a word. Simply turned and walked up the hall, tails pointed and mean.

A full minute passed before I spoke again. "Place smells funny. Too much scent blocker or something. Makes it feel like a graveshack. Like we're standing next to a heap of bodies and the—"

"Sedric...enough."

"Sorry, sir. Don't like to stand. Especially not and wait for some—"

Another hiss. "Where do you think we are, XO?"

"Third Commercial Auditing and Accounting Compound," I said, pointing a thumb over my shoulder. "It was written on the building out front. Not sure what they want with us, but I assume it's part of the new rules. Seems like every time the Emperor sneezes there are rules."

He clutched his snout and shook his head. "You're a piece of—"

"Don't know why the numbers folks want us. We don't have that many numbers. I mean, I see our books. I know how—"

"It isn't that sort of accounting," the captain said.

Wasn't expecting that. "What do you mean? I saw the signs. The list of auditors on—"

"Did you see the cameras too? The mounted guns in every corner?"

"Guns?" I glanced up the hall. "But those does back there—"

"Are trained assassins. At least, in their spare time."

I sniffed. Showed him some teeth. "Captain, I don't—"

"Whatever you do, keep quiet." He pointed his tail at my nose. "Answer only when you're asked, and even then, keep it simple. And legal! Only the legit stuff. Never—"

The doors cracked open. We stared at them.

I was nervous now too. Maybe it was all the finery, maybe the captain's hands, or maybe the tremor in his voice. But my neck fur was on end.

"Come in," a soft, masculine voice said. It wasn't the type of voice I'd associated with a cackling megalomaniac or a shifty backstabber.

I glanced at the captain, then, as was our custom, led the way. I slowly pushed the left door open and peeked inside. I saw a large ornate desk, darkly stained, and lots of shelving filled with strange machinery. Computing power, I guessed. It didn't flicker and glow like the machines on our ship, though. These undulated as if alive. Some of the shelves held bound volumes—heavy, boring reading, from the looks of them. But most of the shelves had those undulating computing boxes.

Behind the desk was a frail-looking rhat. He was blue in color; except I could tell the hue wasn't natural. It was a rinse used to make his sparse hair seem younger. He'd be grey otherwise; I was certain of it.

He had to have been a hundred and fifty. Maybe two hundred.

"Do come in," he said. *High Executive Auditor Tactin,* said the desk nameplate.

I stepped inside and motioned for the captain to follow. He did, but I had to hold the door and almost pull him through.

On our side of the desk were two plush-looking chairs.

Black with golden highlights and nice wide tail notches in back. Nothing that would pinch or squeeze anything. I almost looked forward to sitting in them, despite my nerves.

I took a step forward.

Auditor Tactin fanned his desk with a paw. "Not here," he said.

"What?"

He pointed an aged finger at the corner to our right. "Over there. I want you both back there."

There was a pair of chairs against the wall in that corner. Portable metal contraptions like one would use in an emergency. They were positioned uncomfortably close to a particularly full and low-hanging portion of the shelves. One with a tangle of flexible tubing spilling down like a slaughtered slimeworm hung to dry.

The captain crept up next to me.

"He wants us in the corner, sir."

The captain nodded. "We'll go to the corner then."

I studied the plush chairs and the fragile man behind the desk. "But—"

Captain Wendel was in the corner already. A second later, there was a screech as his posterior made contact with one of the metal chairs.

I shook my head and walked over to join him. My chair lacked a tail notch, so I had to sit such that my tail followed the back of the chair to hang free near my right hip. Not comfortable at all.

There was a hiss followed by a low droning sound. The *Executive Auditor* whooshed around his desk on a hoverchair that made even the plush ones look inferior. Heavily padded with lots of silver. His feet dangled a couple centimeters from the floor. He stopped a meter from us, and after smoothing the front of his buttoned vest, he dropped his hands into his lap and studied us both.

The captain's hands were in motion.

I returned the auditor's stare and tried not to shift in my seat. I wasn't supposed to speak. Say nothing about anything.

The auditor focused on the captain. "You had a shuttle go missing?"

The captain narrowed his eyes but remained silent.

The auditor puffed out his cheeks, then let them dwindle away slowly. "It's a yes or no question, captain."

The captain nodded. Still no words.

"Sir?" I said.

The auditor sighed. "It appears we need some ground rules," he said. "I will ask the questions and you will answer them."

"We're free contractors," I said without thinking. "We have right to—"

The auditor puffed his cheeks again, eyes taking on a new intensity.

The captain hissed.

"I only mean to—"

A bony finger pointed my way. "There are no rights except those given by the Emperor. This office is an extension of his will."

"We're one of the finest ships under contract," I said. "Thousands of light years, hundreds of systems. Enterprises like ours are what keeps—"

The captain's hiss sounded like a servolift that had blown its seal. The auditor and I both stared at him.

Captain Wendel's eyes widened. "Sorry," he said. "My XO gets beyond himself. Just trying to keep him in line."

Imperial auditor Tactin nodded slowly. "The shuttle, captain?"

"Yes, we lost one. Had a horrible accident a few years back. An engine sheer while out on delivery. Thing crashed. Had a few injuries, but the good news is—"

"Registration number 425-C3A-200?" Tactin said, contemplating a screen attached to his chair's right armrest.

The captain glanced at me. Hesitated.

"Captain?"

He stroked the back of his neck. "Don't recall the numbers precisely. It was a long time ago."

Tactin sighed, tapped his screen, and spun it around so we could see it. It showed the image of our missing shuttle, looking like it just left space dock for the first time.

Gleaming and bright.

CHAPTER 2

It was an archival image, taken sometime back when our ship was new. Or so I guessed.

The captain squinted and leaned forward. "Might be one of ours. Seems about right." He glanced at me. "What do you think, Sedric?"

I raised a shoulder. "Could be. Sure. Like you said, it was a while—"

Tactin reclaimed his screen. "That shuttle was involved in a raid last month, gentlemutos. Any idea how that could be?"

The captain's seat creaked as he shifted. "That's not possible, high auditor."

"Right," I said. "Our shuttle was wrecked over a decade ago."

Tactin nodded slowly. "So you know *nothing* about this shuttle or its crew?" He indicated the screen. "The one identified as your destroyed ship? That looks like your destroyed ship?"

The captain shook his head. "How could we? We're honest businessmen, auditor. We—"

Tactin snorted. "Honest businessman, yes." He poked the screen and narrowed his eyes. "And you would never falsely claim the destruction of a shuttle for the insurance payout of..." He leaned closer. "Two hundred thousand rhatzan?"

"That's not unreasonable!" The captain said. "Especially when you consider what the new ones cost. Why, you can almost buy a full interstellar for—"

Tactin held up a crooked paw. "Oh, I'm aware. Aware of it all." He glanced at the door. "I wonder where my assistants have gotten. They've proven helpful in the past. Persuasive for the reluctant." He wiggled his nose and smiled. "Remarkably quick. Remarkably strong hands."

The captain's eyes widened. "We're not reluctant! We're happy to help. We're here to help."

"Ah, so good that you're happy." Tactin took a deep breath but didn't puff his cheeks this time. "Now, about the raid...anything you could share about the umans who carried it out?"

I exchanged a look with the captain. "Umans?"

Tactin nodded. "Yes, at least twenty of them. They brought your missing shuttle to a small commerce depot on the third planet of the Scridlack system. From there, they stole two additional ships, loaded all three with a million rhatzans worth of military and commercial equipment, and escaped. They were pursued, of course, but somehow eluded capture."

The captain stroked his chin. "Maybe I'm misremembering... maybe our shuttle was stolen." He looked at me. "We had a stolen shuttle once, didn't we? Before that job on Ritner Five?"

I didn't want to speak, for fear of digging myself a hole. I suspected the captain was in one already...but the executive officer? He might be let go with a warning. He might even be given command.

I knew a lot about that lost shuttle, though. There was a

lot at stake. A big ball of string that could've unwound all sorts of directions. And some might entangle me.

"Yeah, that's right," I said slowly. "We had a big mix-up back there." I smiled at the auditor. "We were hauling Brennen fog juice. Everything is hazy when—"

Tactin waved at me. "The owners of the stolen ships and supplies are demanding recompense. Since the shuttle belonged to you, the law demands that—"

The captain's snout whiskers straightened. "We're not liable! We didn't raid anywhere! We didn't steal anything!"

Tactin leaned forward. "Are you arguing with the Emperor's reputation, captain?"

The fire in the captain's eyes dwindled and he sank into his chair. "No, auditor, but there's a thing called 'fairness.'"

"We *define* fairness. You can find it in the books."

Captain shook his head. "I don't want to argue with that. I just want to return to my ship. We have business."

"We need an advocate," I said. "Perhaps someone from the historian guild—"

"This isn't a trial, gentlemuto," Tactin said. "There's no trial for sedition and fraud."

I could feel the captain's fear. It scampered across the floor from his feet to mine. "There has to be a concession, auditor," I said. "A way we could change the—"

The auditor's cheeks puffed. "You seek to bribe me?"

"Will that help?" the captain asked.

"It will add ten standard to your imprisonment. Twenty thousand to your fine."

"Then we aren't doing that." The captain said, whiskers drooping.

"Thought never stirred in <u>my</u> head," I said. There were *always* concessions, though. Always ways to tilt the scale. It was the heart of muto justice. "I only want options. Our motives are pure. Let us prove it."

The auditor leaned back. Tapped his lips with a finger. "Will you submit to a head walk?"

"A what?" the captain asked.

The auditor pointed to the shelves above our heads. "Certainly you've heard of a synaptic review?"

The captain gripped the sides of his snout, looking terrified.

"We don't visit the core planets much," I stammered. "Don't know the latest—"

"It's proven technology." Tactin pointed at the dangling tubes. "I attach a condensing mask to your head which gives me the ability to audit your memories." He tapped the top of his screen. "I'll view them right here. If I like what I see, you're free to go. Free to return to—"

The captain pointed my direction. "It was his fault! All of it!"

Generally, the captain was dependable. Loyal to the crew. But a situation like this? Always brought out the worst in him. On the spectrum of flee or fight, he was mostly flee.

Tactin looked at me. "To what is he referring?"

I sighed and glanced at the tubing. "Not what you think. Not even what you could imagine."

The fur on the captain's face was standing now, making it look swollen. "*Him*, I tell you. I didn't know what to do. It was a no-profit scenario. Then he had an idea."

Tactin didn't seem surprised at all. I suspect he'd seen his share of panicked confessions. "Were you working with the umans, then?" he asked. "The raiders?"

I wanted to do what the captain was doing. Blame-shift everything.

I think slow, though. Drove my first wife crazy, the way I deliberate. She worried it would get us killed someday. That's probably why she left.

"Officer Sedric?" Tactin said.

The captain hopped from his seat and sprinted for the doors. When he reached them, he strained at their handles for a good five clicks before realizing they were locked. He swore and pounded on them with both hands.

Tactin looked at me. "This is your captain?"

"He has bouts," I said. "Times his instincts just take him. His feels."

"But you don't?"

"I have feels too, sure." I scratched the side of my snout. "I try to think my way past them."

"Get up, Sedric!" The captain tugged the handles with all his might. "Get over here and help me get us out!"

I regarded him silently. He was my captain, after all. Gotten me through a fair share of scraps over the years. Plus, he'd given me lots of bonuses. Often because of situations like this one.

But I kept my seat, waiting.

"Would *you* like to tell me what happened?" Tactin asked. "Why he's panicked?" He glanced at the door. "Save me the trouble of calling security. Avoid any messes they might make."

"Messes? No, I don't want any—"

"I don't want that thing sucking my brain!" the captain blubbered. "Squeezing my memories!"

How much did the captain know about synaptic reviewers? Maybe more than he'd let on.

"I don't know if I can tell it like it was, High Auditor," I said. "Remember all the decisions. All the feels."

Tactin curled his paws together. "All this over a misreported shuttle? The penalties could be severe, but—"

The captain snickered. "A shuttle! All over that blamed shuttle."

I shook my head. "It isn't over a shuttle at all. Not really."

"No? Then what?"

"Is there recompense? Will it make me clean?"

Tactin sighed. "Sadly, no. A simple confession will change little. There will still be fines and penalties."

I twisted my snout. "What's the point of us being here then? If you've already decided..."

"I'm to interview you before the sentencing. That's the law."

"But our sentence is already decided."

"Generally, yes."

I wasn't surprised. Mutos aren't known for honesty. So, anything we'd tell the auditor was suspect. Especially for such high-priced crimes.

The captain thumped the door a final time before sliding to the floor.

I tapped the shelf above my head. "If I let you use that thing, is there recompense?"

"You'll be a vegetable!" the captain said. "A drooling vegetable. I'll have no use for you."

Tactin made a dismissive sound with his lips. "If we use the machine, I'll believe everything you said,"

"But will you feel it?" I said.

"Feel it?"

"I mean, you'll see it from my perspective, right?"

Tactin nodded.

I cupped my forehead. "Will I be alright after?"

"Only thirty-two percent have ever had trouble with the machine." Tactin shifted then pointed his tail at the door. "Typically, those of a more excitable nature."

I nodded slowly. "Okay. You can hook me up."

Tactin returned the nod. "You'll need you to sign a waiver."

"A waiver?"

"Just in case...something went wrong." He touched his seat's screen causing the seat to drift toward the wall near me. "I'll connect you first." He tugged on one of the hanging hoses and a flexible oval mask dropped from the shelf above. It was a murky brown color, but translucent.

He held the mask out. "Here. Slide this over your head."

I didn't want it anywhere near my head. Wasn't even sure I wanted it in the same room with me. "Looks like a slug formed of tree sap," I said, cringing.

"Come now, it's perfectly safe." He stretched the sides of the mask with both hands. "Pliable and soft." He pointed at the mask's interior. "Hibernation gas is used. You won't feel a thing. You use gas all the time, yes?"

"For travel between stars, sure. But this..." It was all I could do not to shiver, yet I took the mask. It felt rubbery and slightly damp.

Tactin mimicked the procedure to put it on. "Just under the chin, over the snout, and back to the ears."

I sniffed the mask. It had a sickly sweet aroma, reminding me of the first uman I saw dead. I almost gagged.

"Here's that waiver," Tactin said, spinning the screen my way. "A simple tail press will do."

I hesitated, listening to the captain whimper. Smelling that dead animal of a mask.

"He's to blame!" the captain said.

I sighed, pressed tail to screen and then mask to face, stretching and pulling. There were a few seconds of panic, a time when my senses knew I was being suffocated and squeezed. But then, with a wisp, the gas kicked in. I tasted its familiarity and relaxed, but also felt my senses heighten. I swore I could hear the captain's ragged breathing like a roar.

"Now," Tactin said. "Let's talk about your ship—"

I snorted. "You mean the cheese," I said. "It is all about the cheese..."

CHAPTER 3

Our ship, the *Granum*, had a distinct scent. It was somewhere between ocean breeze and winter's eve on the redolence spectrum, with a black tar undercurrent. The smell came from nothing in particular. I'd spent many a lonely evening searching for the source, pressing snout to air-ducts, sniffing around corners and up near ceilings. A fruitless pursuit, it was. Nothing gave off *Granum*-evening-tar-breeze. It just was. Like the brown paint on the ship's exterior or the ident numbers scrawled across its hull, that scent belonged to the ship alone.

It was particularly intense that night. Of anything, that's what I remember.

I was seated in the bridge command chair, legs hooked over the chair's right arm, eyes focused only on my left paw. It had been sore and swollen for a week and I worried it had caught the bumble, despite the doctor's assurances. Bumblepaw was common for ship mutos. Ships spread it like the plague. They're never as clean as they should be. And when the bumble has you...it takes months to shed.

The com officer, Yentiss, was the only one with me. She was seated at a desk below and to the right. Nearly out of view in my current position. Yetiss was a second year intern that somehow resisted the call to sire. She was a quiet doe. Efficient and capable. A bit short on the snout for my tastes, but not unattractive. Good company for a quiet night watching nothing but black screens.

The captain was off duty, doubtless involved in a game at the aft bar. Or viewing one of his favorite cyber-thrills in his quarters. He's a risk-taker by nature. Has a nose for profit too, though, so usually the risks pay off.

We were transporting a full shipment of delicacies to a location the captain had yet to divulge. Rich and heavy foods that no one could resist. The shipment's procurement was an example of the captain's talent. He'd found a planet of simple-tons that feared a rhat-like figure as part of their histories. They'd filled our largest cargo bay with cheeses and cakes simply to leave. A hundred percent profit was a hard figure to beat.

Then I heard a thump. An Emperor-cursing thump from somewhere below-decks. After that, the command chair screen pulsed a heavy red. Often, those sort of alerts are sparked by simple things—proximity warnings or faults in the twice redundant gas matrix. But given the thump, I was certain this one meant work on my part. I wasn't happy, but I was no longer focused on my paw.

"Sedric?" Yetiss said, doubtless afraid I'd fallen asleep. It was a fair concern.

I straightened in my chair and pulled the screen over where I could view it. Took me only a second to analyze. "Science." I said it like it was an obscenity. Because it often was.

Yetiss' turned my way, eyes large and snout—brown and youthful soft-puckered. "I see it too," she said. "Did they blow something up?"

"Probably." I dismissed the warning with a tap and searched for the science connection. When found, it gave me another black screen. No smoke, no fire, but the lost view of a dead sensor. I grunted and shook my head.

"They aren't responding," Yetiss said. "I've checked all their views. All give me—"

I swore. "Those two. Should've gassed them first. As soon as we took off."

"Captain has them doing repairs. Wanted to give them time to—"

"Another risk," I said. "And this one brought us thumps. I don't like thumps."

Yetiss's right paw hovered over her screen. "Should I send security?"

"If they were at full staff, they'd be there already. But since they aren't—"

"So, you want me to call them?"

I slid my screen out of the way and stood. "I'll take a look." The screens from the room's other command posts—one in front of me and left, and two behind—were still pulsing red, projecting a visual heartbeat onto the walls.

The bridge was tight quarters, one of the reasons why the other posts were rarely occupied. The other reason was boredom.

"It might be dangerous," she said. "Still no word."

"We aren't venting anything." I forced a smile. "There's a reason science is far from the hull."

Yetiss nodded but said nothing.

I returned the nod. "Just keep things quiet up here."

"Sure, Sed."

"Sure, Sed, sir," I muttered, partially in jest.

She repeated the statement.

I took a deep breath, noting the intensity of *Granum*'s smell, then walked to the door and the lift beyond it.

Our science facility was a circle of three chambers. One is a processing lab, complete with a maze of long tables and large appliances. The second is a housing chamber for aborted experiments, filled with twisted shapes and stranger smells. The third chamber is the one I headed for—a testing facility that's largely wide open space enclosed by light green walls. It's the most dangerous of the three because, as the name implies, it's where our science engineers perform tests. Also, the most likely to produce a thump.

As I approached the facility, I found the metal doors ajar, and a steady stream of something, possibly smoke, billowing through the top of the opening.

I paused. If I kept going, if I walked inside, what would I be exposed to? I also wondered whether I should activate the hall's emergency klaxon to ensure that security arrived. I wasn't sure if they could handle fire suppression or not. I thought there was an automated system for that. Made me think that the cloud wasn't standard smoke.

Either that, or the science rhats had disabled the system. Just as likely.

I took a tentative step and sniff-tested the air. It had a mild chemical hint, but mostly it smelled like rotten meat cooked at high temperatures. Again, I paused, and slid the handheld com from my belt.

The older of the two engineers—Dontel—backed through the open doors. There was a white mask affixed over his greying snout and a full-length white longshirt over his torso, the front of which was splattered with something dark. His attention was on the room he'd left.

He made a dismissive motion. "Yes, yes, I'll think of something. Do it quick. I'm sure they heard. Someone will—" He glanced at the thinning cloud above and fanned the air. "Oh, what a mess."

I took another tentative step.

Dontel noticed the motion and turned my way. His eyes widened.

"What did you do?" I asked.

He stripped the mask away and smiled. "Ah, Sedric, how nice to see you!" He fanned the air again and stepped my way. "How have you been?"

CHAPTER 4

I couldn't keep the disdain from my face. "I heard a thump." I indicated the doors behind Dontel. "There's... something coming out there."

He glanced back. "Oh yes, that. Not to worry. It isn't toxic. We checked."

"Smells rotten." Not that that was a bad thing. My parents taught me that sometimes "rotten" led to the best treats. Probably all muto parents teach their kids that.

"Not rotten, no," he said. "A little cooked, perhaps..."

I crossed my arms. "What did you do?" Last I knew, they were working on our shuttles. In his youth, the captain had served on a ship similar to the *Granum*. He swore it's shuttle could do twice the speed of ours and so set our scientists to the task.

I suspected the captain was misremembering. Young experiences always seem faster.

Two security officers arrived from the hall on the opposite side of the doors. They wore the dark long shirt, belt, and boots of their position and held pistols at the ready. They stopped near the doors, cupped their free hands over their snouts, and peered warily inside.

A quick response from them, actually. Must've been awake.

Dontel hustled back to greet them. "No reason for guns. It's all quite safe. Under control."

One of the guards, blue-furred and large, looked at me. "Officer Sedric, sir."

The cloud dwindled to a wisp, then stopped completely. I joined the others at the doors and looked within. There was some smoke inside, but my primary focus was the large device mounted to the floor: a silver tube that extended from a purple, pill-shaped encasement. It looked like one of the ship's forward guns.

The barrel was pointed at the far wall. Along that wall, seemingly out-of-place, was a metal filing cabinet. The other scientist, Uzel, leaned against one side of the cabinet, arms crossed. He was dressed in a white shirt and mask too. His fur color was a light beige. There were a dozen heavy cables connected to the gun and a couple lab chairs too.

Uzel waved. "Hello, Sedric! How's life on the bridge? Any vacation stops on our way? We could use a break."

I pointed to the center of the room. "Is that one of the—?"

Dontel grabbed my elbow. "One of the guns, yes. We're only making adjustments. Bringing them up to full strength. Captain's orders."

"But why is it *here*? In the lab?"

"Adjustments! Much easier to adjust here." He indicated the ceiling. "Better lighting. And all our tools are here."

I frowned and sniffed again. The rotten smell was strongest in the direction of the gun. I strolled that way and stepped around the gun, sniffing. It was hard to avoid the cables and the tools the scientists had left. Many of the latter looked ill-suited for gun adjustment—hammers, chisels, and prying brackets. There was a block of food at the gun's base. Smelled like white cheddar.

Dontel waved and pointed to the right, toward the closed door of the processing lab. "If you want to see something truly amazing, you should see the shimmer coats we've been working on."

"Shimmer...coats?"

Dontel's face brightened. "Yes, they make the wearer virtually invisible! Imagine the usefulness. The items that could be reallocated without risk of discovery."

I nodded and glanced at Uzel.

He showed teeth and waved again.

Something guilty in his behavior.

"What was the noise we heard?" I asked. "A large thump."

"There was a noise?" Dontel asked. "I wasn't aware." He walked to the lab door and poked the wall-mounted door control with his tail. After a short wait, the door opened, and he walked inside.

"Dontel!" I said.

"One moment..."

Inside, I could see the end of a black table and a silver, circular machine sitting atop it. I didn't care much for anything in there, though. I was more interested in the thump and the source of the smoke.

As for the smell...it was strongest on the side of the gun nearest Usel. He must be hiding the source.

My eyes rested on the cabinet. It's shelves were full of miscellany—statues, science manuscripts, and small devices. Nothing seemed out of the ordinary necessarily. But why was the cabinet the only furniture in the room? Had it been there the last time I was here? I couldn't remember.

The guards lingered near the door, now looking bored.

Finally, one stepped my direction. "Are we needed, sir?" he asked. "Doesn't look like—"

Dontel bustled out of the lab with a bundle of folded, blue material. When he'd nearly reached me, he shook the material loose and held it up. It was a full body suit, complete with a hood.

"That's the shimmer suit?" I said.

Dontel turned the suit so he could see it. "We've been calling them shimmer 'coats,'" he said. "But 'suits' works too." He twisted his snout. "Yes, maybe that works better. Would you like to try it on?"

"Not really, no." I'd had limited exposure to the science team, but their reputation was inescapable. They'd lost a number of assistants. Not to death, but almost.

"Oh come, it's quite, um..." He noticed the nearby security agent and gave him a once over. "It might fit you." He smiled and swung the suit the agent's way. "Here, please try it on."

"We don't have time—" I began, before remembering how bored I'd been on the bridge. I gave the guard a wave. "Go ahead. Try it on."

He looked puzzled. "Sir, I need to get back. I have to—"

"To what? Sleep?" I snorted. "Come on, this will be more interesting than sleep."

He stuttered, searching for a way out. Failing that, he grabbed the shimmer suit and pulled his feet into it. The suit was roomy, even with the agent's long shirt intact.

I mentioned that to Dontel.

"Well, we want them to be useful for anyone."

"He'd be tripping all over himself."

Dontel's hand found his chin. "Yes, well, science requires adjustment."

I frowned and walked toward Uzel. He held his position, still leaning against the cabinet. "Hello again, Sedric," he said.

"Yes, hello." I examined the case, walking slowly to one

end, and then the other. The smell was evenly dispersed. I leaned closer and sniffed. It wasn't the cabinet itself, but definitely nearby.

Dontel clapped his paws together. "Officer Sedric! Please watch!" He smiled at the agent, now completely engulfed in blue material. "You're free to turn it on."

"How do I do that?" the guard asked.

"Pat the chest, of course."

"Of course." I gripped the left side of the cabinet and gave it a little shove. It shifted half a paw length before Uzel stopped it. With a smile, he pushed it back into place.

The agent touched his chest. He shimmered, sure, but he didn't become transparent. Instead, his snout seemed to shorten and his body glowed red. He looked like a short, glowing, red...uman.

"I can still see him," I said.

"Yes, yes." Dontel smiled. "But it's a revolutionary start."

"It made him red. And ugly."

Dontel nodded. "It will need adjustment."

I glanced at Uzel, who nodded and said, "Adjustment. Science always—"

"Needs adjustment," I said. "Right."

I pushed on the cabinet again. "Could you move, please?"

Uzel looked annoyed. "I don't want to. Leaning here...helps my back. My spine is—"

I hissed. "I'm ordering you to move, does that help?"

"With my back?"

I scowled. "Move it, scientist."

Uzel glanced nervously at Dontel, then shrugged and stepped away.

I leaned into the cabinet. With little effort, I moved it a couple strides. Beyond it was a large, gaping hole. It's edges were fused solid as if from high heat. Height-wise, it was only a head shorter than me.

The captain would be mad. I was mad.

"You shot a hole in the wall?"

Dontel's snout drooped. "What's that?"

I pointed at the hole as I spoke. "You two. Shot. A hole. In the wall."

Uzel backed further away, gazing at the hole as if for the first time. "Oh wow...how did that get there?"

I glared at him.

He smiled. "It's fixable."

"Yes." Dontel moved closer. "We can fix it. We *will* fix it."

The smell was pervasive now. It was coming from the hole. Definitely from the hole. "Why does it smell so bad?" I asked.

Dontel slowly walked closer. "Yes, we had a misfire. Yes, that was probably the thump you heard. But it's only a hole. And the structure of the ship is sound, obviously, so—"

I ducked my head and looked into the hole. Some creatures in the five galaxies would've required extra light. I'd had enough interaction with umans, for instance, to know that they wouldn't have been able to see much more than a dark aperture. But muto eyes are sensitive, and mine were among the best around.

The "misfire" passed through a second supporting wall about a dozen steps behind. Beyond that, there was more ambient light. I could glimpse a tendril of gas coming from that hole. The rotten aroma.

I couldn't recall the last time I'd seen the ship's schematics. I knew the science station was positioned near the center of the ship, but our guns had a lot of bang. How many walls did those idiots get through? How far did the damage go?

"Terribly sorry, Officer Sedric," Dontel said, now standing close behind me. "I see we clipped another wall there. We'll fix that too, of course."

I sneered. "That's more than a 'clip.'" I pointed at the other hole. "Did you follow it? See what else you hit?"

"There wasn't time for that, sorry. We were just discussing how to repair *this* hole when you arrived. Science takes time...and—"

"Adjustments?" I shook my head. "Mighty big adjustment."

"We were only trying to please the captain. He asked us to—"

"I thought you were working on the shuttles."

Dontel looked at Usel. "The captain did say guns, didn't he?"

Usel shrugged. "That's what I heard."

I sighed and looked at the far hole. "I'm glad you weren't working on the engines!"

Dontel rumpled his snout. "It would be a shame if we were working on the wrong thing. Especially with all the other inventions we're—"

I tested the hole's edge with a paw. Still warm. "You two need to get the ship fixed. Get all the walls patched and fix whatever other damage you've caused."

Dontel nodded. "Of course. That's what we intend to do. Do you have to tell—"

I chuckled. "The captain? Are you kidding?"

Dontel's face got serious. "Not kidding, no. Not at all. Why?"

I sighed and stepped into the dead space between walls.

Dontel's head poked through the first hole. "What are you doing?"

"I'm going to figure out what you hit," I said. "And then I may just turn on the gas in your quarters so you—you and your assistant—can take a much needed nap."

"But we have many things to do!"

"Right. Fix the walls first. Then your nap."

"But—"

I pointed my tail at him. "No arguments. No telling what you two messed up here. I'm going to check. I'm hoping I don't have to wake the whole crew to get it solved. But you two? You're going to sleep."

Dontel bowed. "Very good. We'll start working on the wall."

"Good," I said. "But don't seal anything until I'm out."

"Of course not. We won't do that."

I studied him a moment. "You know, don't do anything until I'm back. Just wait right there."

"But we—"

"There. Right there." I remembered the security guard. "And get that poor guy out of the suit before he explodes or something."

"Yes, sir. Right away, sir."

CHAPTER 5

An hour later, I knew the full extent of the damage. I wasn't happy, and the captain wasn't happy either. His curses made me grateful I'd chosen to tell him on the bridge where it was only Yentiss and I.

Scramble or scratch were the two most common crew member responses to an angry captain. A whole ship that's in full scramble mode is an immensely uncomfortable thing. Usually someone gets trampled to death. At a minimum, there's lots of tail loss. Who wants to be on a ship of stumps? Not me.

The captain clutched the command chair back as he stood behind it. "Tell me again how this happened? How one accident caused all this?"

"Well, it didn't touch the hull," I said. "We can be thankful of that."

"But the primary hold!" he said. "Our cargo! The whole uman-infested thing?"

I took a deep breath and noticed the ubiquitous *Granum* smell again. It had a little higher tar mix this time. Or perhaps the smell of rot had damaged my olfactory organs. "The shot pierced the hold's ceiling, sir, then ricocheted a couple times."

"But we can't just seal it up again? It's food, after all. It shouldn't be spoiled. Not like that."

I took the officer's seat next to Yentiss. She was doing okay so far, but it seemed like being near her might help somehow. "It was a high pressure vacuum seal with external dampening. Not only did the shot cook the food, it imploded it. It's a real mess down there, sir." I shook my head. "It'll take days of cleaning...for someone."

"Eject the whole lot to space," he said. "No one needs that work."

"I was thinking maybe the scientists..."

The captain snorted. "Oh, they should have it, no doubt. But we can't afford to lose their service."

I disagreed, but said nothing, hoping he'd come to it on his own.

The captain hopped into his seat and leaned forward. "We have a contract to fill. An important contract."

"Could we go back?" Yentiss focused on her desk screen, poking and pushing. "It will take a month standard—"

"We can't afford the turnaround." The captain swung his screen where he could see it. "What's near here? Anything?"

Yentiss shook her head. "Not seeing anything Empire connected or even sympathetic. We're light years from the boundary. Deep in unclaimed territory." She gave me a pained expression. "Can't find anything in the habitable planet registry either."

"Doesn't need to be in the registry," the captain said. "Only needs to be close and viable enough to have sentients. A society that can produce food. Lots of good food."

"It's a little more complicated than that, sir," I said. "These sentients would have to have similar metabolisms. Similar digestive systems. Similar taste receptors. Not to mention the danger of—"

The captain snorted. "Spare me the details. I know all that."

"Only verbalizing the challenges, sir. We need an advanced civilization. One with motors, at least, because—"

He touched the end of his snout. "What's this?"

I narrowed my eyes. "Your snout, sir."

He nodded. "And what does the snout do?"

"Finds profit," I said, somewhat grudgingly. "Lots of profit."

"Exactly!" He fluttered a paw. "All those needs you mentioned? Pointless distraction. The galaxies mostly eat the same. Taste the same. Even the Llyr like cheese, I've heard."

"The Llyr are plants," I said. "They don't have mouths."

"Another distraction." He focused on his screen and began a rhythm of tapping and poking. "What do we have within a few days' time. There must be something..." Finally, he smiled. "Ah, here we are."

"What?"

"A place we can land." He pointed at his screen. "A planet." He waved toward the front of the room, where a larger, rarely used, display was located. "Here, I'll show you."

The center screen flickered to life. There was a square section in the top left corner that displayed yellow where it should show the black of space. Doubtless a place where the screen's display matrix had been damaged. But otherwise, the central image was of solid, blue circle.

The captain grunted. "I can do better than that. Hold on." After more tapping, a blue planet appeared. It had a single white moon.

There were no large space stations, or space traffic of any kind. In fact, aside from a few touches of green on the surface, the place looked lifeless. "We'll have better luck finding cheese on its moon," I said.

"What?"

I shook my head. "Just thinking aloud, sir. It doesn't look inhabited."

"Ah, but it is! There are signs of sentient life." The image magnified until we could see a large city with a river through its center. "See there. Look at all the sentients."

The buildings looked worse than those of the most backwards planets of the Empire. Made of wood and stone. A strong wind would blow them over. And how much sunlight would they keep out? Not enough.

"Looks awful," I said. "Especially during the day. Everyone running around outside like that?"

Yentiss's eyes went wide. "How do they protect themselves from predators?"

"They have buildings with doors," the captain said. "They'd be safe."

"A frekle would make quick work of those," she said. "Smash right in and—"

The captain made a sound somewhere between a growl and a laugh. "We don't need to worry about predators. We're in a ship. We have weapons." He hopped from his chair and started to pace. "What we do need to worry about is finding the food. Every town would have some, of course, but we're looking for the best. Enough to please royalty." He tail pointed at the com officer. "Yentiss, find us a spot."

"Sir?"

"You have royalty in your blood, don't you?"

Yentiss glanced nervously my way, then turned slightly to address the captain. "Not really, sir."

"You're being humble. I've seen your files. Your grandsire was a baron, or something."

"He married a widowed baroness, sir. Long after his spouse—"

The captain raised a paw. "There you are, in your blood! Find us a place. I'll trust your judgment."

Yentiss shook her head. "I wouldn't know where to begin."

"No tail-dragging, doe, or I'll sell you to a dock hand at our next stop."

"Captain," I said, "you can't—"

He glared at me. "Don't tell me what I can't do! I've slaved out crewmembers before."

"When?"

He wagged his tail. "Before you were here. Maybe ten imperials ago."

Yentiss's eyes locked on her screen, her facial fur bristling.

"Yentiss," I said. "He can't." I shook my snout. "I won't let him."

The captain laughed. "Standing up for the doe, eh? What motivates such honor?"

I stared at him a few moments before shaking my head. I tend to be more scratch than scramble, but usually I'm neither.

"I know you, Sedric," he said. "Know your color." He moved toward my station and leaned close. "There's no blue in you."

There was more blue than he thought, and a fair share of red. But I generally defied color boundaries. The captain brought profit, but he needed someone else to keep it. That's where I came in.

"Here's something!" Yentiss said. The central screen flickered as she took control. A second later, there was an image of a large stone structure with lots of turrets, towers, and stepped walls.

The captain made a humming sound. "What's that?"

"Reminds me of Malafix," I said.

"Of what?"

"The imperial residence on Susstis Five," I said. "The structure has a similar shape, but without the protective shields."

The captain squinted at me. "And how would you know that?"

"I've seen images."

Yentiss nodded. "I think it's royal too." She brought up image after image, each time presenting a similar, but different stone structure. "This area has lots of them."

The captain tapped the side of his snout. "That *could* mean something, sure. What do you think, Sedric?"

I shrugged. "Who builds big? The rich and the royal."

"That's right, isn't it?" His eyes brightened. "I think you struck it, Yentiss. That area right there. That's where we should go."

There was a hundred mutos in our crew, three quarters of whom were in hibernation. Gassed and secured until we reached our final destination. "Do we wake the sleepers?" I asked.

The captain turned and paced away. "That would make things easier. More paws for the finding." His eyes searched the room as he pondered it. Then he shrugged. "Meh. I like the quiet. Let them sleep."

I nodded. "How long to reach it?" I said to Yentiss.

"Only a couple days," she said. "Barring any accidents."

"Enough time to plan," the captain said. "Set a course, Sedric. And scout out a good place to land. Somewhere near one of those structures. Preferably with a city nearby."

I had a surge of trepidation. There were too many unknowns here. Much that could go wrong. "We don't know who built those structures," I said. "They could be any sort of creature. They could have eyes with lasers. Or fire breath."

The captain grunted. "My guess is they're uman," he said.

"Why would you think that?"

"If it isn't something else, it is almost always uman."

I shook my head. "That makes no sense."

He hissed. "You know what I mean. Umans are everywhere."

"But are there any mutos there?" I asked. "If the world isn't in the registry, then it hasn't been surveyed. It's completely isolated. Never seen another sentient. Bad things happen on such primitive worlds. Do I have to remind you of the Teril Massacre? A whole ship stripped by the natives? The crew cut into—"

"We have guns," he said.

"So did they."

The captain eased into his chair again. Despite his apparent confidence, I could smell his nervousness. "We'll be fine," he said. "We have scientists."

"They got us into this."

He shrugged. "Do you have a better plan?"

Unfortunately, I didn't. And breaking our delivery contract would hurt business for years. "We'll have to hide," I said. "Do everything in the shadows."

He nodded. "Yes. We'll hide the ship. Work only at night."

"What if someone is seen?" Yentiss asked, her voice wavering. "If they haven't met other sentients, how will they respond when they see one?" The Teril Massacre was a legend. A story told to scare kits and grownups alike. Certainly, Yentiss had heard it.

"We'll be fine," the captain repeated. "My snout likes this one. It smells right." His voice became resolute. "Now, get us there and quick!"

CHAPTER 6

The days before planetfall were mostly spent arguing with the captain. He wanted the scientists to push ahead on their shimmer suits in the hopes of using them on the primitive planet. I wanted them to finish up everything else they'd started, including the two shuttles and forward guns. They'd left the shuttles in such a state of disrepair, in fact, that we'd be forced to take the *Granum* down instead. Exposing it and all of us to whatever dangers the planet held in store.

The captain also wanted to keep us at a skeleton crew of a dozen mutos. I wanted to wake at least a dozen more, if only to have a backup set to operate the ship.

In the end, the scientists pushed ahead on the suits, and we woke ten more crew members. It was a compromise I could live with.

The other major endeavor was the repair of the cargo hold, followed by its venting and cleaning. That was no easy feat. The more fragile portions of the shipment had bubbled over and burst, spreading rotting food everywhere. Rhats have tough stomachs, but they aren't ironclad. At least five crew-members reported to the doctor. A couple others were returned to hibernation.

Our approach to the planet went without incident, though. True to the long-range sensors, the planet had no space travel. There wasn't even traffic to the planet's moon, or within the planet's atmosphere. The primary mode of global travel, particularly between land masses, appeared to be by wooden boats.

Wood! It was inconceivable. No muto planet had wood-only sea-ships for fear of the monsters that lived beneath the surface. We wouldn't travel by wooden ship anywhere if we could help it.

The captain chose an area north of a half-dozen of the royal stone structures. It was also near the largest city in the area and comfortably south of a large body of water. The body wasn't an ocean, so sea monsters were unlikely, according to the captain.

The body of water did connect with an ocean, I noted.

"It's well enough inland," the captain hissed. "Plus, umans need water to craft the types of delicacies we're looking for. We can't park in a desert due to fear."

The captain was right about the world being populated by umans. Our scans showed nothing but umans and uman structures. So, I went with his instincts on our final landing spot.

Another concern was concealing the *Granum* from uman eyes. Yentiss found a perfectly shaped bare space in an otherwise dense forest. Given these umans didn't fly, there were few better choices—unless we submerged the ship. No one wanted to do that.

Our ship had cloaking emitters too, but even the captain knew it was best not to rely solely on technology. Not when the threat of scientific "adjustment" was always a factor.

Near midnight on the third day, a forest in the middle of Royal Stoneland of the Primitive Planet Uman became our home. It was a quiet spot that smelled a little like the forests on my birth world, Tricx.

The damp musky aroma somehow found its way into *Granum*'s air system and mingled with the ship's usual scent, diminishing the tar, and emphasizing the sweet. It lifted my spirits, making me think this whole adventure might turn out all right.

The captain summoned everyone who was awake to the suspended central platform above the primary cargo hold. The hold was rectangular with grey walls and a shiny, no-slip, black floor. Built above and around the outside of the hold was a latticework of robotic lifts able to stack and transport nearly anything we could fill it with. It also had temperature sensors in the walls and floor. It was doubtless the most environmentally controlled place in the ship...before the scientists shot a hole in it. Still, I was impressed with how good the repair work looked. From above, I could hardly detect where the wall had been blown in, or the splattered, bubbling mess that ensued.

The central platform was square, with safety rails all the way around. The captain found a spot on the side closest to the ship's aft end and leaned against the rail there. The rest of us formed a loose semicircle near the opposite end of the platform.

Beyond and below the captain was the loading door and a half dozen yellow hover trucks. "Our goal, does and bucks," he said, "is to fill the space below with transportable food. The richest food we can find."

"And how are we to do that?" spat one of the newly-woken crewmembers. Named "Krate," he was large and beige, dressed in a grey shirt with a tear in the front.

Without hesitation, I poked him with my zap stick. Zap stick payout is established first officer duty, and insubordination, a punishable offense.

Krate shrieked and went to his knees.

"Good question, gentlebuck," the captain said, smiling.

"We're going to divide in teams and search the immediate area for potential food sources."

Krate groaned and slowly returned to his feet. He gave me a sideways look.

I nodded and showed him my stick.

Krate turned his attention on the captain again.

"There are complications, of course," the captain said. "To start with, we can't be seen by anyone."

There were groans. None that I could easily identify, though.

"Sorry, mutos, it's a uman world," the captain said. "We need to be mindful of their presence."

"They aren't familiar with mutos," Yentiss added. "We need to be careful."

No insubordination there. I was glad. I didn't want to zap her.

One of the crewmembers, an older blue doe named "Dec," held up a paw. I shuffled near her just in case.

The captain recognized her paw with a nod.

"What about stunners?" she asked. "Can we carry stunners?"

A stunner was a step above a zap stick. They were short-range weapon with just enough juice to cause a muto—or uman—to hibernate for a short time. A few hairs often got scorched in the process too.

The captain scratched his snout. "Might not be a bad idea, that." He looked to his right, to where our pair of hapless scientists stood.

Both were dressed in clean, white longshirts this time. Dontel was all smiles, both paws behind his back. Uzel was distracted, eyes gazing at the hold below.

"Do we have enough stunners?" the captain asked.

Dontel rocked obliviously. Smiled. Uzel continued to look below.

I felt the stick in my hand. Took a happy step their way.

"Chief scientist?" the captain said.

Dontel startled and coughed, making a show of clearing his throat. "Pardon, sir. Yes, what do you need?"

"Stunners," I said. "How many do we have?"

Dontel's fur bristled. "How am I to know that?"

Uzel nodded vigorously. "Weapons are a security concern. We craft gadgets. They disperse them."

"How many have you crafted?" I asked.

They exchanged looks. "At least twelve," Dontel said then.

Uzel nodded again, smiling. "And clothing!"

"Clothing?" I looked at the captain. "The shimmer suits?"

Dontel raised his paws. "No, sorry. They're not ready yet."

"But we have two options," Uzel. "One is a long, brown robe."

The captain nodded. "In case we're seen. The robes will help hide us."

"We've seen similar clothing in our scanning images. Wearers will likely go unnoticed."

"Our faces will still be exposed," I said. "They'll see our snouts."

"They have hoods!" Utel said. "Long, heavy hoods." He circled a paw over his head. "Easily hides the whole face."

I frowned. "And the other option?"

"Similar in some respects," Uzel said. "An extended long-shirt, but made of lighter, multi-colored material. Instead of a hood, there's a..." He pointed to the crown of his head. "A separate covering for the head." He smiled.

"And snouts?" I asked. "How will they—"

Uzel smiled. "The head covering has a wide bill. We've adjusted it to be long enough to obscure our snouts."

I glanced at the room below. It was a large space to fill. "And the umans won't notice those adjustments? It won't look—"

"We only work at night," the captain said. "Remember that. Only at night."

I shook my head. With twelve going out, I gave the effort about a ten percent chance of success. But what choice did we have? We'd need to stick with the basics.

"We need to steal," I said aloud. "To find cheeses and desserts and whatever else might pass as a delicacy, take them, and get them back here as fast as we can." I cast a wary eye on the rest of the searchers. Maybe two thirds of them were competent enough to pull even that off. But the others?

I sighed. I should've been more selective in who we woke. "We should go in teams," I said. "That way we can watch out for each other."

The captain frowned. "We don't have many paws here. And there's a lot of ground to cover."

We could wake more, of course, but more mutos would mean more chance of discovery.

I scanned the group again, counting in my head. "We have enough for five three-muto teams, with five mutos staying with the ship. That should be enough." I looked at the captain. "A good place to start, anyway."

He gave me a worried look but nodded anyway. "We'll see how that goes."

The scientists needed to be in the group that stayed behind with the ship. And probably the captain. Not sure about the rest. Krate was a concern, but he was strong and could carry a lot. Best to have him in my team where I could watch him. I checked the hold again. Shook my head.

I'd need to think hard on who went with who. What teams would be best. Then I remembered another issue. "Speech!" I said. "What if we have to talk with them?"

Dontel rocked on his heels. "Translation pellets, of course. We have enough for everyone here."

He meant ingestible translation devices. A large pill that

somehow meddled with the appropriate brain and body functionality to make another language feel right. Both speech and hearing were altered. These devices were a new invention, which I generally didn't like. They gave me headaches long after their usefulness had expired.

Our scientists hadn't invented them, so they'd probably be fine. Didn't look forward to the hangover after, though.

The captain searched our faces. "Is that all, then? Is every detail worked out?"

The only issue I had left was the metal ball that seemed to be resting in my gut. Something wasn't right about all this. I had a job to do, though. I was there to temper the captain, and let his instincts take us to the prize. Whatever that prize might be.

"XO, are we ready?" the captain asked, looking my way.

I nodded. "We have a deadline to meet."

CHAPTER 7

Two standard hours later, those of us designated as "searchers" were outside the ship, awaiting final instructions.

The *Granum* rested on three, seemingly-undersized landing struts—one in the front and two in the rear. I always liked the ship's look from the outside. Roughly rectangular, its shape suggested a utilitarian, no-nonsense approach, one which allowed little flourish or extraneous material anywhere. Even the ship's front, though rounded, seemed only grudgingly so. As if the designer had been zap-sticked to make it happen. Only the sides in the back, where the emitter coils, fueling pipes and control fins protruded, displayed a hint of flair. But again, sparingly—even painfully—so.

It was a clear night, or at least the sky directly over our landing spot was clear. It was a warm night too, making me glad I'd chosen the lighter of the two clothing options. Regardless of how un-rhat-like it seemed, with my legs covered and a long-billed, puffy covering over my head, the getup let a lot more air circulate around my body than the heavier, brown robes would have. The other members of my team, Yentiss and Krate, were dressed in robes and already looked uncomfortable, scratching and fidgeting.

The captain walked down the ship's central boarding ramp to the crowd of searchers, then turned and raised his paws to the ship approvingly. "Ah, my flying tub with fins. Thank you for getting us here safely." He smiled and turned our way again. "Always praise the scow that brought you! They can hear it, believe me."

He pounded his paws together. "Our scientists tell me we're in the planet's summer season and close to its longest day. That means we'll be hampered by a short night, mutos. Less than eight hours left, so make good with your time." He checked the sky. "Tonight should chiefly be about scouting. Finding the best locations for food."

Dontel and Uzel hurried down the ramp behind him. Both had their arms full with large, square containers. About halfway down, Uzel tripped and tumbled forward. The contents of his container—handheld stunners—showered the ramp from where he fell all the way to the ground.

Dontel somehow managed to step around the clutter and make it, huffing and puffing, safely to the bottom. "I have bags!" he said. "Collection bags!"

The captain hissed. "Not so loud. Don't want to attract the locals."

"Or the predators," Yentiss whispered.

I put a finger to my lips, cautioning her.

The bags and hopefully-still-functioning stunners were distributed. I gave Yentiss another glance as I received mine, but she only shrugged and pulled her hood over her head. It barely concealed the end of her snout.

I checked the sky again. There were plenty of stars, but no sign of the planet's moon. That was a good thing. As big as the satellite was, it would cast a fair amount of light.

Enough for an uman to notice a furred snout hidden within a hood? Probably.

My stunner was a tear-shaped device with a single switch

on the front side. Easily concealed within a paw. In addition, it had a wrist and finger loop to help hold it that very place—coupled in the cleft of the paw, with only the business end peeking out between fingers. Not a bad design.

"Any final questions?" the captain said.

There were a couple coughs, but no one said anything.

The captain circled a paw in the air. "You teams should fan out around the ship. With five teams..." He looked at the *Granum* again. "Maybe have one moving from the front, a team from each side, and two teams in the back." He smiled. "Yeah, I think that's right." A wave. "Be on with you."

My team took one of the two positions at the rear of the ship. We followed a planetary direction of northeast, using our natural muto sense to guide us into the forest.

I often wondered how the muto directional sense managed to function, no matter the planet I was on. How my head recognized the magnetic pole of the world, despite the planet's orientation, size, or composition. But somehow it did. In all the dozens of planets I'd been on, tell me to go south and I'll know which direction to put my feet.

If there's anything that suggests a power higher than the Emperor to me, it's that directional sense. Rhats may not know where they're going, but they always know the way.

For some reason, though, Krate kept drifting to the north. Not sure if it was a lingering effect of hibernation, or a faulty directional sense. But it was annoying. Finally, I told him to tail Yentiss and me.

He merely shrugged and fell in behind us.

"I knew you wanted to talk to me alone, anyway," I said to Yentiss a few minutes later.

Her hood pointed my direction, enough that I could see the end of her snout. "What's that, Sedric, sir?"

My head covering fluttered, blocking my view. "Ah, you said 'sir,'" I said. "I have regained your respect."

"Sir?" she said again.

I shook my head. "Never mind." One of the things I admired in Yentiss was her efficiency. She didn't mince words and she didn't waste time. Apparently, that translated to idle conversation, as well.

Still, it would be a long eight hours if no one was talking.

"How far are we walking?" Krate asked.

"We just started," I said.

"Feels like forever." There were a couple heavy footfalls. "And I keep stepping on sticks. I hate sticks."

"We could scurry for a while," I said. "Or bound."

"No...," he said, and then: "Sir."

I'd left my zapstick on the ship. The stunner would suffice if Krate's attitude got too insufferable, but it would knock him out for a while. I didn't want to drag him anywhere.

Ten minutes passed with only the sounds of twigs breaking, and Krate's occasional curses.

"Why did you join the *Granum*?" I asked finally.

"Because I was out of food," Krate said.

Krate had better ears than I expected. "I was talking to Yentiss," I said.

"Okay, sir."

I wrinkled my snout, but kept my eyes forward, hoping to spot the end of the forest. "Yentiss?" I said then.

"My father was a pilot for the Empire," she said. "He wanted my older brother Rezel to be one too." She looked my direction. "But he lost a leg. So here I am."

"Did *you* want to be a pilot?"

She shrugged. "Rezel would've been better. He was great on simulators."

"But he was injured."

She nodded. "Bit by a trenken. On the way back from town..." She held up both hands. "They're two headed, those trenken. Easy to get bit. Except..."

"Except what?"

"They only lived in one small pond near our home, and Rezel knew it." She drug a hand over a tree's trunk as we passed.

"So why was he there?"

She shrugged again. Said nothing. Continued walking.

"He got bit on purpose?" Krate said.

I frowned and gripped the stunner tightly.

Yentiss turned so I could glimpse her eyes. "I think he wanted an excuse to stay home."

Some muto were like that, I knew. Afraid of space, even though the Empire had conquered it. Or just as likely afraid of the creatures that filled it up.

"So here I am," she repeated.

I snorted. I'd lived my life around mental irregularities. Worked for some of them. Often worked around them.

Apparently, she had too.

CHAPTER 8

The trees thinned out ahead of us twenty minutes later. Most of what was visible beyond was solid grey, though.

"Water," Yentiss said. "We walked straight toward water."

We stepped free of the forest onto a gentle grass-covered slope. The body of water ahead was small—its far side clearly visible—so it wasn't the northernly sea that had earlier been a concern. It wasn't that unlike a pond I'd grown up near. That water had had summer contests around it and fish to be caught. Plus, it had been predator-free. Hopefully, this one was too.

"Should've thought of this," I said. "The other rear team will probably run into it too." I looked north, and noticed, maybe five hundred meters away, three robed figures exiting the woods. I assumed that was the others, but they were distant enough that I couldn't be certain. Nor could I really tell which way they were looking. I waved anyway, and pointed more to the north, hoping they'd understand it to mean they should head that direction. One waved back before they turned and walked away.

"What now?" Krate said.

Near the shoreline to our right was a cluster of buildings. "Head toward those, I guess." I pointed. "See what we can find."

"Toward the water?" Yentiss asked.

"We'll be fine." I held up my right hand. "We have stunners." I was more worried about the umans, frankly. I figured there couldn't be any predators too large around or the umans wouldn't be living here.

On my home world, we were more likely to get eaten in a forest than a lake.

I led the way to the buildings. There were three structures, the largest being in the center. All looked completely dark. Part of me *hoped* they were abandoned. The other part knew that abandoned buildings rarely had food. And we needed lots of it. Soon.

Another ten minutes brought us to the shadow of the large building. It was made of light stone and had a dark, wooden roof. Wood boards in the shape of an "x" ran all the way around the top portion. I wasn't sure if those were for support or decoration. Otherwise, the wall appeared seamless. Not even a window to peer through.

"Smells bad here," Krate said. "Smells real bad."

I scurried ahead and placed a hand on the building's exterior. It felt cool and moist. "Cheese smells bad," I whispered. "Maybe it's full of them." I forced a smile. "Maybe we got lucky."

Krate tapped the side of the building. "How do we get in?"

"Not on this side." With a wave, I led them to the corner on our left, and peeked around it.

No door on that side either.

I could see an entrance to a nearby smaller building, though. Its front faced the large building and there was a series of steps leading to its front door. Was that the primary residence? I had no idea. The only uman planets I'd been on were either domed, fully automated, or had lots of towers. The captain clearly hadn't thought this through.

I decided to stick with the larger building. After another check of the small building's entrance and a sweep of the grassy area between buildings, I crept along the wall to what I hoped was the large building's front.

I was pleased to see a door in the wall's center. I waved at the others again and crept to the entrance. The door was about twice my height and three or four times my width. I searched for a control mechanism but didn't find any.

"How does it open?" Yentiss whispered.

I poked the door and felt it rock slightly. It was affixed at the top...and possibly nowhere else. "I think it slides to the side." I checked the smaller building again before waving at Krate and pointing to the door. "The edge there, push that."

Krate complied, applying his weight to the door's edge. There was a heavy squeak, and the door started to move. A few seconds later, the building's interior stood before us.

Krate snorted and grabbed at his nose. "Smells worse now."

Yentiss removed her hood. "Yes, what is—?"

A low moan came from somewhere inside.

Yentiss scurried behind me. "That sounded dangerous."

There was another sound. This time, a higher-pitched squeal.

With a glance over my shoulder, I slowly stepped forward.

"I don't think you should go in there, sir," Yentiss said.

I made a shushing motion and took another step. "I want to check this out." There were more rumbles and moans, but no movement that I could detect. The interior was dark, but I could see where it had been subdivided into small sections. Possibly containment units of some sort. There was no sign of food, but there was much I couldn't see.

The door squeaked again, and I looked back. My team-mates had shut me inside.

"Cowards," I growled to myself.

And something inside answered.

Now I felt a little fear myself, but I bridled it with irritation. "Get in here," I hissed.

More rumbles and bleats from inside. Steeling myself, I walked toward a row of subdivisions.

The front door moved again slightly. Enough for Yentiss to push her snout through. "Sir?" she said. "Sedric?"

I waved her in. "You two shouldn't be standing out there."

I reached one of the subdivisions and peered inside. A large white-and-black animal lay on a bed of grassy material. The subdivision generally smelled like fecal matter, but there was a hint of the wood and field matter in there too.

The others came up behind me. "Is that a predator?" Yentiss asked.

The animal lowed and lurched heavily. Yentiss darted behind me again, but Krate—insufferable Krate—

No sooner had the black and white creature reached its feet, then I heard a clicking sound behind my right ear and saw a stunner's whirlpool-like blast.

The creature, clearly a domesticated servant animal of some sort, let out a clipped moan and slumped heavily to the floor.

Other animals got restless then, lowing and snorting. Stomping their feet.

I spun on Krate. "What were you thinking?"

Krate gestured toward the animal. "It was attacking."

I swatted Krate's snout.

He bellowed, hissed, and lunged for me. His eyes were tightly shut from pain, though, so his attack went wide. There was a heavy "thump" as he hit the front of the animal's stall.

Yentiss yelped.

I pointed my stunner at Krate. Shook my head.

Krate turned my direction, still looking hurt.

"There's room enough in that stall for two," I said.

He massaged his snout. "Why'd you hit me?"

"Because you're dumb," I said. "I have half a mind to take that stunner from you."

"What?"

I pointed at the fallen animal. "If you'd shoot that thing there, what's to keep you from shooting one of us?"

Krate glanced at the animal, grunted, and shook his head. "I was only trying to protect you."

I lowered my weapon hand. I doubted Krate was that loyal, but it sounded good. Especially coming from him. "Well...think longer next time."

Arms crossed, Yentiss walked slowly toward the stall. "You say it's livestock?"

"Sure..." I pointed at the creature's underbelly. It was pink and bloated with four large teats. "See the mammary glands? This one is a milk producer. Like a dokul, or an entier."

"So it's—"

"Right. Means it's where the *cheese* comes from too." I looked at Krate and frowned. "And you just shot it."

"It will be alright," he mumbled. "It's just stunned."

As if in agreement, the creature started to snore, seeming peaceful.

"Don't shoot unless you ask next time." I nodded at the creature. "Still, if they've got milk, they probably have cheese around here somewhere." I circled the interior of the building slowly. I spotted a couple animals like the one Krate shot, but also representatives of other species too. Some longer and taller. Others smaller, with heavier fur.

Hard to know what they all were used for. Maybe to eat. Maybe for other things.

I returned to the first stall again. "No cheese in this building, though. Nothing but animals here."

"Hot," Krate said, tossing his hood back. "Too hot and too smelly."

That got me thinking. I smiled at Krate. "Good observation, mate."

Krate scratched the back of his neck, looking puzzled. "What?"

I made a sweeping gesture. "It's too hot in here for cheese. It needs cooler temperatures."

"So where?" Yentiss said. "The smaller buildings?"

I frowned. "Maybe."

"Where do umans sleep?" Krate asked.

I walked to the door. It was partially open now, with only enough space to squeeze through. I peered out. "In those same buildings, I'd guess."

"They sleep with the cheese?" Krate said.

"Not with it." I scowled and ran my right thumb over the stunner's surface. How heavy would Krate be, really?

Yentiss stepped closer to me and looked outside too. "They store it near them, though. How do they keep it cool?"

"Are they sophisticated enough for cooling units?"

"I don't think so." Yentiss held up a paw. "Listen."

I listened for a full ten seconds but heard nothing aside from the infrequent chirps of nocturnal insects. "What am I listening for?"

She snickered. "No hums. No pounding repetition. All quiet everywhere, Sedric."

I gave her a questioning look. "So?"

"No machines."

I listened again. Sure enough, nothing sounded even remotely like an engine. "So, no cooling units."

"Right. They may not even have ice. At least, not unless there's a way to form it naturally."

I tipped my snout knowingly. The buildings had been a clue, as had the lack of air and space travel. This place, this world, was more primitive than we'd expected.

"No cheese!" Krate said, loud enough I startled and hissed.

"Not no cheese," Yentiss said. "Just not the sort of storage we'd use. Nothing mechanical. Passive systems would work. Airflow or..." She nudged the door further open, and nestling up next to me, stared out. She focused on the other two buildings. "Underground, I think. Below the buildings."

I flicked my tail. "Of course. Cellars! I should've thought of that."

There was a long moan behind us followed by the rustling sound of heavy movement.

"See, that animal is alive." Krate smiled and pointed at the first stall. "It's standing."

I nodded, slightly irritated.

The animal snorted a few times and started to bellow. Soon other animals, doubtless woken from their slumber, joined in. Before long we had a bellowing chorus.

"We can't stay here!" I slid through the door opening and looked around. Directly ahead, beyond a stand of trees and a hundred meters of open field was the body of water. To my left was the smaller building we'd seen earlier. To the right and set back slightly was the third building.

As the chorus of bellows continued, a light came on in the building to the left. With a wave, I darted across the clearing to the rightmost building, and sheltered around its back side.

The others huddled with me a few seconds later. I kept an eye on the lit building.

"We should go back to the ship," Yentiss whispered. "I think we should go back."

"We don't have any cheese," Krate said. "I'm hungry."

I hushed them to silence. A few seconds later, a lone uman

exited the far building. It was dressed in snug, dark leggings and a white shirt and had a light in one hand. The other hand held a long black stick.

A weapon?

What sort of weapon would umans of this planet use? Nothing that threw energy or light. Passive systems. Maybe something that threw rocks or wood. Maybe even metal.

I grunted. I didn't like the looks of it, regardless.

"What's it doing?" Krate asked, using a surprisingly gentle voice. "Is it coming this way?"

I ignored him, focusing instead on the uman. It took about twenty steps toward the livestock building, then paused as another higher-pitched voice called from the dwelling. The armed uman gave a curt answer and waved the stick.

The high-pitched call was meaningless to my translator-enabled ears. I figured it for a name or salutation. The uman's response, though, translated as "I'm fine" and "don't worry."

I suspected the two had a family arrangement. Either sire-bonding or parent and offspring. The one inside was worried. Maybe because it was nighttime, maybe because it had young umans to care for. Or maybe because the armed one was mis-dressed. I had no idea.

The armed uman resumed its trek to the livestock struc-ture. It halted at the door, seemingly surprised.

I looked at Krate. "Did you shut the door?"

"Don't remember."

I hissed softly.

The uman slowly widened the door's opening, and leading with its light, checked inside. After a few seconds, it stepped completely within, out of view. I took that moment to study the building it had left. Did anything there indicate a storage level for cheese? A passive, underground cellar?

There was a percolating, frenetic noise from the building beside me. The sound of multiple animals—avians, I guessed—

disturbed and possibly distressed. I turned and saw only Yentiss. She pointed toward the part of the building that was out-of-view.

What now?

A second later, Krate strode around the corner. Cupped in one hand, was a small, white oval. "They have eggs," he whispered as he drew close. "Those birds in there. We could—"

I slapped his nose again.

He dropped the egg.

Next came a clap of thunder followed by an uman shout. Though I was no longer looking that direction, I had a fair idea what the source of both sounds was: the uman had heard Krate and responded.

Yentiss and Krate stared at me, eyes wide.

There were more thunderclaps and the sound of scurrying feet.

We had only one option now: Run.

CHAPTER 9

I'm not sure how long or how far we ran. I only know that our disguises were a detriment, and nearly got me caught. It was the leg coverings! Sure the extra material hid the rhat nature of our lower extremities, but it also severely limited the speed at which one could travel.

After twenty steps on hind legs, I pitched headlong into a bush that grew in the middle of an otherwise empty field. This bush had thorns that tangled and bit—especially into my lightly colored costume. I struggled, but only got myself more entangled.

If it wasn't for the night's darkness, and the fact that Yentiss sprang to action freeing me, I might have been discovered. Or been shot full of whatever substance that the uman's thunderstick threw.

Yet, though I was sure the uman saw something move—and the duet of thunderclaps that we heard cemented my certainty—I doubted he knew what. To him, we were no more than desperate shadows. Either uman thieves or nocturnal predators. Night creatures that had disturbed his livestock and taken eggs from his fowl coop.

Emperor-be-praised, Yentiss got me free before the uman was in range. She deftly plucked one thorn after another from my frilly longshirt as I rolled away from the bush to the ground. From there, we did our hampered best to get as far away as a muto could. Another downside of the clothes: We were limited to upright motion. No four-limbed scampering.

Unfortunately, Krate hadn't paused a stride since the first shot, and now was far ahead of us. His path was sporadic and difficult to discern, as it seemingly zigged and zagged across the terrain. At one point he'd made a sharp right turn near a stand of trees before suddenly twisting left and traveling at an angle toward the still-distant water. If it weren't for a good sense of smell and bounding ability, I wouldn't have been able to follow him.

Some mutos should never lead.

Finally, leaned over a large rock and breathing heavily, we reached him. His robe was hiked up to his belly, exposing his lower half.

"You're uncovered," I said, checking the area around us. Only a mixture of trees and tall grass. No umans that I could see, though that didn't mean they weren't there.

Krate took a series of deep breaths and waved at his feet. "Makes running easier."

I glanced at my own legs, which were both feeling a bit chaffed from my gown. Why hadn't I thought of that?

I rubbed my paws together. Both felt damp from exertion, as did my tail. I contemplated rubbing the latter's dampness off on my gown, but since blood tends to travel in muto tail sweat, I decided against it. Instead, I tucked my tail around my right leg.

"What now, Sedric?" Yentiss asked. She didn't say "sir"

but I didn't mind. I liked the way she said my name. Seemed more respectful than the title.

"I wonder how the others are doing?" I wasn't sure how many planetary hours had passed since the ship, but my internal clock said over three standard. Plenty of night left.

Yentiss shook her head. "Hopefully better than us."

I nodded slowly and blew the edge of my head covering from my eyes. "We can't come back empty handed."

"Maybe we can take one of the livestock," Krate said. "Make our own cheese."

I chuckled, despite my irritation. Three hours wasted.

I scanned the horizon again. To the south was a larger cluster of buildings. Too many for it to be a single homestead like we'd just left. More buildings meant more chances for food. And, hopefully, more storage cellars. I flipped my snout that way. "Over there, I think. See what we can find."

After a few minutes rest, we started toward the village. Unlike the homestead, this group of buildings had some sort of external lighting. That could complicate things. We'd have to rely on our disguises to keep us hidden, and given we'd just run a kilometer or two, I wasn't certain that was a safe bet.

Still, we needed to find something. Or at least come up with a plan on how to find something.

There were about twelve buildings in the cluster. The lighting was concentrated in only a few places along a primary street. We stuck to the unlit portions. The buildings were a mixture of single story and double story. All had the same stone-and-wood exteriors as the dwelling with the livestock. There was livestock here too. I could smell it.

I noticed uman writing as we scouted the outskirts of the village, on rectangular signs and the sides of buildings. My translator was no help with those. The strings of characters could've been royal edicts or the babbling of a lunatic. I had no idea.

There's something the ship's scientists should have been working on: Ingestible translators that can read. Much more useful than shimmer suits or guns that blow holes in the ship.

I'd never use such a translator, or course, even if it worked for others. Not if it was one of Dontel and Uzel's creations. No telling what the side effects could be. Might grow a second tail or lose your whiskers.

I led the others to the rear of a building near the village's center. Minus any of the royal dwellings that we'd initially been drawn to, the largest building seemed the best choice. It also smelled the best. Like it might house an eatery during the day.

There was a wooden fence surrounding an area behind the building. It had words written on it that I stared at a moment before shrugging and looking for a way inside. I found a gate and a simple metal mechanism that kept it shut. With a little jiggling, I got it open and we went inside.

The smell of food was stronger now. Intense enough that my stomach rumbled.

Krate sniffed loudly. "What is this place?"

The back of the building had a single door and no windows. Near the door was a large, square container, roughly a meter and a half high and three meters long. There were also a couple cables strung from the structure to a two-meter high cross to my left. Square pieces of cloth were laid across the cables, along with items of clothing like my own. All fluttered lightly in the night's breeze.

The cross and cables made me nervous. "What are those?" I asked, pointing.

"Not sure," Yentiss said. "Want me to investigate?"

I waved and moved closer to the nearest cable. The clothing looked damp, but I didn't dare touch it. "Could it be some form of security system?" I pointed to the hanging gowns nearer the building. "Did those have umans in them?"

Yentiss shot me a confused look. "What?"

"You know...walking along, touched the lines, and *pfft!* Disintegrated!"

"Disintegrated?" Yentiss snickered. "And left the clothes?"

"I don't know their technology."

"No machines, Sedric, remember?"

Krate pulled back his hood and leaned forward, looking. "Are you sure?"

"I studied lots of images," Yentiss said. "Spent hours at it before we landed. Didn't see anything that looked like a machine."

"Umans are sneaky," Krate said. "Like the Silents, always sneaking and poking. Messing things up."

"Silents" were a group of covert umans that often interacted with our people. Many of the umans found on rhat planets were employed by the Silent Company. They were one reason the captain kept a rhat-only crew. Didn't want to risk prying uman eyes...or their hands taking his spoils.

At times, they could be useful, though. Especially when dealing with other umans. "Silents might help us here," I whispered.

Krate shot me an angry look. "There's no good time for Silents." His breathing was heavy, and his fists clenched. Even his scent had discomfort mixed in.

I wasn't sure what upset him, but it could've been anything. Torture, extortion, kidnapping—Silent Company wasn't known for being subtle. Or merciful.

"Sorry," I said. "Didn't know they were an issue."

"No Silents," Krate repeated.

I returned my attention to our surroundings. Despite the mysterious cables and the bounding fence, I had a good feeling about this building. There was food there, I just knew it.

Krate took another long sniff and drifted toward the rear

entrance. I hissed at him, but Yentiss touched my elbow. "I think he'll be all right."

I grunted, but waited, content to watch where Krate's nose led him.

The larger rhat stopped a few steps short of the back door and turned instead to the square container there. His snout went over the side, and a second later, his paws followed.

I hissed his name, worried.

Krate brought his arms over his head triumphantly. He was holding...something.

I waved a hand, hoping he wouldn't shout, and hustled forward. Yentiss followed.

Krate held out his find. It had a triangular shape and was light in color. "Cheese!" he said, smiling. "Rich, lovely cheese."

"Are you sure?" I said, but the scent was unmistakable. It was cheese, and the good stuff. Fit for a king.

I peered into the container. It didn't look like a cheese hamper. There were all sorts of irregular objects inside, along with soiled cloths and other food stuffs. There were flying insects too. Black, buzzing creatures.

I noticed more movement inside and leaned closer. "What is...?" It was a small animal. A mammal because it had fur like us. It also had a tail and a familiar shape. "Is that a rhat?"

"Where?" Yentiss scanned the area. "You mean, from the ship?

"No." I directed my snout into the container. "In there!"

She peered over the edge and gasped. "Do you need help?" she asked the creature. "Are you caught?" She slid along the containers edge and pointed. "Oh look, there's another one. Miniature mutos."

Krate shook his cheese again. "I found cheese, everyone."

"Did you not see them in there?" Yentiss asked him.

Krate shrugged. "They're small."

Yentiss tried to engage the small creatures again, but they didn't respond. "Are they deaf?" she asked.

I studied the mammals as they scurried amid the container's contents. One found a bone and started gnawing on one end. "I think they're primitives," I said. "Dumb beasts."

"That can't be, can it?" Yentiss watched the creatures for a moment before sighing. "Maybe...so, the vermin here looks like us? Like small versions of us?"

There was the sound of loud chewing. Krate's "lovely cheese" was significantly smaller now. He smiled and shrugged. "It's good."

Yentiss pulled her robe tighter. "It's a little disturbing. Miniature mutos." She looked warily at the buildings around us. "What if the umans see us? What we really look like?"

"Let's make sure they don't." I noticed a new feature on the building then. Another door, below ground level. I felt a glimmer of hope. "Cellar?" I said, indicating the door.

Yentiss moved forward to look. "Could be."

"More cheese?" Krate finished his find and patted his stomach. "I need more."

"We need to take some back, Krate. And soon."

"Right, boss."

I scowled and walked to the below ground door. It had a single handle and no lock. I gave it a tug and produced a low, scrapping sound. I looked at the others.

"That may not be wise," Yentiss said.

"What choice do we have?"

She shrugged.

I listened for the sound of movement. Any indication that a uman had heard. Not detecting any, I gripped the handle again, determined to open it as quickly as possible. I steeled myself and gave it a big pull.

There was a clipped groan and the door swung free. Beyond it was a short flight of stairs and a room that stretched back out of sight. Perhaps the length of the building. There was the smell of dampness and decay. But there were other smells too. Promising aromas.

I gripped my stunner. "I'm going in."

"We'll come with you," Yentiss said.

"Yeah, boss, if—"

I waved them back. "Just be ready to run."

I raised my stunner hand and crept down the stairs. The scents intensified, as did my nervousness.

The cellar was filled with wooden shelving. The shelves nearest the stairs had an array of odd-shaped objects—ovals and long triangles. I moved closer and took a couple hearty sniffs. The objects were tubers of some sort. Roots the umans used somehow. I took a bite out of a white one, but immediately spit it out. It hurt my tongue; it was so bitter.

The next shelf had circular cutouts in which glass cylinders had been laid. I picked one of the cylinders up. It had liquid in it. A beverage, I guessed. Possibly inebriating.

Appropriate for our clients?

It very well might be. I smiled. It was something.

The next shelf had inedible things: Folded cloths, crates of miscellany, and stacks of flat, round objects that were probably plates. Nothing our clients would care about.

The fourth shelf made my stomach ache and my mouth water. It was filled, floor to ceiling and end to end, with cheese. All kinds, according to my eyes and nose. Oranges and whites, sharps and milds, wheels and loafs. It gave me hope.

We could take all of it, I thought, along with the spirits. Fill our bags, return to the ship, and come back again. There were doubtless other cellars nearby. We'd need a lot of them, but...it was a start.

CHAPTER 10

A side from the cellar we discovered, four more cheese reserves were located by other teams. Two to the east of the forest, one to the south, and another to the west.

More importantly, everyone managed to stay concealed. Our beloved scientists took full credit for that result, claiming their "period accurate" costumes had performed as conceived. They also analyzed the samples the teams had recovered—including the drink my team had found—and ruled them of excellent quality. If we managed to fill our hold with similar products, we'd more than fulfill our contract.

No scouting mission is ever flawless, of course. Put any rhat mischief in unfamiliar surroundings and someone will bang their snout on a tree, step into an unforeseen hole, or encounter a vicious animal. This mission was no exception. Thankfully, none of the injuries required more than a few bandages and the touch of a pain reducer.

The fact that there were *any* injuries made the captain nervous, though. The shadow of the Teril Massacre was ever present.

In that case, a stranded muto ship had been discovered by a primitive indigenous society. Initial meetings were peaceful, with gifts exchanged along with other pleasantries. But some unrecorded event had soured the relationship. The mutos were attacked, their ship destroyed, and their lives lost.

The only evidence a search team later discovered was scattered remnants of the ship, a fragmented account of what had happened, and the skins of the muto crew—sold as blankets in a nearby town.

We had defenses, sure. But what's one ship against a world of potential antagonists? The only creatures similar to us were in a garbage bin, after all, fighting over food scraps and old bones. How harsh did the umans here have to be for that to be the case? Our genetic brethren repressed to the point of barbarism!

So to be cautious, we sent out fewer teams for the second round of scouting. I took Yentiss and Krate again. They had performed adequately the first time, so I saw no need to change.

Together, we returned to our treasure cellar. This time, we brought along a hovering, yet silent, mobile cart and concealed it in the grass outside the village. We had only three hours before sunrise. We wanted to get as much loaded as we could.

The plan worked perfectly to the point that, after an hour's loading, we'd nearly looted the cellar. It was here I reached a decision point. With a cart only half full and a couple hours to go I thought it best to separate. I was certain there were other cellars nearby. Maybe not as stocked as this one, but it was worth exploring. We had a deadline, after all.

So, I sent Yentiss and Krate to look while I finished the cellar alone. There was only half a row of cheese to move—maybe twenty wheels. Following Krate's earlier example, I'd tied my gown such that it went between my legs and wrapped tight around them. It functioned similarly, I thought, to the pants I'd seen umans wear. It was certainly more functional.

During my fourth loading trip, while I was nestled deep inside the room, and stooped low as to get cheese from a bottom shelf, I heard a throat clear behind me.

"Mademoiselle?" a voice said, which to my translator-enabled ears came out as "Miss?"

I wasn't sure how to proceed. I wasn't going to turn and reveal myself to whomever was speaking. But I also wasn't sure the voice was directed at me. Was there a female in the cellar too? Someone who'd quietly snuck in while I was hefting cheese into my bag?

I decided to say nothing. I held my position, and my breath.

"Can you hear me, Miss?"

The voice was lower in register, so I assumed it belonged to an uman male. This voice had another subtle quality, though. A lightness that made me suspect youth. So, a younger uman male, but not so young as to be a pup.

"You're not hiding from me in the dark," he said. "Come out, please. Come on."

He took a couple steps my direction and gasped. "Sacré bleu, where's all the cheese?"

Three things became clear to me then. First, the uman thought me a uman too. Second, he thought me a thief, which I clearly was. And third, he thought me female.

That last bit was a surprise, but it shouldn't have been. Not when the scientists had designed the insipid costumes. They'd given me woman's clothing and either not let on, or not known. I cursed them under my breath.

"See here, Miss. This can't stand. You need to come away this instant. Show me where you've taken my master's supplies, and then we'll go to the constable."

This young man was a servant, I guessed. Doubtless up early to help prepare the day's meals.

And he'd discovered me, a disguised muto from another planet, stealing from his master's cellar. There was a joke in there somewhere, but my panicked mind couldn't find it.

I rose slowly, preparing to run.

Another gasp. "Dear woman, what's wrong with your legs? Your hair is thicker than my own!"

I remembered my gown, how I'd hiked and tied it so I could move. I swore and quickly undid the knot, letting the gown fall over my feet. Much too late, of course.

The man drew closer and laid a hand on my shoulder. It was the worst position I could possibly be in. Cornered underground by a strange and suspicious uman. How long before he became hostile? How long before he called for help?

I'd been quick in my younger years, able to outdistance my siblings. (A notable accomplishment when you're the youngest of twelve.) But I hadn't put that swiftness to use in quite some time. And I'd never tested it with a female gown draped around my ankles.

Another mistake: I should've left the gown knotted.

"Let's be out with you." The man tugged the back of my gown. "Turn around. Come on."

I sighed and slowly turned my head.

The man's eyes narrowed before widening so large I thought they might pop free of his head.

"What in God's name? What are—?"

I ducked right, pulling myself clear of his reach and darted past him. I put some distance between us, even making it to the aisle's end where I could glimpse the doorway of freedom. Then my gown—our scientists' handiwork—caught a foot and pitched me over onto the ground. I landed in a heap, legs akimbo, back against a wall.

He scrambled up on me. Towered over me.

Umans are incessantly tall. Even primitive ones.

He was dressed in dark pants and a short, light shirt. His

hair was brown, and he showed neither the greying nor wrinkles of age. Just as his voice had suggested.

"Are you the Beast!" he said. "The one of Gévaudan?"

What an odd question. "Beast" could be a dangerous predator, but perhaps not. "Gévaudan" defied translation. A proper name, I assumed.

He positioned himself between me and the door.

I wasn't thinking clearly. I only wanted to get away. "Would it help if I was?" I said. "This Beast. Would you let him go?"

He startled. "Mon Dieu!" He crossed a hand over his chest before touching his forehead. A gesture of some sort.

"I take it the Beast doesn't talk," I said.

He answered with something that didn't translate. Profanity, I guessed.

I tipped my snout. "I feel the same way, uman. A whole bag of whatever you said."

I started to stand, but he waved a hand. "Stay there, demon." He plucked something from the shelf to his left, then showed me a long-handled knife with a rounded blade.

Things had gotten worse.

"Are you with the foreigners?" he said. "A bewitchment meant to deceive the Emperor's forces?"

The fur on my neck bristled. "Emperor?" I said. "How do you know him?"

"His forces gather to the south," he said. "Master says they will soon—" His eyes widened, and the knife fell from his hand.

"Uman?"

He slumped slowly forward. Toward me.

"Uman, what—?" I raised my paws and somehow slowed his fall. He was now on top of me, though I wasn't crushed. Wasn't hurt.

Nor, it appeared, was he.

My mind raced. Were fainting spells normal here? He didn't feel dead. He was breathing. I could smell his breath, in fact.

With a grunt, I attempted to push him off. To shove him—

"Sedric?"

The uman's bulk was pulled away and I felt air on my face. I saw my teammates standing over me.

Krate's paw was extended such that I could see the stunner's barrel peeking out between his fingers.

"You shot *him* too?" I said.

Krate shrugged and offered me his paw. "He had a knife. You were in danger."

Waving the paw away, I climbed to my feet. "Give me your stunner," I hissed.

Krate looked hurt. "But, I only—"

I made my stunner paw obvious. "Give it."

He handed the weapon over. I grunted and turned to study the uman, now propped against a shelf. He looked fine—fast asleep—but he was a serious complication now. "What do we do with him?"

"Do?" Yentiss said from inside her hood. "All we need do is go. Get back to the ship before anyone sees."

Krate nodded. "The village is waking. More lights are on."

I smoothed my gown over my legs. Dusted off my paws. "Seems wrong to kill him," I said. "I mean, I don't think he would've hurt me."

"He had a knife."

"Yeah, but he doesn't seem the type." I retrieved the knife from the ground. There was a trace of something on the sharpened edge. A single sniff revealed what it was. "This is a cheese knife." I tested the blade's edge. "And not a very sharp one."

"We should just leave him," Yentiss said. "Get our cheese and—"

"But he's *seen* me," I said. "Which means when he wakes up, he'll tell someone."

"They'll think he's crazy," Krate said. "Rhats here aren't this big."

"And they don't wear clothes," Yentiss added, patting her robe.

I looked at my gown again. My female gown. "Still...he thought I was something specific. The Beast of Gévaudan." I looked at Yentiss. "Know what that is?"

She shook her head.

"Might be something they'd look for," I said. "Hunt for." Leaving him seemed like too big of a decision for an XO to make. "He talked about the Emperor too. That's strange, right?"

"They know about the Emperor?" Krate said.

Yentiss took a step forward. Beyond her, I could glimpse the sky outside. It had lightened considerably. We needed to decide something. *Do* something.

I remembered our half-full hovercart.

"We'll take him with us!" I said.

Yentiss's snout wrinkled. "What?"

"Cart's only half full," I said. "We'll load him on it and take him back. Let the captain decide."

"Are you serious?"

"Yeah." I remembered my bag of cheese and walked up the aisle to get it. I couldn't resist grabbing another cheese round for my trouble and stuffing that into my already bulging bag. With the bag over my shoulder, I returned to the others.

"You want us to carry him?" Yentiss asked, still sounding incredulous.

"Can you?" I lifted the shoulder holding the bag. "Thing's full."

Yentiss sneered, but together, she and Krate got the uman up and positioned between them, with Yentiss holding the feet.

She didn't look too uncomfortable. I guessed Krate was doing most of the lifting. He probably could've carried the uman by himself—and perhaps he should've. But, Yentiss was the type that was better off busy. A gut call that worked out fine.

Ten minutes later the cart was filled with uman and delicacies, and we were back on our way. As we reached the boundary of the forest, I heard a series of pops and cracks to the south. The trees obscured the source, but I guessed it was an electrical storm. The collision of pressure and light.

CHAPTER 11

The captain was outside when we arrived, which complicated my plan. I wanted to get the cart unloaded, get the contents counted and tested, and have an armful of good news to show him before I mentioned the uman. As it was, his fur was already half-bristled when we arrived. And his aroma? Galaxies, was it bitter and dry. I wasn't sure what all had happened while we were away, but it must not have been good.

Thankfully, his back was to us, as he stood facing the woods to the south. That gave me the opportunity to position myself and Yentiss in front of the cart, with Krate pushing from behind. Sure, it was only a few seconds of cover, but it was something. Enough to think of a new plan and rehearse the exact right words in my head.

The ship loomed as a large rectangular shadow overhead. Only the loading ramp's edge was lit, and even that was a soft blue. Barely noticeable. Invisible from any distance.

With whispered instructions, I directed our cart toward the lights. We almost reached them, in fact, before the captain turned, noticed us, and approached.

He pointed his snout toward the east. "We got more injuries. They stumbled across a pack of animals. Hungry, furry things." He leveled a paw near his waist. "Only about this high, but there were lots of them. Eight or nine." He shook his head. "Seemed to have a nose for the team. Lit right into them."

"Will they survive?" Yentiss asked.

"Doctor seems to think so. They got bites on their legs and arms." He shrugged. "Good they have fur, obviously. Partly protected them. I just hope the animals weren't poisonous." He glanced toward our cart, still obscured behind Yentiss and me. "What'd you find?"

I pointed to my bag, which was on the cart near Krate. He handed it forward with a grunt.

I showed the captain the bag's contents. "Lots of cheese," I said. "Cheese and intoxicants."

He nodded, seeming impressed. "Whole cart full?"

"Yep, full," Krate said. "Very full."

I shot Krate a look. He raised both paws defensively.

The bill of my bonnet blew in front of my eyes. I couldn't be tough in those clothes anymore. Thankfully, only the uman knew what sex they were made for. I glanced at him as I handed my bag back to Krate. He was still resting.

"Sedric?"

I tipped my snout to the captain. "Sir?"

"Something more you want to tell me?"

Yentiss shrugged. No help there.

And no delaying it either. "We brought back more than delicacies, sir." I pointed my thumb over my shoulder.

"Eh?" He took a step forward. "What more did you find?"

"A complication, sir. Something that requires your decision."

He walked closer, and leaning, stuck his snout between Yentiss and I. Then he swore. Loudly. "You brought a uman back?" he said. "Why would you do that?"

"He's asleep," I said.

"Was he awake when you found him?"

I nodded. "Krate stunned him."

"He had a knife," Krate muttered.

I sighed and shook my head.

The captain's paws returned to his hips. "So, he had you cornered?"

I could smell the captain's anger. And his fear. "Something like that, yeah. Snuck up on me. Got me in a tight place."

"And no other way but to bring him here?"

I glanced at the others, thinking. "Even if I got away, he'd already seen me. Called me a 'beast.'" I hit on something then that might lower the temperature. "Mentioned the Emperor too, which I thought strange. How would anyone here know about <u>him</u>?"

The captain clutched his snout. "That's strange, yeah." Curiosity slipped into his scent. "Think more mutos have visited? Maybe some of the Emperor's proselytes?

"Not sure. He said the Royal's forces were coming from the south?"

"The south! South of what?"

I shrugged. "I thought you might know."

The captain snorted. "Maybe you should've just ended him."

I gripped the cart's edge. "Couldn't find a reason to, sir. He's young. Somebody's servant. Just doing his job." My hat's bill drooped again, so I took the whole thing off. "Thought you should decide, captain." Felt wonderful to have my head free. And my conscience.

The captain thought a long moment. "No sense in killing him until we know what he knows. Can't have him running around either." He looked at the ship. "Seems a big risk to keep him, though. What if someone comes looking?"

"He could help find more cheese!" Yentiss offered.

The suggestion made me want to ask her to be my sire-mate right then and there. Whisk her away to some quiet planet near the galaxy's edge and have a whole mis—"

"Sedric?" she said, looking hopeful. "Wasn't that your thinking? The cheese?"

I was staring at her. And why wouldn't I? She was a genius, and she was striking. I pointed a finger. "That there, sir. That was our thinking. The uman could help with the scouting. He knows the scent of things here. The best delicacies, the easiest jobs. Could save us days. Weeks, even."

"Weeks!" Krate added.

The captain studied us each in turn, then glanced at the ship again. Snorted. "That might work, sure. Might be just the thing." He nodded. "Good thinking, Sedric."

The uman stirred on the cart behind me, groaning.

"He's waking up!" Krate said.

The captain indicated the blue ramp lights. "You should get him inside," he said. "Have the doctor check him over. Make sure he isn't infected with something."

I gave the cart a tug forward. "Ay, captain." Yentiss and Krate quickly joined me. Together we hovered the cart around the captain toward the bottom of the ramp.

"Infected?" Krate said. "I ate their food. We all did."

"Push," I said. "Come on."

"Notify security too," the captain said. "In case he's trouble."

I repeated my "Ay" and kept moving. I figured we could keep the uman in one of the containment cells for the time being. Rooms commonly used for drunks and unruly crewmates.

The uman groaned again. I waved at Krate and tossed him his stunner.

"What's this for?"

"In case you need to hit him again. You remember how to do that, right?"

"Yes, boss."

We started our way up the ramp. We'd either just made our best decision, or our worst.

CHAPTER 12

After we delivered the uman to the doctor and alerted security about his presence, I went to the storage bay. I was optimistic. Hopeful that the evening's gleanings had made a noticeable dent in the space we had to fill.

Yet, from my spot on the suspended platform, I could barely find the results of our work. No more than a small mound of circles and squares stacked neatly in the back corner of a huge empty space.

The bay's cooling systems were functioning, though. I could feel the frigidity as it rolled with the fog. It was like hovering above a block of ice. It not only chilled my body, it emptied my soul, making me realize how tired I was. With a closing glance and a halfhearted scowl, I left for my cabin.

This was the way I always approached sleep. Not from a set schedule, but from need. The needs of the ship first, and then the body. Slumber came when time allowed, or when I was too exhausted to function.

That night, hibernation gas wouldn't have made me sleep faster.

I awoke only when the room's com unit squawked. I patted my facial fur, rubbed my eyes, and slid a paw over my head and neck. Groaning, I climbed free of my sleep nook.

My cabin wasn't much of a space. Aside from the nook, there was only a small fold-up desk with a tail-ready chair, a private cleansing unit and a mounted-and-scented face brush. The room's colors were green and silver. I also had four times the closeted storage space of other crewmembers, save the captain. One of the few XO perks—plenty of room to store my things.

The com squawked again, and I stumbled my way to the desk and tapped the built-in com screen. It fuzzed and blurred, then the face of security official Cindel came into focus. He was one of three blue mutos on the ship and might've been the only one worth his pay. Thankfully, he was the head of his department.

"Sedric, sir?" he said.

I smoothed my cheek fur again. "Aye. What's the matter?"

"The uman has been yelling for the last hour, sir. Keeps talking about 'beasts' and other things my translator can't handle."

I nod. "Is he healthy? What did the doctor say?"

"Said he was operating at 'uman standard,' whatever that means."

I snorted and glanced at the cleansing unit door. I could really use a good wash. I smelled of the primitive planet's cellars and forests. "Did you tell the captain?" I asked.

"I did, sir. That's why I called you." The hint of a smile.

I sniffed. "He wants me to handle it."

"Yessir."

No surprise there. The uman's presence was my fault, after all. Hopefully, he could help us. Give us locations to check.

"I'll be right there."

"Thanks, sir. See you soon."

I switched off the com, and after a quick snout brushing, went to the containment cells on deck two.

Deck two was the least inviting floor on the ship. The halls were narrow and the color of soot. They also seemed to attract graffiti——despite a ship-wide ban on such expressions and my insistence that the cleaners check often. Always, there was a splash of color somewhere.

The decoration this time was just outside the lift. A caricature of our beloved Emperor dressed in an uman gown similar to the one I'd worn. The list of potential artists was limited to only a few dozen now, of course. Only those who were currently awake.

I didn't have the heart to pursue an investigation. Small seditions can serve as a relief valve in times of stress. Plus, the image of the Emperor in female clothing gave me a connection to the old royal rhat. The idea that no matter who you are, you never know enough. Never know what others are thinking.

The containment cells were a short walk to port from the lifts. As I approached, I saw Cindel seated outside of one, chair propped against the wall and arms crossed. The tip of his tail was stuck in his left ear.

I heard the uman's voice too. Yelling and yelling. No wonder Cindel had an ear plugged. Too bad he didn't have two tails.

Cindel noticed me, and returning his seat to the floor, stood, and saluted.

I returned the salute. Sighed.

"Thanks for coming." He motioned toward the door. "As you can hear he—"

"He's upset," I said. "Can't say I blame him. I'd be upset too if someone grabbed me from my hovel. Specially if they looked like 'beasts.'" The door had a circular viewport that was so smeared with grime I couldn't see anything except the room's yellow hue and a dark, moving figure.

Cindel smiled and saluted again.

I knocked on the door. "Uman!" That had no effect on the situation inside, so I knocked and called louder.

The yelling ceased, and after a short pause, I heard, "Who's there?"

"Um..." I glanced at Cindel, who shrugged. "I'm the master here. Can I come in?"

"Where am I?" he asked. "I remember terrible dreams. Hairy things that poked and prodded. Then I was in this...place. Can you let me out?"

This wasn't going to be easy. I leaned close to Cindel. "I'm going in to try to talk with him. Stay close to the door. Just in case."

Cindel nodded. "Of course, sir."

I knocked softly. "I only want to talk with you. Can we be friendly? Can you stay calm?" I had my stunner in my left hand, of course. I wasn't afraid, but I also wasn't stupid.

The uman was quiet for a full second. "I'm calm," he said then. "You can come in."

"Good," I said. "Please control yourself. I may look strange, but we've met already. We're friends."

More silence.

"Put your hands over your eyes, if it helps."

"No...I'm...I'm calm. I'll be fine."

"Okay. No one is going to hurt you. Especially not me." I reached for the door control. "I'm coming in now." I touched the switch. It flashed green and the door clicked open. I grabbed the door's handle and slowly slid it back.

The cell made my room look spacious. It was yellow with green highlights and had a small version of everything. Small sleep nook to the left, small, fixed seat and table, small rectangular waste and wash appliance in the back rightmost corner. The uman looked large within the room. Massive, even.

He was perched at the edge of the nook, hands gripping

the side. He didn't look panicked, but his eyes were wide. I was the figure of nightmares now, after all.

"What are you?" he asked slowly.

I managed the best interspecies smile I could muster. "You called me 'beast' once, but I blame that on the way I was dressed."

His eyes narrowed. "We've met?"

"Sure..." I waved a hand over my torso. "I had on a light-colored..."

He straightened with recognition. "You're the one in the dress? The thief?"

I bowed my head. "I am. I was stealing your cheese, in fact."

"Are you a rat then?"

The word "rat," didn't translate to the muto word for ourselves. It instead came out "vermin." I understood the reference, though. He thought I was one of those things in the garbage container.

And why wouldn't he?

I studied the ceiling reflectively. It was a brighter yellow than the rest of the room. "Well...yes and no. I'll agree there's a resemblance."

"You look exactly like a rat," he said. "Your feet, your hands..." He leaned forward and squinted. "Even your tail. All like a rat." He frowned. "I thought the beast was a wolf."

I raised my paws. "Listen, I'm not your beast. I don't know the beast. I am a muto. Name's Sedric."

"Sedric..." He studied me a moment, thinking. "Are you going to eat me?"

"Eat you?" I snorted. "Mutos don't eat umans. They're gristly and tough." I waved at the ceiling and door. "On this ship we avoid umans as much as possible."

His eyes widened. "Ship? Are we on the sea?"

I paused at my slip. How much to tell him? I knew from

the massacre of legend, that there were limits of exposure. A threshold of revelation that a primitive culture could endure before things got ugly.

We didn't have anyone with first contact experience aboard. No xenobiologist or archaeologist or whatever specialist was supposed to handle this kind of situation. Yentiss probably was as close as we could come. I for sure wanted to keep the scientists out of it.

"Not on the sea," I said. "Not right now."

That didn't seem to help. He still looked confused. "Where are we then?"

"We're...on a vessel, yes, but that's not important now. We have a mission. A goal."

His eyes widened. "Is this about the conflict then?" he said. "What side are you on?"

My time to look confused. "What conflict is that?"

"The latest one between the Emperor and the invaders."

"About that..." I wagged a finger. "How is it you know the Emperor?"

"Everyone knows the Emperor!" He raised his arms. "Vive l'Empereur, Vive la France, Vive l'Empire!"

I got "Emperor" and "Empire" out of that. I assumed it was a chant of some sort. Primitives were known for their chanting. "Kill the hairy evil!" was the chant that brought death in the massacre case. I wanted to avoid chants. And death.

But what about the conflict he mentioned? Was it a local thing? He couldn't mean the Empire's skirmishes with the sloth-like Jinn Khan or the arthropod Cho' Hraak, could he? We were far beyond those battle-lines.

I wanted to probe further, but again, there was that threshold issue. Better to remain coy. Reveal only what was necessary.

"Listen, we're not here about any conflicts, emperors, or empires. We only need food. Lots of food."

He leaned back. "Food?"

"Right. Preferably cheese, but we'll take cakes and other desserts." I held my paws about a half meter apart. "Even the liquid. The intoxicants in the fluted tubes?

"Fluted tubes?"

I cursed. "I should have brought some examples along." I tried to mimic the shape of the tubes and then bringing it to my lips as if to drink.

"Du vin?" he said.

"Maybe," I said. "Probably. Fermented fruit drink?"

He smiled. "Ah, yes, wine."

I smiled. We were making progress. "Yes, wine and cheese. We need a lot."

He stared at me, then clutching his midsection, giggled.

I studied him. "What's so funny, uman?"

Still laughing, he touched his chest. "I'm Louis," he said. "Please call me Louis. Not uman."

I nodded and said his name slowly.

He smiled. "Yes, you have it. Louis."

I was proud of myself. Who needs an xenobiologist? "Now, Louis, why did you laugh?"

He pointed at me. "Because you're a—"

"I'm not a beast."

"No, I meant 'rat.' And you're in search of cheese. That's funny, is it not?"

I tipped my head. "Why is that funny? Everyone needs food—umans, mutos, everyone. And cheese is good."

He laughed again, then raised a hand. "No offense, Sedric. For me, it is funny."

I suspected the joke had something to do with the garbage container vermin. Some association that wasn't obvious to offworlders like me. I generally didn't like jokes, but I had no choice here. I shrugged my annoyance away. Put on a smile.

"I want to go home, Sedric," Louis said.

I nodded sympathetically. "That's a bit of a problem. You see, my captain wants—"

He clapped his hands. "You said 'captain!' So, we <u>are</u> on a ship."

I hissed with annoyance. There was no doing this well. Xenobiologist or not. "Sure. If you want." I glanced at the door. I could see Cindel's shadow at the viewport. The glint of his right eye. I smiled and waved.

"Who's out there?" Louis asked.

"Security guard. Watching to make sure I'm okay."

"How many of you are there?" he asked. "On this *ship*."

"Only a handful that are active. The rest are—" I caught myself. I probably shouldn't tell him how many of us were in hibernation. I waved my tail. "It doesn't matter." I'd lost track of the conversation. I raised both paws, palms open. "Where were we?"

"You said I couldn't leave."

"Right. Not now anyway. The captain doesn't want umans knowing about us until we're done. And you might tell more umans."

His face whitened. "My master will miss me. As will my spouse."

<u>Spouse</u>? A sire-mate? An unexpected complication. I should've thought of that. Nothing is ever simple. "Can't be helped," I said. "You need to stay here for now. But—"

He surged to his feet. "I don't want to be here! I won't tell anyone. I swear on the Emperor's shoes!"

I waved my paws at him. "Now, hear me out—"

Cindel burst into the room, gun drawn. Louis shrieked and darted toward me. I raised my stunner, but he was behind me before I could fire. Remarkably fast for an uman.

I felt his arm around my neck. It was a good move—solid tactics. He may have been primitive, but he wasn't dumb. Might even have had some combat training.

He hadn't dealt with a muto before, though.

I wrapped my tail around his lower leg and yanked as hard as I could. I heard a gasp and felt the pressure on my neck ease. Next came a thump and a cry of surprise or pain.

Cindel covered me with his weapon. I waved him off and looked at the uman.

Louis's head was beneath the waste appliance, but otherwise he seemed fine. He cowered as if he thought I'd attack.

I smiled. "You forgot the tail," I said. "Umans always do."

He raised both hands and slowly sat up. "I'm sorry. I only—"

"Want to get home," I said. "I get that. But you can't for now. If you want to get the captain's favor, to get him on your side, you can help us find food."

He stared at me, eyes wide. "If I help you, you'll send me home?"

I raised a shoulder. "If we meet our quota, anything is possible."

He nodded, but still looked frightened. Doubtful. "I don't want to steal."

"You won't have to," I said. "Only tell us where to look. We'll do the rest."

"Can I think about it, Sedric?"

"Sure," I said. "But that's the best offer I can make. At least, for now. I'm sort of improvising here."

"I wasn't part of your plan?"

I snorted. "None of this was part of my plan. I'm reacting based on the information I have before me." I put out a paw to help him up. "Just like you did when you wandered into that cellar." I shook my paw, urging him to take it.

But he didn't take my help. It was too soon for that.

I shrugged, lowered the paw, and left.

I hoped he'd see straight to help us. I could always threaten him—try to scare him. But having been an executive officer for five years, I knew that those tactics had limited appeal. Sure, they'd work in the short-term. But long-term I'd have to watch my tail, because someone would want to slice it off, or use it to swing me out an airlock.

Better to be frank and as open as possible. If I could make the uman an ally, everything would be easier.

That's one thing the mission could've used more of: Easy. We needed a lot more easy.

Perhaps this was where it started.

CHAPTER 13

The next night's gathering added little to our food reserves. Sure, some delicacies were acquired, but it was piecemeal work. A bag here and a cart there. Not enough to meet our contract, and consequently, not enough to please the captain. He was in a particularly foul mood, in fact, partly due to the uman's refusal to help.

"He's nothing but baggage now, Sedric!" the captain said. "Another mouth on a ship that needs food!"

Another factor in his disposition was the cloaking cells. We'd been using them off and on since landing, primarily during the daylight hours when the chance of discovery was greater. Unfortunately, like much of the technology on the *Granum*, the cells were unreliable. Not only had their pull on the ship's resources increased, but their effectiveness had seemingly decreased.

The first indication was when local birds started nesting on the *Granum*'s exterior. They were detecting something—a solid object in an otherwise empty clearing—then flying in close, seeing the ship, and building upon it.

Four-legged mammals started to linger in the clearing, as well. They looked the ship's direction and moved their heads back and forth as if transfixed by a bright light. Some ventured toward the mirage and came right up to the ship. We even found creatures perched on our loading ramp—possibly aware of the foodstuffs that had passed that way. Or finding morsels that had been dropped or misplaced.

"We're creating a colony of beggars!" the captain cried. "Smelly, dirty vagrants."

The scientists were eager to look at the cloaking cells, of course, and so dropped every other experiment and project to focus on them. That made me nervous. A divided science team was a nuisance. A focused one? Dangerous.

Yentiss and I were on the bridge the third night of gathering. Given we'd been involved in bringing the "useless" uman aboard, the captain ordered us to remain on board. Instead, he had two sleepers woken to replace us outside, which—if the goal were to preserve resources—didn't make a lot of sense to me. But little on the *Granum* did.

The captain hadn't restricted Krate from gathering, though. Krate was too big and strong. Useful for when the search teams located the giant stash of cheese that would free us from this planet. And the captain's grouchiness.

I sulked in the command chair. My left paw ached again. Curiously, it only bothered me when I was on the bridge. I almost suspected that the pain was in my head now. That the stress of the bridge, the inherent wait for something new to fall on my head, was the root cause.

I would've asked the doctor about it, but I didn't much trust him either.

Yentiss was at her station, running diagnostics for the fourth time. The ship was as ready to go as ever. We had a dozen system warnings tied to components that had been "enhanced" over the years. Nothing dangerous, but also nothing that could be addressed without the scientists' help.

On the central screen was the view outside. Much of that view was obscured by a bird's nest—a raptor, by the looks of the creature's beak and claws—built within a forward sensor nook. The bird was within her nest, staring out at the forest. Occasionally she'd turn toward the sensor as if something about it bothered her. She even pecked at it a few times.

"Do you think it has an egg in there?" Yentiss asked.

"No idea," I said, scowling. "I hate birds."

"I think it's interesting," she said. "Watching life develop."

"You'd feel differently if we were beneath the sea." I pointed at the screen. "If that was a trenken out there spawning."

Yentiss glared at me. "Like the one that bit my brother, you mean?"

Alluding to the manner of her brother's loss was impulsive. Hurtful even. Our situation drug it out of me. "I was wrong," I admitted. "Unprofessional." Sighing, I straightened in my seat. "Be patient with me, diligent communicator. It won't happen again. "

She narrowed an eye, but after a moment, a smile appeared. "It better not."

I returned the smile.

The bird looked our way now. Beyond it was the darkness of the forest. I wanted to be where darkness, the infinite darkness of space, was around us again.

One of our teams was scouting a "royal" structure that night. A large stone complex that was a long walk from our hiding spot. I hoped it brought us a trove of cheese. We needed more cheese.

I stood and started toward the door.

"Where are you going?" Yentiss asked.

"I want to check on something," I said. I felt restless and confined.

Her snout curled downward in a pout. "Leaving me alone here?"

"Someone needs to..." I waved a paw at the screen. "...run diagnostics..."

"Sedric!"

I'll admit, Yentiss was growing on me. Dangerous business for someone in my position. Too much flirting and I'd find myself on a planet somewhere with a mischief large enough to crew a battleship. "Sorry, Yent. I have a—" I raised my left paw. "Sore paw. And I think it's telling me something."

"What?"

I shook my head. "Something is wrong about this place. We need to get done and leave."

She lifted a shoulder. "The captain has a knack for profit."

"I know. But right now, his knack is making my hand sore."

She turned to face me. "Do you need help?"

I raised both paws. "Just stay here, okay? I'm going to—"

The lights on the bridge flickered. Next, the bird squawked—and beating its wings furiously—shot into the sky.

The view beyond the nest was a lot clearer. Why? Because the tail-bent external lights were on. And not just the narrow spot beams, but the boundary floods that illuminated the ship's exterior.

"Those idiots!"

"Who?" Yentiss looked between me and the screen. "Oh..."

Every hair on my body was on edge. "The risk of those two messing with the cloaks." I wanted to gnaw Dontel's and Uzel's heads off, I was so mad.

With a parting wave, I stormed off the bridge. I didn't know where the scientists were, but I'd have their tails. They were messing with something somewhere that caused the externals to come on. Where might that be, exactly?

My first stop was the science deck, where I found Dontel wearing one of the shimmer suits. The suit had been modified, though, because he looked like a short *green* uman now. Except his feet. Those were still red.

He welcomed me with open arms. "Ah, Sedric. I have so much to show—"

"Where's Uzel?" I asked. It was strange hearing Dontel's voice come from a green and somewhat-hard-to-follow uman mouth. Uman features are so subtle and unappealing.

"Uzel? I believe he's working on—"

"I know what he's working on. *Where* is he working on it?"

He pointed toward the door. "Ah, deck four. The entrance to the cloaking array is there. Why do you—?"

"All I needed," I said, turning.

"But Sedric, I—"

I couldn't look at him anymore. I made a slicing motion with my tail, straightened my long shirt, and left.

Three minutes later, I stood outside an open access port along one of deck four's exterior hallways. It was about a meter square and at floor level, meaning I had to get down on all fours to peer inside. There was no doubt Uzel was in there because I could hear his voice—his singing voice—echo through the hole. It was bad enough to make me want to avoid the confrontation altogether.

I used a nearby wall-mounted communicator to contact Yentiss on the bridge.

Her eyes brightened when she saw me. "Sed—"

"Are the lights still on outside?"

She glanced upwards. "Yes."

I growled.

"Sedric?"

I shook my head. "That's all I need for now. Thanks." I hovered a finger over the com cutoff.

"Wait!"

"Yes?" I said, squinting at the screen.

"One of the teams came back. There's more umans, sir."

"More? Where?"

"Don't know the details. Only that there are more of them on board."

"What idiot—" I caught myself. If something had gotten stunned, Krate had to be involved.

The captain would lose his tail with anger.

One mess at a time. I needed to get the lights off first. "I'll look into it," I said, closing the line.

I banged on the wall above the access port. Uzel still sang through the tunnel beyond, and after ten attempts to reach him, it was clear he couldn't hear me. So, I entered the port.

Now, mutos are supposed to be comfortable in tight spaces, but I, for one, am not. Blame it on childhood trauma. I got stuck in the roots of a wexi tree once while chasing one of my siblings. I screamed for hours.

This wasn't a wexi tree, of course. I knew that. It was only a small access tunnel that led further into the steamy bowels of the *Granum*. What made it worse as I slunk my way toward the singing, was the fact that it was neither clean nor straight. Something on the floor crunched as I moved through it. Also, slender wires and cables dangled from overhead. Harm me? They wouldn't, no. But I didn't like the way they drug over my head and back. My tail perspired and my toes narrowed. My every move made me want to turn, shake myself, and bolt for the exit.

I attempted to calm my nerves by calling the scientists' name. "Uzel!" I shouted, over and over. After a half minute of crawling through eggshells and tentacles, his name grew harder to force through my chest. Like I didn't have the strength.

My anger at the scientist hadn't abated, but my reason for wanting to see him was less concrete. More about salvation than condemnation.

When I finally reached Uzel, I was nearly on my stomach. He was nestled into an alcove where all the wires and cables seemed to converge. There must've been a thousand wrapped around him. I couldn't see his head, he was so obscured.

"Uzel...," I squeaked out, and somehow managed to hit a lull in his song.

He grunted and the bundle of wires shifted to reveal his face. "Sedric? What are you doing on the floor?"

I pushed myself up on all fours. "I'm not. I'm simply—" I thumped the floor with my paws. "The lights are on!"

He searched the tunnel around us. "Lights?"

I sucked in a breath and pushed a little closer. "Outside! The lights *outside* are on!"

His eyes widened. "Well, that's not very good, is it? Someone could see us. Maybe Dontel should—"

"You!" I pointed at the wires around us. "Here!"

He scanned our surroundings again. "You know, there might be a..." He brought a paw to his snout. "Yes, most certainly there's a light conduit through here somewhere. Do you think—?"

"Fix it."

"Is that an order? Because he explicitly told us to—"

"Fix. It. Now."

He stared at me a moment. "You don't look so good, Sedric."

I raised my sore paw and pointed back the way I'd come. "I'm fine. I'm going out now. Get the lights off. Right now."

His eyes brightened. "Ah! I know where the problem is now." He reached into the nearest clump of cables, selected a single strand, and squinted at it. "Yes, this is compromised. And that would mean..." He grabbed a tool from the ground near him.

I didn't wait to see what happened. I merely turned and, as best I could, and started to slink my way out.

A few seconds later he called my name and said, "That should fix it!"

"Great," I said, though I wasn't sure he heard me. All I cared about was reaching the hallway before I passed out.

After that? The next problem.

CHAPTER 14

My next stop was at the medical bay where, according to Yentiss, the three umans were being checked over. The bay was a circular room with four evenly spaced examination nooks for patients and a smaller circle of machines and doctoring devices in the center. The full spectrum of diagnostic and treatment automations.

The *Granum*'s lone doctor—an aging yellow fur—stood near the machines, as did his competent, silver-furred nurse. Both wore green longshirts.

Also present were the members of the gathering team, of which, Krate was one. The other two were amber-furred midship-mutos named Feelix and Cantie. They were bright and generally hardworking. They should've more than compensated for Krate's blundering. But apparently, they hadn't. All three were in their robe disguises.

The umans occupied three of the examination nooks. Due to their height, they looked a little cramped, but that didn't matter. They were unconscious.

They were dressed alike—dark blue pants and coats with white straps that crossed over the center of their chest. On their shoulders were red, puffy devices that I guessed were decoration. Two of the three had large, black elongations on their heads. If I didn't know better, I would've thought those genetic defects.

The reason I knew better was because Krate held one elongation in his hand. What the purpose of such a thing was, I could only guess. But I'd seen a lot of strange decorations in the past. There was always a reason, though often it was no more than "we like how it looks."

Krate waved the head deformity at me. "I didn't break this off," he said. "It's a hat."

The hat was furry. Perhaps part of a religious observance. Or an attempt to mimic another, more-hirsute, creature. I had no idea.

I skipped to the important question. "Why are there more umans, Krate?"

"It wasn't me," he said, looking uncomfortable. "Feelix stunned them."

I looked at Feelix.

Feelix trembled, then cleared his throat. "They surprised us, sir. They were hiding in some bushes."

Cantie nodded. "Guarding something. A large metal gun, sir."

"Gun?"

Another nod. "A simple cannon, sir. Discharges a metal ball. Fueled by gunpowder."

I squinted at her. "How do you know that?"

She twisted her snout into a half-smile. "History, sir. A similar weapon was used in the massacre of—"

I groaned. "Not that again. We aren't repeating that here." I hadn't known that gunpowder weapons were used in the massacre. I should've studied more history.

I felt a shot of pain in my paw and squeezed it away. "So, why did they have it?" I asked. "The cannon?"

"They're part of an army," Krate said. "We thought they were going to attack the ship—especially after we saw light in the forest. Why was there light?"

"Not worth discussing," I spat. "So, you stunned them because of the lights?"

Krate pointed at the other two. "*They* stunned them."

"Right. But they got stunned." I glanced at the sleeping soldiers. "And now they're here."

"We couldn't leave them," Krate said. "They saw us!"

"Did they know you were rhats?"

Krate looked at the others. "Don't know. Probably. They got a good look at us."

I pointed at the wall. "But it's dark outside. And they're umans!"

"There were lights."

I recalled the access-way and Uzel immersed within the wires. I felt ill. "Right," I said. "The lights."

Cantie slid the hood from her head, revealing a circle of brown fur atop the amber. "They're not the only soldiers out there, sir."

My paw throbbed again. I glanced at the doctor, now studying one of the center machines. What would he say about my soreness? Given my luck, he'd probably want to amputate.

"Did you see more?" I asked.

"A cannon crew wouldn't be alone," Cantie said. "There'd be others. Probably some on foot and others mounted or transported."

"See?" Krate said. "Lots of umans. That's trouble." He patted his chest. "We were looking out for the ship, sir. We did good."

"You brought trouble on board," I said. "Not so good." I drifted toward the nearest patient nook. The one with the uman without his hat. His real head fur, what little there was of it, was dark red. There was a bruise on his left cheek too, possibly from where he'd hit the ground. I poked at his left shoulder puff, then pawed through it a bit. It wasn't hiding anything or even protecting anything. Purely decorative.

I scowled and approached the doctor. His attention was on the machines. The nurse's attention was on him.

"Are they safe?" I said.

"Safe?" the doctor asked. "Certainly not. No uman is safe."

"For us, I mean. Any danger of—"

"Infection?" He snickered. "Of course not. In my time as a physician, there's never been a uman to rhat jump." He pointed at my right paw. "What's wrong with your paw there?"

I realized I was massaging it and stopped. "Nothing." I flexed it for good measure. "Feels fine. Just a nervous tic."

He narrowed his eyes. "And why would you be nervous, XO?" He exchanged looks with the nurse and both chuckled. "Anyway, the umans are in acceptable health. They should pose no difficulty. Containment is your problem."

I hated that. The smugness. Hated it.

The captain entered the bay on all fours and at full scramble. After a quick scan, he stood and straightened his longshirt. "There are more umans here! How did this happen?"

I opened my mouth, but he waved my explanation away. "No matter. We need to phase 'em. Dump their bodies somewhere."

"Sir?"

His paws found his hips. "We have a good thing going here. Crews scrounged a lot of cheese last night. The nearest fortified structure was a windfall. It's like a small village inside. Foodstuffs were easy to get to."

"How much stuff?" I asked.

"Four carts full."

I couldn't help but think of the storage bay. How very large it was. "How many carts do we need?" I asked.

He shrugged. "I leave the counting to the accountants." He paced toward one of the other nooks. "I only know we're adding to it. More nights like tonight and we'll..." He searched the room again. "...well, except for this disaster." He pointed at the nearest hat-wearing patient. "What's wrong with its head? Looks infected."

"Part of the uniform," I said. "They're soldiers."

"Soldiers!" He kneaded his paws together. "They brought back soldiers! The umans have to go, Sedric. Have to go now!"

As much as I would've liked that problem to go away, I wasn't one for wanton killing. Especially when the victims weren't an active threat. "They might be useful," I said. "For informational purposes. If we stay here and finish, I mean."

"We <u>have</u> to finish," he said. "There's no other way. Not enough time." He waved toward the door. "We have a schedule. A week at the most. Otherwise...it's not good." He rubbed his paws harder. "We should wake the rest of the crew. Let them swarm in all directions."

I got a mental picture of hundreds of my subordinates, all wearing robes and dresses, swarming out to meet an army of long headed umans armed with cannons and swords. And right in the middle of the conflict, right when concealment was most important, the rhat robes light up brighter than a binary system because a scientist crossed a wire.

"Shoot all the lights," I muttered. "The furry lights."

"What?" the captain said.

I shook my head. "I'm against sending more out. At least, not yet." All eyes were on us now. This wasn't the sort of conversation we normally had in the medical bay.

"What do you propose, Sed? How do we solve this?"

Cindel from Security entered the bay, made a cursory sweep of the room, then fixed his eyes on the captain and me.

With a nod, he walked straight for us. He addressed the captain with a "sir," then looked at me. "Officer Yentiss said you might be here."

My paw throbbed again. "Yes? What is it?"

"The uman wants to talk ." He pointed a thumb toward the door. "The one in containment, I mean."

"Louis?"

"Right, him. Says he wants a deal."

"Deal?" The captain wrinkled his snout. "Are we negotiating now?"

"I left him...options," I said. "I'm hoping he can help."

"Help how?"

"Locations, complications...soldiers. I don't know. Something."

The captain scratched at his chin, thoughtful. "That's good thinking, Sedric. That's why we have you."

I nodded. "And the other umans? Can we contain them for now?"

The captain checked the examination nooks, then scowled at Krate and the others. "Do we have a place to put them?"

"There are a couple more containment cells," Cindel offered. "Maybe they can share? I like to keep at least one cell free for—"

"Yeah, that's what we'll do," the captain said. "Contain them in case whatever plan you come up with requires them, Sed."

"Thank you, sir. I'll—"

"Now, get on with your negotiation."

CHAPTER 15

Louis was seated at the desk this time, with hands clasped together and resting on the desktop edge. Seemingly relaxed. Seemingly thoughtful. A sophisticated repose for a primitive.

I took only a few steps into the cell and stopped.

Cindel remained in the doorway behind me, preventing the door from closing. "I should be here with you," he said. "For your safety."

I raised my sore left paw. "This should be a civil discussion." I fixed Louis with a smile. "I'm right, yes? Civil? No trying to grab me?"

"No grabbing." Louis patted the desk's surface. "I'll stay right here."

I told Cindel to wait outside, and he left, grudgingly.

"Are you well?" I asked. "Had enough water and food?"

"Yes, thank you."

I nodded. "That was a good move before." I pointed at the waste appliance. "There before I pulled you over."

"Yes, your tail was unexpected."

I smiled. "That's my life. All unexpected." I touched the edge of the desk. "Are you trained to fight?"

"I was an officer in the previous war." He smiled and shifted in his seat. "Hoping to stay out of this one. Maybe start a family."

I nodded. "Very good. I've been told you want to bargain."

"I would." He shifted again. Looked past me towards the door.

"You realize your position." I indicated the room. "You're on my ship, filled with my beasts."

He nodded. "And you have a desperate mission, monsieur. One I can assist with."

"I wouldn't call it 'desperate,'" I said. "Important, maybe." I smiled. "And what do you demand for your help?"

He raised two fingers. "Only two things. First, I want my freedom—"

I was disappointed in his technique already. Asking for the impossible? So uman. "As I mentioned before, I can't let you—"

"Not freedom from the ship," he said. "Freedom *on* the ship."

"*On* the ship?" I noticed his sleep nook. Its coverings were tight and straight, as if he'd never used it. "That's worse than setting you lose outside. You aren't..." I sighed. "I don't think you can handle it. There's much different here. Things you'd find unfamiliar...overwhelming." I wagged a finger. "Plus, you'd get into trouble. Mess with something that could hurt you, us, or the mission. I can't have that."

His eyes widened. "You made me fall asleep. Certainly, you could do that again if you needed to?"

"I could, but it wouldn't be good for you. Plus, it's a hassle. Having to hunt you down and all."

He nodded slowly. "And you like to avoid hassle."

I grinned. "Which on this ship, often proves difficult." I patted the desk surface. "So that's nonnegotiable, I'm afraid. What was your second request?"

He pointed at me. "I know this is no sea ship."

I opened my paws but said nothing. What could I tell him? That we were part of a civilization that spanned galaxies? Hardly.

"I don't think it travels on land either," he added.

"And why would you think that?"

"No beast of legend uses such a device."

"No?" I shrugged. "Perhaps your legends are wrong."

"I don't believe so. I think you are of another sphere as described in Cavendish's *Blazing World*."

"Blazing what?"

He looked surprised. "You don't know of this story? It was published decades ago in England. A young woman dispatched to another world where she meets animals that can talk."

I snorted. "And you think I'm one of those animals?" I had no idea where "England" was, but I assumed it was a nearby place. Possibly filled with storytellers.

"It's all that makes sense to me."

Louis was brighter than I'd originally thought. Using only his limited experience, he'd stumbled upon a theory that wasn't that far from the truth. Surprising for a primitive. I sort of liked him, despite his uman-ness. "Tell you what. I won't let you wander around unattended. But I will let someone give you a tour." I pointed toward the door. "Maybe Cindel out there. Would that suffice?"

He stared at me a moment, eyes narrowed. "Perhaps," he said then. "But I have another condition."

"Your second request, yes. What is it?"

He shrunk in his seat now, seemingly shy.

"Louis?"

He took a deep breath. "I would like my wife to join me. On this ship."

"What?"

"She's all I have, Monsieur Rat, and she's probably worried sick. She always prepares my evening meal. I don't know what she thought when I didn't return last night. Beside herself with worry, I'd guess. Fears me taken by the allies or conscripted into service." He gave me an imploring look. "They <u>all</u> worry, Sedric. The women."

I wrinkled my snout. "Louis..."

"It's just one more person. This ship is large. Anne is small. She won't take up much space. Have you no spouses on your planet?"

"We have spouses, yes." I thought of Yentiss then, despite having...nothing with her. My head fur stood suddenly on end, so I smoothed it with my right paw. "The captain's already angry about the three umans we just picked up. There's no way he'll allow another—" I stopped myself.

I'd done it again. Shared too much.

"More like me? On this ship?"

I snarled, angry with myself. I was terrible at interrogating. I'd never make it as a Silent.

Louis startled and pulled away.

"My apologies," I said. "I meant no offense." Finally, I threw caution away. "Eh, maybe you know them."

He raised an eyebrow. "Know the umans? I might."

"They had an interesting way of dressing." I described the three umans clothing as best I could.

Louis listened attentively, and by the end of my description, his eyebrows were raised. "That's...um..." He leaned back. Crossed his arms over his chest. "Interesting."

I snorted again. "Interesting how?"

He smiled. "It means I could help you. Help you quite a bit."

I chuckled. If Louis had a tail, it would've been three meters long and filled with gall. "Taking the hard side now, huh? I could have you skinned, you know."

His face paled, but his voice remained firm. "What a waste that would be, Sedric. A foolish and dangerous waste."

I turned and walked slowly toward the door. Waiting. Testing.

Watching at the viewport, Cindel noticed my approach and quickly opened the door. "Is there a problem, sir?"

"No problem, no." I smiled to myself. The fact that Louis wasn't charging my back meant he was beyond simple survival now, beyond fear. Mentally joining us—this ship filled with mutos. Interesting, Louis. Interesting indeed.

I looked at him again. "One of my crewmembers thinks the umans are soldiers. Are they soldiers?"

"Maybe *I'm* a soldier," he said, smiling. "How would you know?"

"Fair point," I said. "I'd forgotten I can't trust you. Not really. Even if you say you'll help, I don't know that you will."

"Nor I you."

A bit of an impasse. But impasses can be useful. A way of refining the negotiation. Clarifying the important parts.

My ship was in a bind. There were too many unknowns, and no easy way to figure them out without a native. I had a seemingly-willing native aboard, who only wanted to see the ship and his wife. Was that price too high?

Was <u>any</u> price too high?

I scratched my chin. Studied Louis.

He raised an eyebrow but said nothing.

I pointed my tail at him. "All right, we'll play it like this. Tell me about the soldiers and you'll get your ship tour."

"And my wife?"

"As to that...it will be a trick getting it past the captain. Not saying we couldn't do it. We probably could." I glanced at the room's yellow ceiling and walls. "You could share this space, right? If we were to move that direction?"

He sat forward. "Of course, yes. Easily."

I nodded. "Very good. The soldiers get you a tour. More food—and I mean, lots of food—gets you your wife."

He looked pensive. "How about soldiers, then tour, then wife, then food?"

"You give first, then I give?"

He nodded once. "Yes. Like that."

"Done," I said.

He stretched a hand across the desk. "Shake on it?"

I frowned. I wasn't inclined to touch the uman, despite assurances that he was neither infected, nor a danger. Something about paws with no fur. They're sickening.

"Sedric?" He pulled his hand back. "Is there a problem?"

With a grunt, I put out my right paw. "There's no problem. I'm just not used to agreeable umans." Our appendages touched. It wasn't altogether bad. Warmer than I expected and rougher. He was a worker, that Louis. It was a good sign, I thought.

I thought a lot of things.

CHAPTER 16

The next thing Louis wanted was to see the soldiers. When I explained that they were still incapacitated in our medical bay, he said "All the better! I can have part of my tour and help at the same time!"

I couldn't argue with the logic. The next twenty minutes was spent transporting him from the confinement deck to the medical bay. It was an unbearably slow trip. We couldn't walk a meter without his primitive mind noticing something it'd never seen before.

He rapped his knuckles on the wall outside his room, before putting an ear against it and rapping again. "These walls," he said. "What are they made of?"

"A composite material," I said. "A fusion of metal and synthetic. Blended at the subatomic level, I guess."

"Metal?" he said. "Like a blade or a pot?"

I tipped my snout. "Not like that, really."

"Then what?"

"You'd need to ask the scientists, and even then, I don't

know that you'd get the right answer." I waved up the hallway, toward the bank of lifts. "We need to go that way."

The lift was equally distracting. He focused on the lights that ran around the top of the room first, getting up on tiptoes and pressing close. Staring deep into their transparent shell. "Where does it come from?" he said. "The light. I look for the flame but can't see it. There's only light—like you've captured one of the stars. Or a firefly's tail." He tapped the light's exterior. "There were similar spots of light in my room. I studied them for a long time. How is it done?"

"I don't know. Bound electric cells, or something." I waved my hands. "Power flows into a container and it lights up."

"Power?"

"Yes. The juice. It flows into the—" I shook my head. "I can't explain it." I reached forward and worked the lift's controls.

Louis watched that process attentively. "There were little drawings there," he said then. "They just appeared and disappeared."

"Deck numbers," I said. "Nothing complicated."

"But where did they come from, those numbers?" Louis gave a little yelp as the door slid shut, then stared at that a moment.

"Who shut the door? Was it someone outside I couldn't see?"

I was beginning to regret our arrangement. "Mechanics," I said. "Machinery. You have machines, right?"

He shook his head slowly. "It's like magic, but I don't think it is." He pointed at the control, the doors, and the lights. "All this is normal in your world."

I scowled at him. "You're talking to a large rodent here. You could be..." I touched my head. "You could be crazy. You know what that means? A diseased head?"

He smiled. "Oh yes, monsieur Sedric. Very much so. I had an uncle who went crazy. Lived with the pigs for three years before he died."

"Pigs?"

"Yes, swine. Do you not have them? They are livestock. Pink with floppy ears." He put a hand above his knees. "Roughly this high?" His eyes widened. "Or perhaps your pigs talk and walk about?"

"We have lots of strange," I said. "But not that." I recalled the first structure we visited. The one where Krate stunned an animal. "I think I know the creature you mean. Think I saw some earlier." I didn't mention other alien races that bore a resemblance to lesser creatures, like the ant-like Phants, or the Jinn Khan sloths. It would've only lead to more questions.

The lift stopped at the medical bay level and we got out. Thankfully, we had only a short walk to the bay itself. We passed a couple of crewmembers along the way, which resulted in long stares from all involved. I told everyone to knock it off and get to work. There was some joy in that.

"Colors," Louis said then. "You're all different colors."

"Umans have different colors," I said. "I've seen some."

"Not so many," he said. "I haven't seen the same color here yet."

"You will." I leaned close. "Don't make much about it. Some are sensitive that way."

He nodded. "Yes, monsieur rat."

"And could you stick with 'Sedric?'"

"Certainly."

The doctor was standing over one of the umans when we arrived, but otherwise, little had changed in the med bay. The nurse lingered near the central machines and the umans were asleep in their nooks. Their furry hats had been removed, though.

The doctor regarded Louis a moment, before motioning us near.

He pointed at the unconscious uman. It had light-colored hair but seemed unremarkable otherwise. "I was wrong in my assessment before," the doctor said. "This one has parasites."

I took a subtle step back. "Where?"

"On its head. Ugly little creatures. Very small."

I felt the urge to scratch my snout. "Can they get on us?"

He frowned. "Possibly. Everyone should be checked." He nodded at the sleeping uman. "I'd like to keep this one for observation." He pointed across the room. "The other two can go to confinement. They're clean."

At that point, I did scratch. "I will tell security. Make sure they get everything set."

Louis's eyes shifted from one prone uman to the next. "They are sick?"

"They have bugs," I said. "At least, one of them did."

The doctor nodded. "Comes from exposure to the outside."

Louis nodded, looking nervous. "I would like to talk to them."

"Sure. We're moving them soon. We'll have them near you." I'd mentioned that already, of course. "Talk all you want."

He nodded again. "They're the Emperor's soldiers. I don't know why they're here. They should be further south."

The only Emperor I knew shouldn't have had any soldiers nearby, but I suspected that wasn't who Louis was talking about. This world must have its own tailless version.

"You think there are more out there?" I watched as the nurse attached one end of a hose to the central machine, then carried the other end to one of the uman patients. A scanning device of some sort.

"I'd guess there are many," Louis said. "The Emperor's fighting the allied coalition. He has thousands of troops. Tens of thousands."

My left paw started to ache again. "You mentioned this Emperor before," I said. "Is he a local ruler?"

"His Imperial and Royal Majesty," Louis said. "Emperor of the French and King of Italy. Mediator of the Swiss Confederation and Co-Prince of Andorra."

"Impressive title," I said. "We have an Emperor too. His title is longer than that one. Compensating for his tail size, I think."

"I don't understand."

I shook my head. "Yeah, you wouldn't. Your Emperor have a shorter name?"

"Of course. Napoléon Bonaparte."

CHAPTER 17

The name suggested someone with a shorter-than-normal tail to me, but I kept that thought to myself. Louis seemed to be a fan of his Emperor and it would do no good to get on the wrong side of the uman help. Deal or no deal.

Louis studied the nearest soldier, the one with dark hair. "It will be difficult to get information from them," he said. "They're conditioned not to talk about troop movements. On penalty of death."

"But you're one of them," I said. "Surely they would—"

"They don't know that," he said. "I could be working for the British for all they know." He indicated the medical bay walls and ceiling. "Not to mention where we are. They're going to distrust everything."

"We'll make sure they don't see us," I said. "That they only ever see you."

"How do you hide your metal walls, though? Your lights without flame?"

"Don't know," I said. "Maybe with cloth?"

He looked at the patient nooks, frowning. "Maybe you shouldn't wake them at all."

I studied the soldiers. "The captain wanted to kill them and bury their bodies. I was hoping to avoid that. Seemed like a waste."

Louis's eyes widened. "In cold blood? Members of the Grande Armée?"

I waved a hand. "Nah, I wasn't going to let him. I only need a way to get clear of this whole thing. To make it all work out."

He nodded. "You could put them to work, Sedric. Certainly, on a ship this large there must be something to do."

"There's work, sure." I shrugged. "They could help with the unloading. Especially if you find more food."

"I have an idea, but..."

"Yeah, your wife. We need to grab your wife."

The nurse approached us, snout curled with annoyance. "You're disturbing the patients."

"That hardly seems possible," I said. "They're sleeping."

She narrowed her eyes and huffed.

I snorted, then indicated the door. "Let's go to your cell," I said. "We'll discuss strategy on the way."

He followed me to the hallway. Again, his eyes drifted to the lighting. Kid was like a moth.

"I need to go outside," he said then.

I chuckled. "Not likely."

He raised a finger. "Please, listen. If I go out, I can study the troop movements. Maybe figure out where they are headed. Then I'll know what to suggest to you for a food source."

"Louis..."

"I'll help with my wife too. She'll be easy to capture if she sees me. I can explain—"

CHAPTER 18

There was a sucking sound and the feeling of something being lifted from my face. Then I felt—not smelled but felt—the presence of sleep gas all around me. It was like a bubble around my head, threatening to drown me in its ethereal slumber.

Gradually, I realized there were cracks in the bubble. Places where fresh air slid through. I felt it tickle my forehead, then across my nose and snout. Finally, the air seemed to be hovering over my eyes. Swirling around, bumping and poking. Wanting to come in. Wanting my eyes to open.

"Can you hear me, Sedric?" A strange voice. Not the uman, Louis. Not the nurse or doctor.

"Wake up, you traitorous scum. Wake so I can beat you."

That voice I recognized. My captain. The *Granum* captain.

I forced my eyes open and peered at my surroundings. I was surprised by the spindly, blue muto in front of me. His chair hovered above the ground, and in his right hand was what looked like a dirty bag.

"There now, you're all right," the muto said. "Do you remember where you are?"

I searched my surroundings. It was a spacious office. To my left, heavy shelves, overflowing with machinery and manuscripts. Transparent tubing cascaded down from a lower shelf, ending with the bag the blue muto held. I focused on him for a second, feeling his name rising to the surface. Percolating like a bubble of indigestion. "Tactin," I said finally.

He waved the dirty bag. "Precisely good. I knew you would be fine. Rarely are mutos affected." He rested the bag on the arm of his chair. "I'm questioning the usefulness of this exercise, however. We've covered your ill-advised landing on a primitive planet, along with the minutia of your role as the executive officer. I've heard nothing that relates to the loss of your shuttle, or the fraudulent insurance claim thereof." He glanced at the captain, still sitting on the floor near the door. "I'm inclined to transfer you both to the inquisitor's office for further investigation."

The captain brought his paws to his face and moaned. "See what you've done, Sedric! Now they'll dock our tails and pin our ears."

Tactin frowned. "How does that one captain a starship?"

"He has his moments," I said.

Tactin wheezed a sigh. "I've seen nothing in your memory to support that claim. Crew discipline is atrocious. The antics of your science team, the unorganized attempt to fulfill your contract, the mingling with savages..." He wheezed again. "While it makes for good comedy—none of it follows protocol. Particularly the conduct code set forth by his Imperial Majesty, and the commonwealth he governs." He puffed out his cheeks three times quickly. "Such matters are beyond my jurisdiction as accountant."

"There's more!" I said. "Lot's more."

Tactin's eyes widened. "So I fear. More buffoonery."

"Not my buffoonery!" the captain yelled. "See how my officers betray me! See how my XO makes deals that lead to ruin."

There was a knock on the door. Swiveling his chair that direction, Tactin answered. A moment later, our female escorts entered the room. Their expressions were as dour as the last time I'd seen them, making my memories of Yentiss seem all the better.

The captain shook his head. "Don't take us yet. Let Sedric—"

Tactin raised a hand. "Relax." He indicated the does. "They only brought us lunch."

The red-furred doe—the one with spectacles—tipped her snout. "Should we bring it in?"

Ten seconds later, there was a large cart heaped with cheeses, meats, and breads in the center of the room. The aroma was incredible. Almost enough to make me leap from my chair and gorge. I resisted, but my mouth watered uncontrollably.

The captain shot to his feet, hurried to the cart, and finding a small plate there, began to fill it. Occasionally, a morsel would go straight to his mouth, though.

The accountant's cheeks puffed slightly. "I find myself curious about the soldiers. Who did they fight for?"

"The French," I said.

Tactin fluttered his whiskers.

"One of the nation-states. Seemed we'd landed in the middle of a decades-long dispute."

"And the cause?"

"A mix of boundaries, ego, and food." I watched as the captain returned to the floor near the door, plate heavily laden. "As far as I could tell, anyway."

"So there *were* more soldiers?"

"Oh yes," I said. "Lots more."

"And did you take this Louis out to look?"

"He didn't need to!" the captain said between bites. "The trouble came to us." Another bite. "It always came to us."

Tactin waved toward the food cart. "Please, help yourself." He slid the head walk mask from his armrest, letting it dangle in midair like a web-trapped insect, then hovered to the food tray himself. He made his selections with some deliberation, a single item at a time.

I followed Tactin's process as best I could. I returned to my seat with a plate that was a near duplicate of his—equal portions of yellow cheese, red meat, and brown bread. All three were savory.

Ten minutes passed. They weren't silent minutes, however, because the captain's consumption was loud and perfunctory. As if he were eating his last meal, which, perhaps, we both were. I had no idea who the inquisitor was, but the captain wanted to avoid him at all costs.

A minute later, the captain belched, put his plate on the floor, and stood. "You have a waste outlet nearby?" he asked, patting his stomach. "I think I need to—"

Tactin waved a paw. "Around the corner outside. My assistants are still there. One of them will show you."

The captain's tail straightened nervously, but he nodded and walked to the door. A few seconds later, the room was quiet again.

Tactin sniffed. "Is it true that trouble finds you?"

"Always on the *Granum*," I said. "Always." I sampled a piece of meat. Smiled. "Amazing we held it together."

"But at that time. Did the soldiers—?"

I nodded vigorously. "Oh yes. Thousands poured in from the south." I looked at the ceiling, attempting to remember the specifics. "French troops lead by a General Rapp attempted to stop the allies somewhere to the northeast of us. They advanced to the city of Hagenau and then to the forest that shared that name." I took another bite of meat. "Which was precisely where we were."

Another cheek puff. "Well, that's distressing. What did you do?"

"Besides pray the lights didn't come on again? Or that someone didn't accidentally engage our weapons?"

He chuckled. "Yes, besides all that."

The door opened and the captain returned. His eyes found the food tray again and I could see him weighing what was proper in this situation. Whether he should show control—for now, at least—or blindly eat more. With a glance at us, and a shake of his head, he returned to the chair near me. "Maybe I should let you plug me in," he said to Tactin. "Let you see how it really was."

"You doubt the veracity of Sedric's memories?" Tactin said.

"He makes me look like a slug! Like I was sitting in my cabin eating cheese!"

"Were you?"

The captain's snout wrinkled. "Of course not!"

The accountant took a bite of bread. "I assure you..." He pointed at the dangling mask. "The machine is incredibly accurate. Certified by the inquisitor's office." Another bite. "But, if you wish to dispute its findings, we can send for someone from that office and have them—"

"No," the captain said. "I only think..." He glanced at me. "Well, it's Sedric's perspective. Slanted."

Tactin bobbed his head. "But no less true." He collected the mask and held it out for the captain.

The captain's snout puckered into a look of disgust. As if he'd eaten a bad egg.

"What's the matter?" Tactin nodded my direction. "You've seen how safe it is. Your XO is perfectly—"

The captain's paws came to his mouth and his cheeks puffed. There was a clipped retching sound.

"Emperor's bones..." I muttered.

The captain hurried to the door, rattled the handle until the escorts let him out, and disappeared.

Tactin cackled. "Well, that was fun. This is the best interview I've had in weeks." He looked at me. "Now, where were we?"

"The advancing soldiers. How they were headed for our hiding place."

"Ah yes. Quite interesting." He took a bite of cheese. "You were right in your concern over the massacre. I was the junior accountant for that event in my youth." He frowned, squinted at his chair's screen, then touched a couple times. "A terrible affair, that. Little profit in it."

"I'd guess."

He scowled at the screen before waving away whatever concern it presented. "So...the soldiers? How did you respond?"

I studied the mask's tubes. "There's quite a bit more," I said. "Especially to get to the shuttle."

He tapped the mask. "You'd like me to experience it with you?"

"I think I would, yes."

"I find I would too." He raised the mask. "You have a unique perspective."

I ate a final bite of bread before taking the mask. Then, with a closing smile, I slid it over my snout. I took a deep breath, tasted gas, and felt the mask tighten over my head. "More cheese," I whispered. "Lots more."

CHAPTER 19

The captain seemed to dance his way onto the bridge, he was so animated. His steps were uneven, his paws wrestled with each other, and his tail flicked every which way.

I stood to relinquish the command chair, but he waved my offer away, choosing to pace instead. He glanced around the room, noting first Yentiss at her post up front, and then Louis in the seat next to her. "Why is the uman here?" he asked.

My stomach lurched. Louis's presence went against protocol, sure, but after a couple days of having him around I'd grown used to him. His wide-eyed demeanor and subtle humor. It was like having a kid. A tag-along child of my own.

And, despite the inconvenience and the danger, I was glad we'd snatched Louis's wife too. She seemed more docile than him. She hadn't left their room yet.

She hadn't seen a muto without a disguise yet either. She thought us part of some religious group. Regardless, Louis was happy and helpful, so I considered that a win. Our only resource in an otherwise unknown landscape.

"Sedric?" The captain pointed at Louis. "Why?"

The central screen showed an infrared image of the woods beyond the ship at a distance of about a kilometer. There were no animals in the image. No animals around us anywhere anymore. There were plenty of bright spots, though. Plenty of warm bodies. And these bodies all carried weapons.

"Louis has an idea where we can go," I said. "A place he thinks is safe."

"And our mission?"

"It has lots of food sources too," I said.

The captain clutched his hips. Looked at Louis. "That so, uman?"

Louis nodded. "Ye-yes, sir." Louis's encounters with the captain thus far had all been confrontational. This was no exception.

"How do I know you're not taking us to a bigger trap?" the captain asked.

I indicated the screen. "Is there a bigger trap than that?"

The captain sneered and spit. "Go on." He approached the command seat and waved at me. "Find your place."

I happily complied, taking the seat nearest the wall on the command chair's right. Its desk was functionally similar to the captain's. He often let me pilot the ship from there. I wasn't certain how this particular takeoff was going to go, though.

The captain pointed at the screen. "How long until they can shoot at us?"

"We're already in range," Louis said, eyes flitting between the captain and me.

"What?" the captain said.

"The Emperor's cannons can shoot nearly two thousand meters, sir."

The captain swore.

"They probably won't," Louis said. "Not with all the trees."

Yentiss manipulated her controls and the screen shifted to other parts of the woods. First the north, then the east and west. Aside from a few scattered animals, the infrared showed little activity in those locations. "No other encroachment, sir," she said, giving a reserved smile. "Just the one army."

The captain shifted in his seat. "Well, that's something." He looked at me. "And where would the uman have us go?"

"North of here," I said. "Closer to a large body of water."

Yentiss gave me a wary look.

"But not too close," I added. "About a hundred kilometers away."

"Yes, the Channel," Louis said. "It—"

"Sounds exposed," the captain said. "I don't want to keep the cloaks on at all times."

"We won't be seen," Louis stammered. "There's another forest—Bossu Wood—it should be—"

There were a series of snapping sounds, followed by a solitary "ting!" from one of the external speakers. The captain swore again. "What in the darkened sun is that!" he asked.

There were more snaps and one of the external viewers seemingly went dead.

"Someone's shooting," Louis offered.

"The cannons?"

"Rifles, sir." Louis stretched his arms apart, then cupped one hand as if to show a gun stock. "Handheld devices that shoot—"

"I know what a gun is, uman. Why are they shooting at us?"

I manipulated my own screen, checking power levels and system resources. One never knew with our scientists. Nothing looked out of the ordinary, though, thankfully. "Our cloak is functional. They shouldn't be able to see us."

"They may be shooting at game," Louis said. "And we happen to be in the line of fire."

"It's nighttime," Yentiss said. "How are they seeing anything?" She rumpled her snout at her screen. "Our lights aren't on."

"Is everyone on board?" the captain asked.

"Yessir," I said. "All gathering parties in and accounted for." I hadn't let any go out, in fact. Not tonight.

The captain put paws on his controls. "I'm going to take us out."

I consulted my screen again, checking all entries and exits, but specifically the main ramp. The ship looked tight. "Everything's closed up," I said. "Systems normal."

The captain nodded. "Show me where I'm going," he said. "I want a good look at it."

"Sure." With a glance at Louis, I searched for our stored overhead images. When I found one nearest our location, I pushed it to the central screen.

Louis hopped up and pointed at a section of forest below a curved coastline. "That woods there," he said. "There's a large farm nearby." He nodded once. "They'll have lots of cheese, along with the means to—"

"Get that location locked down, Yentiss," the captain said. "I don't want to fly past it." He squinted at his screen and worked it with both paws. As he did so, his tongue escaped the right side of his mouth. Something he often did when he piloted.

Something flashed red on my screen—a warning from the exterior sensors. I scrolled back to that portal of readouts. One of the exterior hatches was now open. Port side, third deck. A hatch typically used for emergencies. "Gnaw my knees," I said.

"What's that?" the captain said.

"Small situation, sir." I attempted to close the hatch from my control deck. "No luck," I said, frustrated.

"We have an open door!" the captain said then.

All I could think of were the scientists. If they were trying to leave, I just might let them go. But I doubted it was that convenient.

"Get it handled, Sedric," he said. "We need to go."

"I'm on it." I stood and made my way to the door.

From there, it took me about five minutes to reach the offending hatch. I expected one of the scientists at work, or at the very least, telltale signs that they'd been there. What I found instead, was a worried security guard, a red named Derris, crouched just outside a closed airlock. "What's going on?" I asked.

His eyes widened. "Sir!" He pointed his tail at the airlock. "In there, sir. Sorry, I couldn't..." He shook his head. "She's quick, sir."

The airlock door had a round viewport, similar to those on the containment cells. "She, who?" I put an eye to the port. Thankfully, this one was clear, and the airlock beyond, completely visible.

The small, silver room was little more than a couple storage lockers for suits and a bench. At the far end was the exterior hatch. It was open, and a uman woman, dressed in a blue dress and bonnet—an outfit similar to the one I'd wore—was standing at it with one leg hanging out. I couldn't see her face, but that didn't matter. It could only be one person.

"How did Louis's wife get here?" I asked.

"I opened the door," Derris said. "And she ran out."

"Why in the Emperor's name would you do that?"

"I was told the umans had the run of the ship," he said.

I growled at him. "That has never been the case." I pointed at the viewport. "Especially not this one. She just got here." I worked the door control, but nothing happened. So I tried it again. It only flashed red. Mockingly. "She locked herself in?"

"Yes sir."

"And how did she know how to do that?"

Derris only shrugged.

I was beginning to doubt that primitive umans were limited in what they could achieve. In fact, I doubted that any of our technologies were beyond their ability to eventually figure out. My assumption about the threshold of technological exposure, however, seemed right on the mark. I was fairly certain that Louis's wife had reached that threshold. Possibly as soon as she'd woken up.

"How far up are we?" I asked.

"About ten meters," Derris said. "Not far. I was about to override the—"

"Not far for a muto," I said. "But for an uman?" I shook my head. "She'll break herself." The lock had an override on the external control, but what good would it do to unlock it and barge in? That seemed more apt to drive her out. How much help would I get from Louis then?

The wall com near the door squawked and the captain's face became visible. "Why isn't that door closed?" he asked.

I stood in front of the com. "I need Louis," I said. "His—"

"No time," he barked. "We've been hit a dozen more times. Get that door closed. They're dinging up my ship."

"But—"

"Get. It. Shut." The com went blank.

Sighing, I checked the porthole. The uman female was still near the exit door, but both legs were now inside. So, she wasn't completely blind with fear. I just needed to reason with her like I had reasoned with Louis.

Except Louis couldn't have jumped to his death. Big difference.

"You have a stunner on you?" I asked Derris.

He nodded and brought out the weapon.

I took it, tucked it into the back of my belt, and adjusted my longshirt to conceal it. "Here goes nothing."

I tapped on the door. The woman shrieked. "Go away!"

I explained who I was and that I wouldn't hurt her. It sounded a lot like the speech I'd given Louis. I remembered the uman doe's name then. "Anne, right?"

"Ye-yes. That's right."

"Okay, Anne, I need you to shut that door. We have to move, and we can't until—"

"Move! How can we move!" She bent out over the opening again. "There are no legs on this thing. No wheels."

It was the most helpless I'd ever felt. A closed door and an uman who might stumble to her death at any moment. "It would take too long to explain," I said. "It's a long way down, Anne. I don't want you to fall."

She looked my way, and I could see that her eyes were reddened, her face streaked with moisture. "This place is a nightmare," she said. "Endless halls and dark creatures."

"I'll admit," I said. "It's all a bit unusual."

"It is hell!" she said. "That's the only thing that makes sense. I've died and gone to that dark place." She looked out the hatch again. "I always thought it was down and not up."

The word "hell" translated into the muto word for the collapsed sun of our home world, a source of electromagnetic gibberish that scrambles guidance systems and plays havoc with muto minds. It had destroyed a thousand ships over centuries. A place without hope. To wit: I understood perfectly.

"It isn't like that," I said. "Not at all."

"How would you know? You're one of them! One of the dark things!"

"Yeah, I get that a lot." I looked at the floor, noticing a place where the surface was cracked. "But listen, you'll be alright. Your husband is here—"

"Louis is dead too?" she wailed. "I knew it! When he didn't come home, I feared—"

"He's not dead." I glanced at the wall communicator, then at Derris. This was taking too long. I had maybe three seconds before the captain called again. And the soldiers outside couldn't be far away.

I studied the interior door controls. I needed her to be reasonably safe before I overrode the door. Since it was an airlock, the control had additional options. What were they?

I scratched my chin. I could adjust the pressure inside, but with the external hatch open, that might inadvertently send her out. Not an answer.

There was a range of gas options. Typically, if someone were going out the airlock for a spacewalk, not only would the pressure be adjusted, but so would the oxygen levels. At least for air-breathers like umans and mutos. An increase of oxygen might give her a headache or make her drowsy. A decrease could knock her out.

But again, with the door open, that was a hit-or-miss proposition. It'd take too long to make it work. And did I want to risk making her disoriented?

What else did I have? What could I—

Then it hit me. Gravity. I could adjust that either way. But which to use? Too much could hurt her, but lighter gravity seemed risky too. Couldn't have her just flying around.

I checked inside again. She was about a step from the door. Fair enough. Heavy it was.

I whispered my plan to Derris. He nodded and moved up beside me, standing with an eye at the viewport. I returned his stunner, just in case.

The wall communicator chimed, and I heard the captain's voice. I ignored him as I worked the airlock controls. Within seconds, I had the gravity at three times normal. Next came a yelp followed by a "thump."

A thump was good. It meant she was still on the ship.

"She's down," Derris said.

I started on the door override. A few seconds later, the door snapped open and Derris rushed inside.

I heard a scream and the sound of the stunner. Then I heard the exterior hatch close.

"Sedric!" The captain from the wall communicator. "I'm taking off! Hatch be—"

I shook my head and entered the airlock to check on Anne. She looked fine. Asleep, but fine. I gently picked her up, and with Derris in tow, carried her back to her room.

CHAPTER 20

There was a sense of comfort when we finally brought the ship down again. The forest Louis had suggested, Bossu Wood, was denser than the one we'd left. In fact, we had to blast a few trees from overhead in order to have a clearing large enough to land in.

Louis assured us that the gun flashes, if seen, would only add to the forest's mystique. "Some think Bossu was part of Brocéliande once," he added.

"And what's Brocéliande?" I asked.

Following my encounter with Anne, I'd returned to the bridge. Louis and Yentiss never left, per Captain's orders.

"An ancient forest filled with magic and mystery." Louis spread his arms. "It's featured in several books, most relating to the legend of Arthur." He smiled. "Another reason for us to be here. Many fear Bossu and will stay away."

"What about soldiers?" the captain asked. "Will <u>they</u> stay away?"

Louis cleared his throat. "The Emperor's men are said to

be fearless. But they will be wary, I think. Their leaders should be too."

The captain nodded. "And this farm you mentioned?"

"It's large. There will be many dairy products."

The captain looked at Yentiss. "How much time until sunrise?"

"Almost two hours, sir."

He looked my direction. "Is that enough time, XO?"

I gripped the edge of my desk. "Seems unlikely, sir," I said. "It's a bit of a walk."

The captain wrinkled his snout. "We don't have much time. We'll be late..." He stared at each of us in turn. "We won't like it if we're late."

It felt like the temperature controls had failed, suddenly dropping the room to freezing. Something about this job was off. Too much tension for a simple food run. Too much urgency. "Why won't we like it?" I asked.

"The clients," the captain said. "They aren't the kind you should disappoint. It's bad for business."

Louis noticed the temperature change too. "We...we shouldn't waste any time then," he said. "I can go to the farm with you. In the morning."

"Morning!" The captain laughed. "You can't go in the morning!"

Louis gave me a confused look. "But you have disguises."

"You saw us," I said. "How convincing are they?"

"Especially not in direct light," Yentiss added.

"I could negotiate with the owner in the morning, though," Louis said. "Get him to—"

"Negotiate!" The captain cackled.

Louis nodded. "The owner is known to me. If we bargain—"

"We've been stealing," the captain said. "Stealing has worked fine so far."

I smoothed the back of my neck, surprised at how stiff the fur felt. "The cargo hold has a lot of empty space yet, sir." I waved a paw Louis's direction. "There have been... complications."

The captain patted his armrests, thinking. "So, we send the uman to negotiate..." He squinted. "But how will we be part of it? How will we watch?"

The central screen showed a view of the world outside. Already the sky color had lightened. I shook my head. "I don't know, but those disguises won't—"

The captain clapped his paws together. "The suits! The ones the scientists have been working on!"

"The...shimmer...suits?" I asked.

He pointed my direction. "The very same. Their wondrous suits."

I noticed the *Granum*'s odor again. Its sea-breeze and tar smell seemed to have more tar in it this time. "Those things don't work, sir. They make the wearer look like a bright red uman. And an ugly one at that." I waved a paw at Louis. "No offense."

"That's fine," Louis said. "I don't think much of your appearance either."

"No, no, the suits work now," the captain said. "I've seen them."

I doubted him, but only nodded and said, "That's fortunate."

He squeaked happily. "Yes, our gifted engineers have come through again. Not sure how many suits are functional, though. Two at least." He pointed to Yentiss and I. "You two. You're adequate. Take the uman out."

I was tired, frankly. The last thing I wanted was to be the test case for a new invention. But there'd be no arguing the captain out of it.

Ten minutes later, Yentiss and I were in the science deck's

greenish testing room. There was a hint of sulfur in the air. Just enough to sting my nose. Another large piece of equipment occupied the floor space this time. A curved structure with wide, transparent sections. I worried it was part of the *Granum*'s interstellar engines.

Yentiss shielded her nose with her right paw. "What have they been doing in here?" she said, waving her other paw in front of her face.

I approached the curved object and walked a half circle around it. It was twice my height and at least as wide. "Nothing good. Never anything good."

I called the scientists' names. A few seconds later, I heard a rustling sound in the attached lab and a "Hello?" in Dontel's voice. There was more rustling before the greying scientist appeared at the lab door. His facial fur was pressed flat, making me suspect he'd been sleeping.

"Ah, Sedric! What can I do for you?" He rubbed at his face, but the fur maintained its position.

"Are the shimmer suits ready?" I asked.

He smiled. "Ah ha! Yes, they are. They are." He disappeared into the lab again. There was more rustling, and he returned carrying two bags. He handed one to Yentiss. "This will fit you perfectly, my young doe." He regarded me a moment before handing me the other bag. "This...will be close enough." He scratched his cheek. "Perhaps a little snug."

I opened the bag, expecting to see the same blue suit I'd seen demonstrated before. The suit was grey now, though, and glistened. Like it was both reflecting and emanating.

I brought it to my snout and sniffed. Minty? Unexpectedly fresh. "And these things work now? With no...side effects?"

"You'll be perfectly concealed." He clasped his paws together happily. "Go ahead. Try them on!"

I shared an apprehensive look with Yentiss, then emptied the bag and started to pull the suit on. It slid on easily, and afterward I could feel...its presence. It was warm and light, yet it had substance. Mass. I felt a subtle tingling sensation too. Enough to question what it was doing to my body.

After I had the whole thing—hood included—in place, I checked on Yentiss. Her suit seemed to fit perfectly, while mine...was a little snug around my tail.

"What do I feel?" I asked. "The tingling?"

"Nothing to worry about."

I slid my paws down my arms. "But it feels...potentially dangerous."

Dontel nodded. "Well, the suit radiates, of course, but—"

"Radiates!"

"It's not harmful, Sedric. I assure you. Would you like me to show you? I have a scanner that—"

I shook my head. "I suppose I'll have to trust you." I searched the suit for its control but didn't see anything. "How do I make it go again?"

Dontel patted his chest. "Just give it a gentle tap. Pat the chest, Sed."

I did so. The tingling increased to the point I felt warm. All over. I looked at my lower paws. They were blurry, but I could still see the individual toes. I looked at Yentiss again. She was a rhat-sized blur too. Not transparent. Blurry. "I can still see her."

"Of course you can," the scientist said. "You have a suit on. And so does she."

"What?" I patted the suit's chest again and the warmth reverted to a slight tingle. My suited extremities became crisp and clear.

Yentiss, on the other paw, was completely gone.

"Ah, okay," I said. "We were...on the same level."

"Precisely," Dontel said. "If you're both suited and powered on, you can see each other. Otherwise, you might blunder into each other. How embarrassing would that be?"

I activated my suit again and studied my shimmer, then Yentiss's. The thing actually worked. I couldn't believe it.

"Well?" Dontel said. "What do you think?"

I made myself visible and motioned for Yentiss to do the same.

She reappeared and pulled the hood from her head. "That was exhilarating!" she said. "Invigorating and wonderful." She smiled at Dontel. "I've doubted you before, but this—" She pinched her right sleeve. "Is incredible."

The scientist glowed. "Thank you, Officer Yentiss," he said, bowing his head.

I nodded, reluctantly. "I'll admit I'm impressed too."

He bowed again. "That fills my heart with joy, Sedric."

I looked at Yentiss. "Let's gather Louis and get outside. See what he can do."

I felt a glimmer of hope. Louis, functioning shimmer suits, and a promising new location—maybe things would be all right now. Maybe we'd reach our quota and get off this backwards planet. Get back to our clients.

Whoever they were.

CHAPTER 21

Before an hour had passed, Louis, Yentiss and I were making our way through Bossu Wood, headed southeast, toward the farm.

The forest was a beautiful place, filled with towering, green trees and an occasional gentle brook or winding game path. Despite my lack of sleep, I was happy to be there, in that exact moment, beneath an alien sun with those two. Even if one were a primitive uman, and the other, only a moving shimmer in my peripheral vision.

"I don't understand how they work," Louis said. "These invisible suits. Do they rob the sun of its power?"

"I don't know how they work either," I said. "To be honest, I'm surprised they do."

"Why is that?"

I snorted. "Because the scientists are often… unpredictable."

Louis nodded. "I know someone like that. The owner of the inn where we met." A pained expression crossed his face. "He's given to much drink."

I snorted loudly. "I don't think that's the case with the scientists. Though it would explain some things."

Louis looked between Yentiss and I, still with that strange, uncomfortable, expression. "Could you turn your suits off for a while?" he said. "It feels like I'm walking between two ghosts."

"Ghosts?" Yentiss said.

"Dead people," Louis stretched his arms wide. "Their spirits still lingering in our world." He frowned. "Do you not have spirits?"

"Not in close proximity, no," I said. "But I believe the Apolastic church teaches such a thing."

"Well, it's like I'm talking to the wind here. Please, stay quiet when we get to the farm. You will scare someone to death."

"Huh..." I nudged Yentiss. "A potentially useful ability."

Louis chuckled. "You may be ugly, Sedric, but you're funny."

Twenty minutes later, we reached the forest's edge. The view beyond was one of rolling grassland, crisscrossed by narrow, dirt roads. Buildings and stands of trees dotted the countryside. The former were light in color with dark blue or black roofs. The roads were empty of traffic.

Shielding his eyes, he searched all around us, before indicating a distant grey roof. "That's the farm there." He bit his bottom lip and checked our surroundings again.

"What are you looking for?" I asked.

He nodded slowly. "Just making sure there are no signs of infantry here. Of either side." He pointed east. "We're near the border of France and Allied lands."

I searched the area too. I saw only solitary animalpropelled vehicles and a few pockets of pedestrians. All were distant.

The landscape displayed an array of colors. The scents

were wonderful too. A glorious glimpse of the area's summer months.

Again, my spirits lifted. We just might be okay.

"You fear the soldiers too, then?" Yentiss said.

"Oui, I'd rather not encounter any." Louis started to walk again.

Yentiss followed, as did I. "Why?" she asked.

"Many reasons," Louis said. "For the destruction it brings, but also for the chance I might be stopped. A young man, alone, in the early morning..." He smiled softly. "I could be pressed into service again."

"You're not alone, though," she says.

"They wouldn't know that," Louis says. "And they shouldn't know that!" He looked Yentiss's direction. "They would kill you both."

We had stunners with us, of course, but they wouldn't help against an army. It was best to be wary.

We walked an hour over mostly even ground. It would've been a pleasant journey, were it not for the tightness of my suit. It kept riding up to kink my tail, forcing me to reach back and adjust it. Only Yentiss could witness my movements, of course, but that was enough. I'm sure she thought me infected with the scritch.

Stupid suit. Stupid scientists.

The farm was larger than I expected. The central building—the "barn" itself—was simple in construction, but massive—at least a hundred meters long. It had four red exterior walls and a dark grey roof. The barn formed one side of a larger square of structures, all made of the same material—bricks from clay and rock. I would've thought it a fortress had Louis not called it a farm. It was a smaller agrarian version of the region's castles.

A dirt road led directly to the farming complex, but also split to go around it. Yentiss and I walked either side of the road as Louis followed it. I was still a little uncertain about him, so found my right paw hovering near my belt. Near where my stunner rested.

After a few minutes' walk, Louis pointed at the ground near Yentiss and then near me. "You should get off the road," he said. "Your steps are showing."

I glanced down, noting the small disturbance of dust my every step produced, and glanced behind us. There were three trails in the road's dirt. A dead giveaway.

I nodded at Yentiss and moved right into the grass. I was still creating a trail, but at least it wouldn't draw attention to Louis. It made it harder to watch him, but I comforted myself with the fact that we still had his wife on the ship. I wasn't sure about all his motivations, but I knew he loved Anne. And we had her.

A short time later, an animal-drawn wagon exited the farm entrance. Louis raised a hand, and when the cart drew near, the driver yelled "Ho there!" and slowed the vehicle somehow. The animals—"horses"—grunted their displeasure but obeyed.

Unfortunately, Yentiss and I were out of earshot. Frustrating, because I wanted to know everything the young uman was saying. Still, their mouths moved so fast I doubted my translator could've kept up. Louis never looked our way. It was nerve-wracking.

Yentiss must've felt it too because she grabbed my paw and held it tight. My XO instinct was to pull away, but my buck instinct? It thought contact with the female was more important than the chain of command. We were in a dark nebula here, after all, where everything was unclear.

To distract myself, I studied the contents of the cart. It was obscured by a blanket, but whatever was beneath that was large and unevenly proportioned. It wasn't grain or cut grass. It was something dense. Something heavy.

I took a couple steps forward, dragging Yentiss along with me. I leaned toward the cart and sniffed.

The aroma filled my snout so vividly I almost coughed. Cheese, glorious cheese! Multiple kinds and flavors. Wonderful, get-us-out-of-trouble, cheese.

I glanced at the driver and readied my stunner. If I stunned him, we could take the wagon to the edge of the woods and unload from there. That was, if the uman Louis knew how to control the thing. I wasn't sure I could, but I had enough reason to try. A full wagon of reasons.

Yentiss gave my hand a hard squeeze. I looked at her and she shook her blurred-but-beautiful snout.

I raised my equally-blurred shoulders. What? Why not—

She pointed at Louis. The young uman was smiling now, as was the driver. They pressed hands together, and the driver pointed toward the farm proper. Then he shook the horse's reigns and the wagon started to move away.

I gasped, raised my stunner, and started to follow.

Yentiss jerked me back. I shook free of her paw and moved ahead anyway. We needed that cheese!

She scampered in front of me and pulled her hood back, exposing her face.

CHAPTER 22

Louis's eyes widened and he hurriedly moved in front of Yentiss, just as the driver glanced our way. Louis smiled and waved the man away.

The driver waved back, seemingly oblivious.

When the wagon was a couple dozen meters away, Yentiss slid her hood on again.

"Why did you do that?" I asked.

"You were going to shoot him!" she said.

I pointed toward the retreating cart. "It was a wagon-load of cheese!"

She shook her head. "Not enough."

Louis nodded in agreement. "I've toured your cargo bay, Sedric. You'll need a lot more."

I shook with frustration. "We have little time now. And there are soldiers—"

Louis pointed at the farm's entrance. "The driver told me who to talk to. He said they'll be happy to discuss supplying us given the coming storm. There's lots more where that wagon came from."

Yentiss put a paw on my elbow. "This will work, Sed, I can feel it."

I grunted and shook my head but remained quiet the entire time it took us to walk inside. Even when Louis went off to find the man he was to talk to, I waited patiently with Yentiss near the entrance. Trusting that the young uman would return with good news.

I had little choice, and I hated it. Beyond the entrance was a wide expanse—a courtyard formed by the surrounding rectangle of buildings. In that expanse was a fair amount of activity. Uman females manipulated small devices made of wood and cloth. Small fowl ran around the yard while small umans pursued, squealing with glee. There were pens filled with bleating, horned animals. Uman men opened large doors to lead animals from one building to the other. On the far side of the rectangle was a building that I suspected was a dwelling. It was more ornate than the others and had more windows. There were colorful plants near one of the doors.

Yentiss and I sheltered in the shadows of the large barn. Even invisible, it felt more comfortable to be hidden from the morning's light. The shimmer suits worked flawlessly. So much, that I'd almost forgotten where they'd come from. But I felt vulnerable, nonetheless. A muto has three favorite defenses: swarming, scattering, or hiding. We could do only one here.

"This was a bad idea," I said finally. "If he betrays us, we'll be exhibits in the local zoo. Or killed outright."

"He's given no signs of deceit." Yentiss said. "No indication that—"

"He has no loyalty to us either," I said. "No reason to want to help, except for his wife." I watched cautiously as a young uman dressed in brown pants and shirt, manipulated a mechanical device—which I later learned was a "wheelbarrow"— past us and through the exit to the road beyond.

"Maybe he doesn't even like his wife? Maybe he wants to be rid of her? Get her imprisoned on a ship of monsters and—"

"Sed..."

"Well, I don't know!" I said. "Don't know how a primitive mind works."

I noticed a small, dark animal approaching from the courtyard. It had a useful non-uman snout, but it wasn't a "rat." If I were to guess, I'd say it was canine, or perhaps a small equine. It was walking slowly, sniffing at random spots along the way—another animal here, a uman there, the corner of the building. Odd behavior but amusing to watch. Only when it drew near did I get nervous. A few seconds later, it was loping straight for us.

"I think it sees us," I whispered.

"What?"

I drew Yentiss further into the shadows, fully out-of-view of the courtyard. "That!" I said, pointing.

To no avail. The animal came around the corner, sniffed a place on the ground, and followed an unseen trail right to us. It snorted my suit-covered lower paws and legs, before looking up at me and whining.

"That thing will give us away!" I said softly.

"Be still," Yentiss said. "Maybe it will leave."

The creature had no intention of leaving. It sat back on its haunches, opened its mouth, and tipped its head inquisitively. Its tongue dangled from one side of its mouth and it panted, watching.

"What's it doing?" I asked.

The creature dropped to its front legs and yelped. Repeatedly.

"This is not going well," I whispered.

A man approached carrying a large metal cylinder. A container of some sort. He wore blue pants and shirt with a beige hat that seemed to be made of dried grass. He seemed to be headed outside, but when he heard the animal's cry, he slowed and stopped. "Jacques? Why are you here?"

I looked at Yentiss, and together, we retreated a pawful of steps, drawing closer to the barn.

The animal followed, squatted down, and did a hopping move left and then right.

The man drew closer, stepping more into the shadows. "What's gotten into you, Jacques?"

Yentiss shook her head at me.

Wide-eyed, I nodded and raised my stunner.

The animal circled us, whining and panting.

The man noticed something. Possibly the end of my stunner, because he said "Quoi!" and stepped closer still.

I shot him, then I shot the animal. Both dropped to the ground. Thump and thump.

I had little recourse.

Yentiss let out a cry of surprise. "Why did you—?" She pulled the hood from her head and fixed me with a stern look. "You're as bad as Krate," she hissed. "Shooting everything."

"What choice did I have?" I motioned toward the animal. "Come, help me drag them out of view."

She grumbled, but finally relented, taking the tail-end of the animal. We carried it around the exterior corner of the barn and into long grass that should hide it from all but the wariest observer. We hid the uman similarly.

"Are we taking them back to the ship too?" Yentiss asked.

Dread entered my gut. Despite our success in relocating the ship, something was not right here either. Something bad was going to happen. I just knew it.

The man's hat had fallen off, revealing a completely bald scalp. Was he diseased? I located the hat and placed it carefully over the man's face and head. It was more pleasant to look at.

Louis reached the corner of the barn and softly called our names.

"Back here," I said.

Louis walked our way. His eyes widened when he saw the two bodies. "Did you—"

"Stunned," I said. "How was your talk?"

His face brightened. "Very good, Sedric. They will trade us for as much cheese as they can make. There are wagon-loads ready—"

"Trade?" I said. "What could we possibly trade them?"

Louis shrugged. "Certainly, your scientists can—"

"Our scientists?" I snickered. "What could they...?" I glanced at Yentiss, then studied the nearby buildings. All made of primitive materials. Stone and clay. I sighed. "Anything we gave them would be beyond their understanding. And dangerous to leave here."

"They could use a method of creating steam," Louis said. "When I was on your ship—"

"What?"

He nodded. "Many of their machines are powered by steam. But fuel is costly and scarce. If you could find a way to—"

I scratched my chin. "Steam, eh?" I looked at Yentiss again. "Yeah, something like that might be doable. Easy enough that they couldn't mess it up."

Louis smiled brightly. "Excellent!"

"I mean, it would have to be small and self-contained. With all the important parts hidden." I rubbed my chin again. "I wonder if they could make it short-lived? Maybe have it dissolve after a few weeks?"

"You can do that?" Louis said.

I waved my hand. Of course, only Yentiss could see. "Sure. We have a crate full of disposable forming powder. Haven't had much use for it until now."

Louis clapped his hands. "Let's get back and get started then."

"And they'll give us how many wagons?"

"As much as we need," Louis said. "As much as they can make."

"That's a deal I like," I said. "A deal the captain will like too."

"What about them?" Yentiss said, pointing at my two stunjobs.

"They didn't see us," I said.

Louis nodded. "Oui, that's good. They will think it was the sun. Or the vapours."

"Vapours?"

Louis shrugged. "Sometimes people faint. Usually women, but sometimes men too."

I had no idea what the uman was talking about, and given our surroundings, I doubted he knew much about the microscopic world. His primary concern, given all he'd seen in our ship, was heating water. I was surprised he hadn't asked for lights, but perhaps that would come.

I shook my head. "All right. Let's get them their water heater."

CHAPTER 23

Within a few hours, Dontel and Uzel had formed something that would heat water efficiently for a couple months using nuclear batteries they scalped from a broken lab burner. It wasn't much to look at—little more than a thick, silver plate—but it got the job done.

After a nap, I went with Louis to deliver the heater. Though I remained in my shimmer suit, and partially hidden, I could tell the farm owner was enamored with his new toy. Especially after Louis demonstrated its full usefulness, placing a pot of water on its top surface and bringing it to a boil in seconds. When asked where the marvel had come from, Louis simply said, "the Americas" and that seemed to be explanation enough. I later learned that "the Americas" was another country, often known for technological wonders, particularly in the area of steam power.

In exchange, the owner agreed to have two full wagons of cheese ready for us by nightfall, which was the sort of response I hoped for. It would take more than two loads to meet our obligations, but along with what we'd scavenged already, it would get us halfway.

More negotiations with the farmer and a few more night-time deliveries and we'd have everything we needed. I was sure of it.

The captain seemed confident too because his mood improved dramatically. "Time off and a bonus," he told me. "Enough to win the finest sire you can find." He lowered his snout and winked. "Enough to keep her too."

I never had that level of enthusiasm, nor did I believe he would—in the end—be as generous as promised. But it was a pleasant dream. After our mission was complete, I could've used some time off ship, preferably in a place of luxury. The grease-baths of Relgus, or even the food fountains of Cenene.

Regardless, the captain made me part of the cheese recovery mission too. It was a simple task. The wagons would be delivered to the road closest to the woods, where Louis would meet them. The deliverymen would return to the farm on the horses they'd used to pull the wagons. The next morning, the emptied wagons would be waiting for pickup.

There were questions about the drop off and delivery process, of course. Specifically, why the delivery had to be done at night.

"The buyers work during the day," Louis answered. "It's the only time they can gather the cheese."

That explanation proved sufficient. The farmer's delight with his new heater and the promise of more wonders helped to quell additional curiosity.

So, that night, along with a crew that included Krate, I set off to meet Louis. We dressed in shimmer suits and brought with us three hovering carts and a lot of good will. Finally, our luck was improving.

We reached the wagons without difficulty. Both were covered with cloth, but there was a high mound beneath those covers. For mutos, there was little disguising what the wagons contained. The aroma was thick and heavy.

For many seconds no one said anything. The only sounds were grunts of pleasure and long draws of breath. A couple mutos wobbled and had to grab the wagons' sides. Lactose intoxicated.

Krate raised his snout, breathed deep, and coughed. "Better than mud when your toes sweat."

I shook my head, but slapped Krate's back anyway. "Come on. Let's get this back."

Some of the crew moaned, wanting to bask in the aroma a few moments longer. But I wouldn't allow it. We had work to do, and even the nights were dangerous now.

The first trip, loading our smaller hover carts and transporting the contents to the ship, went without incident. There were a few times when someone tried to sample the boon—and in fact, a few succeeded—but after the necessary reprimands, snacking was no longer an issue. Plus, there was some comfort in knowing that the umans had produced desirable food. If my crew wanted it, then our clients would too—and maybe wouldn't notice if we were a few kilos short.

I only wanted to be done. Despite his newfound optimism, the captain insisted that we needed to leave in two days, regardless of our take. That wasn't much of a window to finish in, even if things went perfectly. And they never did.

I'd asked the captain what would happen if we failed to return. If we shirked our obligation and hid in parts unknown. He only shook his head and rubbed his hands together nervously. That worried me. It suggested that whoever our clients were, they had influence enough, or assassins enough, to make life uncomfortable. We needed to deliver.

As we left the woods for our second load, my feelings of hopelessness returned. The road where the wagons were parked was visible from the wood's edge. Even from a distance

I could see there were multiple umans there now. Nearly a dozen, in fact, along with some horses. Half of them carried some form of handheld lighting. It danced as they moved, creating uneven shadows on the ground around them.

And they were approaching the wagons. Our wagons. Our cheese.

I held up a paw and hissed the crew to silence. "Louis has company."

"Did the farmer come back?" Krate asked.

"I don't think so. There's too many." I was concerned about Louis, sure, but also about the cheese. What were all the umans doing here? It was nearly midnight.

I looked at the others—Krate, Feelix, Cantie and Derris— all shimmering versions of their former selves. Invisible to anyone else. One positive I could cling to.

"What now, sir?" Feelix asked. "Do we go back?"

I shook my head. "We need that cheese. And we need Louis."

"But he's uman," Cantie said. "Among his own." He pointed at the wagons with both paws. "If we go down there? They may hear us or see our tracks."

"We have a hundred meters yet and we know how to be quiet." I got down on all fours. "Let's get close enough to listen." I was about to bet on the suits and our stealth, I realized. Typically, the latter was better than any uman—primitive or no. If a muto doesn't want to be heard, he rarely is.

Everyone mimicked my posture. The grass was long enough to conceal us, even were our suits to fail. That was something.

We scurried toward the wagons in single file. The closer we got, the more anxious I became. I knew uniforms now when I saw them. I recognized the telltale pattern of bold colors and stripes. I didn't know which side the umans ahead were on, but I had no doubt they were soldiers.

A half dozen surrounded the wagons and Louis. Another two milled about the road and grassland beyond. These latter variety were mounted, so had the advantage of a higher point of view, along with speed of movement.

Krate touched my shoulder. "Aren't those—"

"Yes," I whispered then held up a cautioning paw. We were less than twenty meters away now. In this situation, I wished the crew hadn't ingested translators. Untranslated, we could've spoken freely, our voices sounding like soft squeaks and clicks to the umans.

I settled for short sentences and a hushed tone. "They're armed. We need to be careful. " I looked at each muto in turn. "No loud noises. No sudden movements. We're here to listen."

Everyone nodded. Everyone—even Krate—seemed to understand.

We crept closer still. Soon I heard Louis and a heated voice questioning him. I held up a paw again.

"Then you are a spy!" the heated one said. "A Bonaparte spy."

"I'm a simple farmer," Louis said. "From yonder farm. This is my—"

"It's food!" the interrogator said. "No one delivers pong at night, except sympathizers. Where are the French troops you're supplying?"

French? I glanced at the sky, now full of stars. Hadn't the soldiers on the *Granum* been French? Wasn't Louis French?

The soldiers nearest me had their backs turned. Squinting, I studied their uniforms. They were different then the men on the ship. The striping went different directions, and the primary color was red. Not blue like the French soldiers.

"*Sacré bleu,*" I whispered, copying something Louis often said. "They're the enemy."

The lead mutos—Krate and Feelix—gave me a questioning look.

I shook my head. Lowered myself to the ground. What should I do now?

"I know nothing about the French army," Louis said. "I'm to make a delivery to an inn in Quatre Bras. 'Le Rat Volant.' Perhaps you've—"

There was a thump, as if someone had been struck. "There's no such place," the harsh uman said. "You made that up."

"I didn't," Louis said, softer now. "I will take you there if you like."

The interrogator chuckled. "And lead us into a Crapaud ambush? I think not." Next came the sound of movement. "If you won't tell us what we want to know, you'll be tossed in a black hole for a French spy."

Black hole? I didn't like the sound of that. I rose up on all fours, and when that didn't reveal enough, I got up on my back paws. There were two soldiers on our side of the trailing wagon. Two others lingered near the lead wagon. Three more were in front of that wagon with Louis. One of them restrained Louis's arms. Another held a light for the third. I noticed a new bump on Louis's face.

The third soldier, whose uniform was slightly different than the others, manipulated a rope in his hands. After a minute of this, he showed it to Louis. The rope had a tight loop in one end. "All we need is a horse and a proper tree to hang him."

Louis looked past me, toward the forest from which we'd come. "I'm no spy," he said. "I'm a free man. A model citizen." He started to struggle.

The rope-holder chortled. "If you were a bang up citizen, you would be a swaddy for one side or the other. Since you are here, alone, in the dead of night, I can only assume you <u>are</u> a swaddy in smalls." He motioned to one of the mounted men.

The man nodded, galloped over, and took the rope. He

joined another mounted soldier near a small cluster of trees. They selected a large tree and fed the rope over its lowest branch.

My companions stood now too. Krate's snout was tight in anger. Feelix and Cantie looked worried. Derris appeared to be counting umans.

Digging into my belt, I took out my stunner and raised it up where they could see.

Everyone nodded and brought out their stunners too.

We were invisible, after all. We could stun ten umans before they knew what hit them. I waved Feelix and Cantie toward the more-distant mounted men, then shrugged the other two toward the nearby soldiers.

I crept between the wagons to where Louis was being held. I contemplated the best course of action before finally deciding to attack those holding Louis. From there, the men holding Louis would be easy to take out. The other soldier—the talker—would be harder since he was shielded by the others, but I could be fast when I wanted to be. This time, I wanted to be.

After a quick scan, I shifted my position again. Enough that I could see the other rhats. Feelix and Cantie were in position near the trees. Krate and Derris looked ready near the rear wagon. I leveled my stunner at the nearest man and raised my free hand as a signal.

There was a strange hissing sound. Then the soldier-in-charge looked straight at me. "Bumpers of belch! What is that?"

CHAPTER 24

Following the hiss, there was a blinding flash of red. It was so bright and unexpected that, at first, I'd thought I'd been hit by an unseen weapon. Only after I blinked a few times and my eyes adjusted did I realize that I hadn't been hit by the color—I <u>was</u> the color.

"The suit," I muttered. "The Emperor-forsaken shimmer suit." For some reason, Dontel's creation had reverted to the ugly-red-uman mode. Not only was I visible, I was hideous.

Everyone was looking at me, a beacon of color in an otherwise somber night. Thankfully, all the uman soldiers seemed frozen in place. Startled to inaction.

"Attack!" I yelled, while stunning the soldier nearest me. As he was the one holding the light source, my action had the added benefit of darkening the area. Adding more confusion. I next shot the soldier restraining Louis. The former grunted and quickly joined his compatriot on the ground.

I heard the crackling sound of other stunners behind me. Those of Krate and Derris. Another light was extinguished. There were grunts and shouts.

Louis turned my direction. I raised a paw in greeting, but he shrieked and ran for the forest. "The red man!" he said. "He's here!"

"Louis?" I said, watching him go. *Red man?* What was that about?

I hesitated long enough for the uman officer to draw his sword and level it at me. "Who are you?" he shouted. "Who do you serve?"

I chuckled. "I serve mostly myself, uman. Unless there's a waitress at the table. In that case, I—"

I heard a thunderclap and felt something knick my right ear. I dropped to all fours and looked in all directions. Feelix and Cantie hadn't been as efficient in their stunning. One of the horses was on the ground, but the soldier it belonged to had a gun aimed in the direction of my still invisible mutos. He swept it back and forth, trying to aim at something he sensed, but couldn't see.

The rifle of the remaining mounted soldier was pointed at me. He must've been the one who'd fired.

The officer made a quick sidestepping move, sliced his sword back and forth, then lunged at me. I hopped left, but still felt his weapon bite into my side. He drew back, but the sword's end remained lodged in my suit.

I tugged hard and the suit tore, exposing much of my right side.

The officer cried out. "What manner of magic is this? Does Bonaparte command the beasts now?"

"There's that beast again." I reached for my stunner, but found it missing. I'd dropped it somewhere. Probably when the uman stabbed me.

He shouted and dove at me again. This time I simply reacted, leaping like any rhat would in similar circumstances. The effort took me completely over the uman's head. I landed, softly, in the grass behind him.

There was another rifle shot, followed by two stun shots in quick succession. I glanced in the direction of the sounds, the trees where the mounted soldiers had been, and saw Feelix standing over the body of one soldier. Cantie was near the other—also downed—soldier, paws raised in a show of triumph.

I wanted to scold him, but I heard motion behind me, my opponent, and quickly leapt again. There was an outrush of breath followed by a word that I suspected was profanity. I turned and smiled. "Missed again!"

The uman shook with anger or fear. I didn't care which.

"Now I know the rumors are true," he said. "Napoleon consorts with demons."

I snorted. "I don't know this Napoleon, but if he's anything like Louis over there." I pointed toward the woods. "He's probably not so bad." I smiled again. "You should've left him alone." I noticed my suit was now flickering. "Bones, I think you broke my suit." I growled and slapped my chest, causing the suit to shut off.

The uman gasped and surged forward. He stopped short of me, though. Didn't try to cut me.

"You're an interesting one," I said. "Not brave, but certainly not—"

There was a stunner's cackle. The uman made a gurgling sound and slumped to the ground. His sword fell with him.

I shook my head. "I was making a point there, Krate."

Krate stood at the edge of the rear-most wagon, stunner raised. "Sorry, Boss. I thought he was going to—"

I waved a paw. "Nah. That's all right." I checked our surroundings again. Only mutos were left standing. I sighed with relief. All looked good.

I retrieved the sword from the ground. It was lighter than I expected. I swept it back and forth a few times like I'd seen the uman do. It was the first time I'd ever held a long blade—especially a metal one. I'd encountered a few swords in our travels, but those were easily overcome by my pistol. Even the light-casting models. I shook the sword again and shrugged. "I think I'll keep this." I slid it under my belt. Not bad. Not uncomfortable. I'd store it in my quarters with the few souvenirs I allowed myself. Typically things that almost killed me.

I frowned at the uman soldiers. "Now, what do we do with them? Can't leave them like this." I waved toward the woods. "If we do, they may come looking for us later."

"Just like the massacre," Krate said.

"Yeah, don't want that."

"You can use them as slaves." It was Louis's voice, coming from somewhere beyond the wagon.

I raised a paw that direction. Louis's silhouette became obvious there, not ten meters into the long grass. "So that's where you got off to." I snorted. "You're fast when you want to be."

He drew close enough that I could see his face. His injury was still evident.

"He got you something good." I motioned toward the fallen officer. "That guy."

"If that's the worst this war brings me, I'll be all right." Louis smiled. "Thank you for saving me, Monsieur Sedric."

I shrugged. "The captain would be mad if I'd lost you. We *need* you."

He chuckled and waved his arms. "Clearly, you don't."

"Not for the scrapping, maybe," I said. "But for the rest." I wrinkled my snout. "Why'd you run off like that?"

"There's a rumor about the Emperor," he said. "That he follows the advice of a demonic red man. I thought you were him."

"A demon?"

He nodded. "A spiritual creature. Evil and dark."

"Couldn't be good and light, eh? Always beasts and monsters with you umans."

"Sorry," Louis said. "Just trying to be honest. Why did you look like that?"

I waved a paw. "Bah. Suit must've malfunctioned. Figures mine was the one that went." I glanced at the sky. It was noticeably lighter than before. "Anyway, we have work to do. Cheese to get on board."

"And the men?" Cantie said.

I shrugged. "Guess we're taking them with us."

CHAPTER 25

So now we had eleven umans on the *Granum*, half of whom were involved in a territorial dispute with the other half. It was a potentially dangerous situation. I didn't count Louis as part of the danger, of course, because he felt like part of the crew now. But the rest? What were we to do? Drop them off somewhere where their dispute didn't matter?

It wasn't long before the Captain got wind of the situation and called a meeting on the bridge. He invited the heads of all the departments, which meant that, along with Yentiss and I, Cindel of security, Dontel of sciences, the doctor, and Fedwi of support services—meaning cooking and cleaning—was there too. Cindel wasn't generally a problem, but the other three? Always had their own agendas.

It made for a tight fit too. The bridge was built for five. Seven pushed it to its limits—particularly when some of our number clearly hadn't used their cleaning soaps in a while. I suspected Dontel and Fedwi of being the main reducers of the air quality. Dontel was known to forgo cleanliness in pursuit of his inventions, and Fedwi was generally lazy. I strained my snout to detect the ship's usual smell. It was present, but oh-so-faint.

Yentiss and I stood near the center screen. The other heads formed a tight circle around the command chair. There was less than a meter between me and Dontel to my right. I hadn't mentioned the malfunction of my shimmer suit to him yet. There hadn't been time.

"Should Louis be here?" I asked. Not that I wanted more bodies in the room, but it felt like any decision about the umans ought to have some sort of representation.

The captain was on the opposite end of the room, near the exits. Unable to pace, he simply rubbed his hands together nervously. "No, I only want crewmembers here for this."

Yentiss exchanged a look with me. "Might I ask why, sir?" she said.

The captain's eyes widened. "Because we have hard decisions to make. Decisions our uman friend might not like."

I laid a paw on the nearest console. "What decisions?"

"The umans!" he said. "We can't keep them." He looked at Fedwi. "Tell them, Fed!"

Fedwi had tan fur and a narrow snout. He was also twice the size of anyone else present—a by-product of his perpetual proximity to food. Even now, his paws rested on the shelf of his midsection. "We can't feed them," he said. "Even with most of the crew still asleep."

"See there?" the captain said. "It's simple. Umans eat a lot. We only have so much food."

"We have half a storage room full of—"

The captain waved me to silence. "That doesn't count, and you know it. That's for our customers."

"We'll gather more," I said. "Keep some back for the umans."

"There's no time for that," the captain said. "We'll be lucky not to miss our delivery window as it is."

"What do you propose?" I ask. "We can't turn them loose. They've seen too much."

Dontel got a concerned look. "I thought they were stunned." He glanced at the doctor. "That they've been kept sedated."

The doctor nodded. "Yes, all but Master Louis and his wife."

I shook my head. "The others saw too much even before we brought them aboard." I recounted our encounter with the soldiers, along with my malfunctioning suit.

"What did you do to it?" Dontel said.

"Do to what?"

"The suit! You must've done something to make it go red." He looked at the captain. "They are foolproof now. We tested."

I snorted. "Foolproof!"

Dontel sneered and raised his snout. "It appears someone here is a science denier."

I chuckled. "You call what you do <u>science</u>?"

Dontel made a clucking sound. "What happened to you, Sedric? You weren't always so hostile toward technology and—"

"Hostile? I'll show you—"

"Science-denier!"

"What the—"

The captain hissed. "Knock it off!"

"I'd love to," I said. "Love to knock it right off the ship."

The captain shot me a look. "Sedric!"

I raised a paw. "My apologies. I over spoke. Been a busy couple days."

Yentiss touched my left arm, sympathetically.

"I was up all night loading," I said.

"Can we get back to the issue at hand?" the captain asked.

"Yeah. Sure."

He looked at Dontel. "That okay with you too?"

Dontel gave a surprised look. "I was never at odds with anyone."

I wanted to throttle him. I really did. But I somehow held my myself back.

The captain panned the room. "Now, does anyone else have a suggestion? For what we do about the umans?"

"We dispose of them," Fedwi said.

"Again with the killing?" I said.

Yentiss shook her head. "I don't want that."

"There's no need to waste them." Fedwi patted his stomach. Smiled at the captain. "Uman meat is delectable if properly prepared. Our clients likely wouldn't—"

Yentiss's whiskers drooped. "You can't be serious." She looked at the captain. "Tell me he isn't serious."

I leaned close to Yentiss and whispered. "He makes our food too, remember. Make you wonder."

The captain rubbed his hands together. "We aren't phants here," he said. "We won't be eating intelligents."

Fedwi raised a finger. "But we—"

The captain scowled. "Nor will we be serving them to others."

Fedwi shrugged. "Only a suggestion, sir. I assumed the situation was dire."

"It is." The captain looked at me. "Desperate."

The doctor raised a paw which the captain recognized. "As much as I'm against killing in principle," the doctor said, "there's a new problem that might make extermination a better route."

"And what's that?" the captain asked.

"Parasites, sir."

"Eh?"

The doctor nodded. "The umans are carrying tiny parasites called 'poux' or 'lice.' We've been sterilizing those we discover, but..." He looked at his lower paws, as if in shame. "Some of the crew has gotten infested too. I fear an epidemic. If the vermin spread to the sleepers... It could be difficult to contain."

"What does it do?" the captain asked. "This parasite? Does it kill? Incapacitate?"

"It carries diseases."

"Uman diseases?"

The doctor nodded. "Yes, and the risk of a cross-species jump is low. But there's still danger in the parasite's spread, sir.
"

The captain stroked his chin. Nodded slowly. "And the symptoms?"

"Primarily itching, sir."

A few of those present started scratching, but all the rest looked uncomfortable. I imagined the parasite's presence on my skin too. Even my left paw, my bumble paw, didn't ache now, but only itched. Incessantly. I fought for many seconds before finally giving in.

"They can be stopped, right?" I said, scratching. "There's a treatment?"

The doctor nodded. "Yes, but their spread will be impossible to contain if we keep bringing on carriers. These lice prefer to live in the furred regions of the body. And unlike umans, we have lots of fur."

The captain looked at me. "Sedric?"

"Sir?"

"I'm looking for a reason not to exterminate the umans now. There seems to be many reasons to do so."

"What if we dropped them off somewhere?" Cindel offered. "Took them to another part of this world?" He glanced at me. "Would that work?"

As head of security, Cindel rarely was in the limelight. Rarely had to speak to anyone aside from those in his detail. It was evident in how he held himself now. He was rigid, with one hand rubbing his belt as if fishing for a weapon. He cleared his throat and attempted to stand taller. "I mean, if left in a foreign environment the chance of the umans telling anyone what they were exposed to seems negligible. They'd be foreigners. Possibly crazy foreigners."

It wasn't a bad idea. Good enough to buy us another couple days of peace, anyway. Get us out of this meeting. "I like it," I said. "Good compromise."

"It limits the amount of food loss," the captain said. "Which is something. Doesn't fix the parasite problem, though."

"Perhaps I can help with that," Dontel said. "We could build a delousing system into the suits. One that would protect the wearers." He smiled. "Then we'd just have to make everyone a wearer for a time."

"We're going to need more paws," I said then. "Louis has arranged a lot more shipments. Enough to reach our goal on time."

"You're proposing we wake more?"

I nodded. "And give some thought to something Louis suggested last night."

"What's that?"

"That we use the captured soldiers as labor. They could help load the ship, for instance."

The captain drew quiet, contemplating.

"It would make security's job easier too," Cindel said. "Watching them all in one group versus spread about the ship. We could contain them in the cargo holds. Have guards stationed overhead."

The captain nodded. "Can the umans handle our equipment?"

"I don't see why not," I said. "They've already proven remarkably adaptable. The farmer had no trouble with the—"

"I like it," the captain said. "Gives everything and everyone a purpose." He looked at me. "And this farmer has more food coming?"

"I think if we keep supplying him with trinkets, he'll bring as many wagons as we wanted."

The captain smiled and clapped his paws together. "That's what I like to hear, Sedric. A way out of this mess."

Yentiss gave my left paw a squeeze this time. It was a little painful, but it was a good pain.

"What if we encounter more umans, sir?" Cindel asked.

"What?"

Cindel glanced at me. "Just observing the trend, sir. Since we appear to gaining umans here, are we going to keep gaining them? I need to know for staffing, sir. Watching a few dozen is one thing, but if it becomes hundreds or thousands—"

"Thousands!"

Cindel shrugged. "My job to be thorough, sir."

The captain scratched his snout. "No reason not to add a few if it seems appropriate. I mean, as long as we have a place to store them and work for them, no reason to waste—" He glanced at Fedwi. "—good help."

There were nods of approval all around. Only Fedwi and the doctor seemed disappointed.

It was the best I could hope for from such a meeting. There were a few intangibles. A few variables that could jump the wrong way, but I was relieved. One more day and we should be free. Able to deliver our goods and be off to something else.

I couldn't wait.

CHAPTER 26

Following the meeting, I went to my quarters feeling good. I was exhausted, sure, but my perpetual goal—the ship's safety and preservation—still seemed possible. The next day would find us filling our climate-controlled cargo bay. Then we'd drop the umans—Louis and wife included—somewhere else on-planet, leave this primitive world to its wars, and make our delivery.

The experience hadn't been as trouble-free as I might have liked, but it hadn't been all bad either. Any mission that the ship flies away from is a success in my book. Everything beyond that was what we called "long-tail." An unexpected bonus.

I crawled into my nook, pulled my coverlet around myself and dropped into dreamland. I could've been gassed, I slept so soundly. Even the noises that invaded the early morning hours became part of my sleeping adventures. Bangs and thumps were the attacks of dangerous creatures. Things with little fur and dangling appendages. Spider-like and vicious. Bounding, striking, evils—all taken down by my sword.

Only when my wall com chimed did I awaken, and even then, it took a full two minutes for me to fully come to my senses. My first question was why the chime seemed to have an echo. As I stared listlessly around the room, at its blue walls and grey ceiling, I could hear the chime's low tone, and then, an answering thump. A deeper rumble.

Next came the sound of someone banging on my door.

I grunted, shook my head, and slid free of the nook. I had a silver longshirt hanging on wall hook that I pulled on. I glanced nervously from the com screen—flashing red—to the door. What to answer first?

Finally, I waved a paw at the com and shuffled to the door. Yentiss was in the hall, eyes wide and fur bristled. "Something's happening outside, Sed. Captain wants you on the ramp."

I nodded, took a step back, and checked the com. It no longer flashed. "Is that what the call was about?"

"Don't know," she said.

I squinted at the screen. It said, "Missed message from the Captain." I shook my head. "Apparently so. Let's go."

Minutes later, Yentiss and I walked down the ship's main ramp. It was still early morning, the sky still dark. There was a lot of action below. Along with a parked cart and crewmembers unloading it, there was a group of muto's around the captain— Cindel and a couple other guards. All looked concerned. other mutos were scattered about the periphery of the clearing. Some scurried into the woods, others away from it.

But everywhere, there was a nervous energy.

"What's going on?" I asked aloud.

Yentiss shook her head. A moment later, a portion of the sky to the south lit up. Next came a series of booms.

"Is that a storm?" Yentiss asked.

I grunted, keeping my eyes fixed on the sky in that direction. It lit up again two seconds later. More heavy thumps. "It's a storm alright. The worst kind."

We reached the group with the captain. The latter scowled when he saw me. "Where's the uman?"

"Louis?"

He gave an exasperated sigh. "Louis, yes. Why didn't you bring him? Didn't you hear my message?"

"No...ah..." I glanced at Yentiss, who nodded. "I'll go get him," she said then. She bounded back up the ramp, reaching the top with only a few hops.

The captain sneered. "He needs to get here quick." He indicated the woods east. "The umans are up to something over that way. Lots of them according to the transfer team." He pointed toward the cart. "They scattered at the first sound, of course. Thankfully, they brought the cart with them." He sighed. "Left some cheese behind." He looked at me. "I have the scientists working on suits. We need that cheese. Whatever we can get."

I knew that, of course.

"I've stationed perimeter guards," he continued. "I want to make sure we don't get found here. Not before—"

There were more distant booms, followed by a staccato that could've been uman rifles. I searched the star-filled sky in all directions. Despite the early hour, it already felt warm. There was little wind.

"How many umans are there?" I asked.

He shook his head. "Haven't seen, but I've been told thousands."

Thousands?

The captain glanced past me.

I followed his eyes to the ramp where Yentiss was now descending with Louis. The former's tail flicked back and forth, keeping pace with her steps.

When they reached us, the captain grabbed my shoulder. "Take the uman east and see what he says. Get his lay of it."

"I'm right here, sir," Louis said. "I can understand you."

The captain glanced at Louis, but only shook his head. "We need information," he said to me again. "As much as we can get." He squinted. "Wait...you don't have a shimmer on."

I glanced down at my longshirt. "I was sleeping," I said. "If I—"

The captain growled. "There's a box of 'em around here somewhere. Get one on." He looked at Cindel. "In fact, everyone should have one on."

Cindel nodded. "Yes, sir."

"Can I go?" Yentiss pointed at Louis and me. "With them?"

The captain scowled but said "fine."

A few minutes later, Yentiss and I were shimmer-suited and in the forest again. I felt fortunate this time because my suit fit perfectly. The captain might be angry, our mission might be in jeopardy—we all might die—but at least my suit had plenty of room for my tail.

"Your captain doesn't like me," Louis said.

"It's umans in general," I said. "Nothing personal." I didn't mention that our cook thought umans were food. I doubted that would help.

"But you came to <u>our</u> planet," Louis said. "To take <u>our</u> cheese. You knew humans were here."

I smiled, though I knew Louis couldn't tell for my suit. "Nothing personal there either. You had what we needed."

Louis paused at a tree to pat its trunk. "How noble. Are all of your kind out only for themselves, then?"

Yentiss placed a paw on his back, causing him to startle. "Sorry," she said. "Not all of us, no. The captain is—"

"On a mission," I said. "The place we're taking the cheese...well, there's something going on there. Something that has him...nervous."

Louis looked at the sky. "But there are other humans out there?" he said. "Like me?"

"Sure," I said. "Lots of them."

"I would like to meet those humans," he said.

"Well, I don't know about..." We reached the edge of the forest and I let my voice trail off. To the east, many kilometers from our rendezvous spot with the wagons, was a moving wall of light. It was too dark and distant to make out individuals, but it was clear by the number of lights and their wavering distribution that they were held by individual umans. Thousands of them. An army.

Yentiss gasped and brought a paw to her mouth. "Whose army is that?"

Louis shook his head. "Too far away to be certain, but coming from that direction, I would guess them part of the Coalition forces."

"Not your country?" Yentiss said.

"But wait..." Louis shook his head. "I believe they're mounted."

The morning's light broke over the horizon beyond the troops. After a few seconds of watching, I could discern new details. "They're riding horses," I said. "They have red overcoats."

"Are you sure?" Louis said.

"I can see them too," Yentiss said. "Red and riding horses."

"They are the Emperor's Lancers." There was the sound of hope in Louis's voice. "This battle will be won."

There was another round of booms, this time from the south. It was difficult to find the source, but I saw flashes of lights that direction too. Another advancing army?

"That must be the Coalition," Louis said. "Possibly the British, though perhaps the Prussians."

The names meant nothing, but I nodded anyway. That those were enemies of "France" was all I needed to know. Two forces at war were converging on our spot and we still had a cargo hold to fill. Did we dare leave early? Would the captain even allow it?

I grunted. "We may have no choice."

"No choice, monsieur?" Louis said.

I tapped my chest, deactivating my suit.

Louis's eyes widened as I reappeared. Then he smiled. "Much better," he said.

"Unless I miss my guess," I said, "we're about to be in the middle of something here. Something violent."

Louis nodded. "Oui. That would appear to be the case. The soldiers from last night an advance guard." He frowned. "We didn't slow what was coming. I hoped by taking them, we might."

"What's coming?" Yentiss asked.

Louis put a hand on a nearby sapling. "The aggressors haven't said much. They wouldn't, of course." He pointed toward the distant wall of lights. "But I suspect they were searching for the Lancers." He looked to the south. "And were part of that force over there. Or maybe not. Maybe others are coming too."

"Others?"

"I've lost track of the armies against Napoleon," Louis said. "The Prussians, the British, the Netherlands..."

I snorted. "Not that different from own Emperor. He has many enemies." I put a paw on a tree too, feeling its cool strength. "Not sure he has friends either."

The tree did nothing for what I felt inside, though. We were swirling a collapsar now. I looked at the parked wagons. One was still half full. "We need our cheese, Louis. How are we going to get it while in the middle of a battle?" I looked toward the south again. There was a creek and a small rise there that the road to the farm circumvented. "What else is down that way? Beyond the hill."

"More villages. Another small forest with a bridge."

"And the armies?" I said. "Would they be using the roads to travel?"

"For the most part, yes."

I looked at Yentiss. "I wonder if we sent a crew down there to block the road. Maybe drop a tree or damage the bridge."

"That would slow the engagement," Louis said. "Yes."

"Maybe give us enough time to get our supplies out and be done."

"Perhaps."

I nodded. "Okay, I'll send a team to do it. Maybe send the scientists too. If there's one thing they know how to do, it's mess things up." I felt pain in my left paw then, and flexing it, worked the pain away. We still might have a chance.

CHAPTER 27

As soon as we got back, I organized a team, led by Cindel and including Uzel, to see about blocking the road to the south in some way. They went armed with stunners, carrying small munitions, and completely obscured by shimmer suits—the last a necessity given it was now fully morning.

In the meantime, another portion of the sleepers—near two dozen—were awakened and set to the tasks of unloading and scavenging. We had no more time for bartering. We needed outright pillaging and packing.

Along the way, more umans were acquired. Some through happenstance—like how we'd found Louis—but others were more deliberate. In one case, a team had accidentally frightened a trio of, as Louis labeled them, "farm maidens." The mutos, properly clothed in shimmer suits, were liberating pies from a rack where they'd been left to cool when one of the maids happened upon them. She witnessed the pies, seemingly hovering in midair, and let out a tail-curling shriek. When the other two maids rushed to see what the problem was, the muto crew stunned them all.

The crew could've left the females behind, of course, but one of them—Krate again—felt guilty for scaring the umans. He also wondered if it was safe to leave them alone, since he knew little about uman females. Perhaps the stunner had injured them?

So, we acquired our first female umans. This distressed the captain, as they weren't as useful, he surmised, to the task of loading the cargo bay. "Can't carry enough," he said. "Plus, they distract the men." The latter disadvantage was enough to make the captain want to hand them over to Fedwi to be disposed.

Yentiss argued that killing creatures that got the men's attention might lead to full-out rebellion. Not only would we have to waste time disciplining them, we'd get less work accomplished.

The captain wasn't convinced, and with a concluding wave, marched toward the women's cell, seemingly inclined to dispose of them himself.

Yentiss and I followed.

It was here that Louis's wife, Anne, showed her merit. She happened to cross paths with me in the hallway, a box of clothing in her arms. When she asked me why we were there, I gave her a quick summary.

She dropped the box and hustled after the captain, dogging him with "Kind sir, wait!" and "Your excellency, please!" until he stopped and looked at me. "Why does this one bother me?"

"I want to talk with you, brave captain," she said.

The captain found it difficult to continue addressing me, as Anne seemed to be ever in his line of sight, shifting in a tight circle around him. Finally, he relented, and leaning forward, looked squarely in her eyes. "Female uman! What do you want of me?"

She curtsied and fanned her face with a hand. "Only to inform you of things to which you might be ignorant."

"Such as?" the captain hissed.

More fanning. "The worth of a woman, of course." Returning to her dropped box, she retrieved a pair of brown pants. "I made these! Stitched together from a few of your sturdiest blouses." She held the pants up and flipped them so he could see both sides. "As good as you could find in any market. Probably better."

The captain snorted and pushed the pants away. "I care nothing for togs. Especially uman togs."

"Of course, you don't, sir." She flourished a hand over the captain's grey longshirt. "Your people require little in the way of covering. But, the umans you've taken do and will. They don't have the fur the Creator has given you. They need protection and warmth."

That brought a paw to the captain's chin. "You make a good point. You can make them some as needed."

"Of course," she said. "But also there's the food you're searching for."

"The cheese?" he said. "What of it?"

"I know how to make that too, along with other delicacies—foie gras, flammenkueche, choucroute—all require only the right equipment."

"We have a cook," he said, glancing at me. "His name is Fedwi."

"And I'm sure he's a fine one," Anne said. "But he's used to cooking for you. Not for umans. And not like Earth."

The captain nodded. "Again, it's good we have you to—"

Anne gasped. "But, kind sir, I *can't* do it alone. Not for all the umans on this ship."

The captain seemed to contemplate this. "Eh...you need help?"

Anne smiled and pointed at me. "I'm told the Lord God has brought me help. Or was Sedric wrong when he said there were three young women on board now?"

The captain gazed up the hall, to where the three women

were held. "He's not wrong. I was just going to see them. See if they needed anything."

Anne brought her hands together and smiled. "Excellent. Let me go with you. I'll see if they can help."

"Er..." The captain glanced at me. "I can do that. I can ask."

"Yes, but you'll only frighten them." Anne placed her hands on her chest. "I can talk to them as a uman female. Use my instincts."

The captain's paw still hovered near his snout. "And you can convince them? Get them to help you make the things you mentioned? The food and coverings?"

She nodded slowly. "I'm known as a persuasive woman. Louis says that I grip notions like a dragon."

"A what?"

She fluttered a hand. "Only a figure of speech, sir."

Another grunt, then he raised an arm toward the female's quarters. "Come along, then."

Anne winked at Yentiss and I, before tucking a hand into the captain's elbow. "Can I hold onto you, please?" She pointed at the floor. "These hallways are hard on my shoes. They want to catch for some reason."

The captain didn't resist. I almost laughed aloud. Yentiss was equally amused.

Before the hour was through, the captain had decided that any uman we acquired was of some use. A fortunate turn.

A few hours later, Cindel's team returned with news that they'd made the road to the south temporarily impassable. It had been dangerous work, as the force that was amassing there was formidable. Tens of thousands, Cindel estimated.

I didn't like the sound of that, but Louis thought the battle would pass us by. He couldn't think of anything worth fighting for in the area. None of the cities were large enough to be considered strategic or decisive in any way.

When I asked him what he thought the nearest area of worth would be, he only shrugged. "There's a small hamlet north of here. A crossroads, really, named 'Quatre Bras.'" Another shrug. "Not sure why anyone would want to go there, though."

CHAPTER 28

Through that day and into the evening our scavenging continued. Four more loads from the farm were delivered. Carts of food were stolen from area businesses and residences. We were making progress, even as the sounds of war were everywhere. The entire crew was activated to help. Some helped with the collection, but more and more helped with overseeing the captured umans.

Why?

Because over the course of the day the numbers of captured slaves ballooned from a few dozen to over a hundred. No one could go out without returning with a few umans, it seemed. The reasons were varied and manifold, but no matter the crew or their mission, the end result was more—male or female, it didn't matter—umans in our storage bay. More to feed, clothe, and manage. The managing was the most difficult, as we now had groups from all sides of the conflict, and none of them spoke the same language!

I later learned that the scientist Dontel had become

intrigued with the social dynamics of the uman male to female ratio, and so covertly bribed some of the external teams to bring back *more* of the latter sex to see how they altered overall slave dynamics. Consequently, the number of females grew forty-fold.

I couldn't tell whether the females helped reduce conflict or not. I don't know that it was important to the scientist, though. I think he only wanted to study. Not improve anything. Not help his beleaguered XO in any way.

Eventually, I had to distract the captain from all the umans being collected. I presented him with a list of issues the ship faced—the inability of the umans to talk to each other being one—and let him wrestle with the solutions. Such "high level" problems were his preference, so he leapt at the chance to solve them. That freed me to deal with the low-level stuff, of which, there was plenty.

The biggest problem was still food acquisition. Though steady, there still wasn't near enough. If we had weeks we might have made it. But only days? And with soldiers ever on the periphery? Impossible.

Louis and his wife suggested we bring some of the necessary materials to produce the local cuisine onto the ship. That instead of stealing and bartering, we could try making the stuff ourselves.

I liked that idea, and in my modern mind, completely missed what "necessary materials" might mean. It wasn't until the overseer of the scavenging missions—Gritly—found me in the cargo bays' screen-filled control room that I truly understood.

The views were of controlled chaos. The primary cargo bay—the climate controlled one—was about three-fifths full of collected delicacies. Row after row of boxed and bound cheeses and wines. It was a lot of food. An amazing amount given what we'd been up against. But a frightening amount still needed to be found. There were crews of workers—supervised umans and rhats—continually stacking and unloading.

The ancillary bay was where the umans were being housed. It now looked like a makeshift village. Or rather, two villages—one on each end and in opposite corners. Cloth material subdivided these "villages" into individual living areas for the men, women—and in some cases—couples.

Gritly was an older blue, with patches of grey mixed into his facial fur. He wore a black longshirt with a holstered stunner on his left hip. He waved as he entered the overlook. "Where you want the animals, Sed?"

I growled at him. "They're umans, Grit." I pointed below. "They might be primitive, but they're still intelligent. Let's not—"

Gritly snorted. "Not talking about the umans. Talking about real animals. The bovine and the other..." He wrinkled his snout and stooping, put a paw a meter from the ground. "...four-legged things with horns." He straightened slowly. "You know, the ones that make that irritating *bleet-bleet* sound?"

"Goats," I said. "I think they're called 'goats.'"

He smiled. "Yeah, that's the name." He pointed a thumb over his shoulder. "Got some of them 'goats' too."

I glanced at the walkway behind him. "Where?"

He glanced back too, then shrugged. "Down by the ramp. Outside. The whole lot of them."

"Are they stunned?"

Gritly snorted again. "Didn't need to. We only tied ropes around them and led them here. Sometimes on carts."

I wasn't sure what to say. I thought about the farms we'd visited. The whole *bleeting* and *mooing* lot of them. Now present on my ship?

"Louis said that's what you wanted," Gritly said. "Was he wrong?"

I checked the screens showing the uman "settlement" again. Was there room for animals there too? It was a large bay. Maybe. Maybe in one of the corners.

"Sed?"

Shaking my head, I looked at Grit. "By 'materials,' I thought he meant primitive machinery. Things needed to make cheese."

"They need cows and goats, Sed. That's where the milk comes from."

I snorted. "I know, but I expected..." Another head shake. "Does it even matter anymore?"

"There's machinery too if that helps. Down by the ramp."

I spent the next hour overseeing the creation of an animal pen and a small cheese factory. With Louis's mediation, I got some of the umans—from both sides of the conflict—to help with the construction. The process taught me two things.

One, that having a uman representative was a continual benefit. Louis's ability to calm beings that would otherwise be frightened or distrustful of "giant rats" couldn't be overstated. He was adept at finding the bright side of a difficult situation and helping others to see it too. He said it was "the Christian thing to do."

Second, that many umans preferred slavery to us to the situation they'd just been in. If given the choice of fighting a war they questioned and transporting food for giant rats, they were fine with the latter. As long as they were fed and sheltered, it was merely a measure of servitude alliances. And some of them—quite a few of them—*preferred* us! Even after they knew what we were. Even after they'd seen us!

Strange galaxy.

After leaving the cargo control room, I returned to the bridge. Yentiss was the only one present, seated at her usual station up front. She gave me a sad smile when she saw me.

I raised an eyebrow and eased into the command chair. "Everything all right?"

From prior experience, I knew that shipboard romances rarely worked. Aside from the risk of others—the captain, primarily—knowing and disapproving, there was the complication of working together and, given any disagreement, not being able to flee. Sure, the *Granum* was a large ship by muto standards, but by spurned doe standards, it could never be big enough. No ship ever was.

Still, there was a lot more to Yentiss than I'd originally thought. Hidden levels. After this job was over, if we survived, I might go against my better judgment. Might ask her to split a cheese round at the ship's cafeteria. Or spend time in the rear observation deck. Watch the stars move against the vacuum of space.

"I'm fine," she said. "Just thinking about the umans."

"Hard not to think about them now. Hard not to <u>see</u> them. Hear them." I took a long breath, taking in the *Granum*'s now-familiar scent. "Hard not to smell 'em either."

She looked at the central screen, where the ship's exterior was visible. Every few seconds, a portion of the sky above the forest would brighten. Proof that the uman battle was still in progress. "All the fighting amongst themselves," she said. "So many sides. Seems needless."

I snorted. "Fighting your own kind? Yeah, don't get much of that in the Empire. Rats fighting rats."

She nodded. "Right. We don't."

"We have all those other enemies to fight. Can't waste time fighting each other when the Jinn Kahn are banging on your door." I remembered the sloth-creatures tendency for deliberation then and added: "Slowly. *Slowly* banging."

She stared at the screen again. "I wish we could help them. Let them see the futility."

"Louis said their Emperor listens to a short red man. Maybe if you dressed the part, you could convince him."

She flared an eyebrow. "Are you picking on me?"

"Not at all." I shrugged. "I'm tired. Tired makes me irritable."

I leaned closer and lowered my voice. "And to be honest, the umans don't worry me near as much as the ones on the other side of this. Those we're supposed to deliver to."

Her eyes widened. "Why?"

"I think they're syndicate," I said.

Yentiss gasped. "Why would the captain deal with—"

"Debts." I pointed toward the ceiling. "This ship, for one. Captain still owes on it. Plus, he likes to gamble. Caught him gaming with some shifty characters back on Lutis Five. Think maybe they're the reason we got this job."

"But that would risk us all," she said. "We could become slaves...or worse."

I nodded. "Makes it hard to sleep, yeah. Especially with a half-empty cargo bay."

"What are we going to do?"

"We're going to fill it," I said. "Even if we have to make the stuff ourselves. I just hope we—"

The screen showed another flash, bright enough to illuminate the forest from one end to the other. Among the tree silhouettes, I saw something that stopped me cold. "Oh...no..."

Yentiss looked toward the screen again. "What?"

"How soon can we lift off?" I tugged the chair's control screen over where I could see it.

"There might be teams out," Yentiss said. "Should I sound an alarm?"

My screen showed that a number of systems, including a

starboard engine, were offline. "What is science up to now!" I said. "They've got us stuck here."

"There were some scheduled—"

I swore. "We need to get all paws outside," I said. "Immediately."

"What?"

"You heard me. As many as can be spared. From every department."

Yentiss's paws hovered over her controls. "What about the captain? Should I—?"

"He's busy." I stood. "Direct all the loading crews to meet me at the main ramp. Have them bring stunners and suits."

Her paws started to move, sending directives, activating com notices and message runners.

"Ship cloaks should be at full power." I checked my screen and found the cloaks were on-line. With a few swipes, I increased their power. It would spike engine use and might dim the lights in places, but it would keep the ship hidden. I sent a terse message to the science team too: *No more maintenance!*

Ten minutes later, I was outside in my shimmer suit. Milling around the under-ship area was about fifty crewmembers. I gave a low hoot and told them to quickly gather around.

The widest section of the ship—that reserved for the cargo deck—was directly overhead. As the crew formed a semi-circle in front of me, two mutos ran out of the woods from the north. Security chief Cindel and one of his subordinates. Their fur was puffed with anxiety. Not surprising given what I'd glimpsed.

Cindel hurried right up to our group. "We're about to be overrun, sir."

I nodded. "How many?"

He shook his head. "Hundreds. Possibly thousands."

"They found a way around the blockade?"

Another head shake. "Coming in from another direction, sir." He pointed back and to the left. "Northwesterly."

His subordinate raised a mobile com unit and swept a paw west. "They started off that way, followed the forest line for a few kilometers, then started to infiltrate the woods itself. We suspect they're trying to intercept the French troops to the south."

"They're headed right through here," Cindel said. "We have maybe ten minutes."

That was what I feared. What I prepared for. There was only one way we'd survive this, and it would probably cost us lives. Hopefully, it wouldn't cost us the ship.

I turned toward the crew. "All right, we have a dangerous situation here. I'm hoping everyone brought their suits and stunners because we're about to play the biggest game of scatter and scurry we've ever played." I gestured toward the woods. "Uman soldiers are coming our way. There's not enough time to leave, and we're not quite ready to anyway.

"The primary incursion is from the southwest, but we should form a perimeter just in case. The *Granum* is at full cloak, but someone could easily blunder into our struts. We don't want that." I glanced at the ramp. "We need the ship closed up too." I touched Cindel's shoulder. "Go make sure that happens. Emergency ins and outs only."

Cindel nodded. "Right away, sir." He pushed through the group to the ramp.

There was no more time for instruction. We had to get moving.

I notice Krate among the gathered crowd. That would help. If anyone could stun an uman, it was him.

I smiled grimly. "They have guns, remember. They are slow and difficult to load, but umans are surprisingly good at the process." I raised my stunner. "Stun and move on. Stun as many as you can. Look out for each other. And stay hidden!"

I waved toward the woods. "Let's go."

CHAPTER 29

A circle quickly formed around the ship. The bulk of the crew, roughly two-thirds, I assigned to the north and west—the sides likely to see the most umans—and instructed them to fan out from there. The rest were to hold a position about twenty or thirty meters out. Far enough to catch any umans that came their way, yet close enough to the *Granum* that they could fall back and defend, should the need arise.

I went with the group to the north. We started shoulder to shoulder, creeping through brush and tall trees, but within a few minutes, I could barely see the shimmers of those to my right and left.

Could we stop hundreds of men? I had little hope. But there was no time to ponder our chances. There was only action, bolstered by muto stealth and whatever protection the suits afforded.

It was the most anxious moment of my life, and the most penitent. I wanted to pray but wasn't sure to who. Not the Emperor, nor the darkened god of his ministers. I had no faith in science or political power. No hope in the steadfastness of my crew or even the blind luck that steered our captain's path.

So, I prayed to the Creator God of Louis and his wife. I was on their planet, after all. It seemed appropriate somehow. My team needed the quickness and resilience those two umans had shown. I hoped their God gave it freely.

At a hundred meters out, I heard the clamor of uman voices. I hissed at the mutos on both sides of me, a signal for them to halt and pass caution along. I heard the echo of hisses for many seconds. I could almost feel the breaths of communication throughout our circle. Along game trails and between thickets. All the way around, a command to stop and prepare.

Despite the suit, I found myself hunkering down, crouching beside a fallen tree. The tree was large enough that the crew member to my right, Stradds, shared it with me, his shimmer registering about ten meters away. I had my stunner up and ready. I marked a line of narrow trees ahead as my "stun line." A place where the umans must not advance.

The sky above was deep blue now, the morning sun having risen somewhere behind us. It reminded me of how little sleep I'd gotten. Would I see peaceful slumber again? Certainly not after this excursion. And possibly not after we'd left for space either.

I gnawed the inside of my mouth to banish my lethargy. To prepare myself

I heard umans thrashing through the brush ahead. Emperor's bones, they were loud! Not only did they talk excessively, they seemed to trample every twig and bend every branch. Some of them swung their swords in an attempt to cleave through the underbrush. I heard every swish and whack.

I glanced at Stradds again. His stunner was leveled, and his head shifted nervously left and right. As if hoping to see that which could not, as of yet, be seen. I waved my weapon at him and pointed to the length of my stun line.

He nodded, seeming to understand.

Aromas filtered through the suit's fabric, telling a story all their own. Dozens of umans approached. A thick concentration of them. They were dirty and tired, with days of sweat and grime on their bodies. I sensed hunger and thirst—but also fear. Anxiety was an overcoat.

The area was as unknown to them as it was us. They were simply following orders, involved in a war for various reasons. Many of them had little choice. Few liked where they were, though some did. Some would shoot at anything that moved. The most dangerous prey.

I gripped hard on my stunner. No uman could reach our ship walking. Afterward? We'd see.

There was a string of twig snaps just ahead, and the first soldier stepped across my line. His uniform was different than those we'd encountered so far. Entirely grey, with a stripe of black crossing his midsection from his left shoulder to beneath his right arm. His hat was dark with a black plume jutting straight up.

Was he part of another army? A *third* army?

I had no idea. Nor did I care.

I fired without hesitation. The man let out an "oof" and pitched headlong onto the ground.

"Hey there, what's the problem?" said the soldier immediately behind him. "Did you stumble?"

I shot that one too. He fell atop the first.

There were gunshots and shouts. Then I heard the clicking sounds of stunners on both sides of me. Crouched and nervous, three more umans broke through my line. They glimpsed their fallen comrades, then looked cautiously in all directions.

"Are they dead?" one man said as another knelt over the bodies.

Stradds shot the standing man. I shot the others. Three more umans in our pile.

"Easier than I thought," Stradds said, smiling.

More umans were coming, and a pile of five would surely alarm them. I waved at Stradds, hopped the fallen tree, and hovered over the men. "We need to move them," I said. "Get them back where they aren't so obvious."

Stradds nodded, and together we drug the men back toward the fallen tree and hoisted them over. From there, we spread their bodies out, concealing them with the underbrush as best we could. They were surprisingly light, which helped.

"Must not be eating much," I said.

"No banquets on a battlefield." Stradds winked. "Know that one from experience."

"Right." Some members of the crew had served in the Emperor's wars. Stradds was doubtless one of them. I shook my head. "Maybe you should be leading this, Stradds. I don't know anything about—"

He waved a shimmering hand. "No expert here. Only a survivor." He looked at the trees ahead. "The umans aren't expecting us." He lifted both shimmering paws and turned them over. "And with this." He winked again. "Ain't really fair."

There were more stunner clicks and the crack of gunfire. Stradds yelped and dropped to the ground. Blood seeped through the chest of his suit.

I swore and scanned left, in the direction of the shot. Five soldiers were in a clearing there, and one was looking straight at us. I checked to make sure my suit hadn't changed color. It was fine, but Stradds...poor Stradds.

"There," the staring soldier said. "Noticed something over there. A shadow."

I fired on him.

He convulsed and fell. His companions screeched and fired in all directions.

I dropped flat and covered my head. The shots continued,

one after another. Finally, when it drew quiet again, I rolled to my right beneath a bush and waited. I chanced to look a few seconds later.

The soldiers were still there, grouped around their fallen friend. Three of them were reloading, while the fourth was bent over the one I'd shot. "Can't tell what's wrong with Brone," he said. "He's warm, but just lays here. Could it be the typhus?"

Stunning "Brone" clearly wasn't the best strategy. I needed to be clever. Especially with four soldiers primed and ready to shoot.

I crept to where Stradds still lay. The end of his snout felt cool—normal—and his body was still warm.

There was a large pool of blood, though. The suit was still functioning, still hiding most of him from uman eyes, but it couldn't keep blood from seeping through the hole and becoming visible.

A soldier started to walk my direction, gun raised.

Emperor's bones, what to do? The soldier would find Stradds if I left him where he was. The blood would appear like a glob of red, hovering above the ground.

I raised my stunner. I had to shoot the soldier. What else could I do?

Shooting him would only reveal my position, though. Invite more gunfire.

Could I simply cover Stradds? Hide the blood?

I was invisible, after all. Still hidden.

I got on all fours and positioned myself over Stradds' body. I didn't go all the way to touching him, for fear of marking myself, but I got as close as I could. And waited.

The soldier approached cautiously. He looked about Louis's age, possibly younger. His hair was dark and his features narrow. There was dried mud on the lower portion of his pants. Bloodstains on his left shoulder.

He surveyed the fallen tree, then looked beyond toward

me. He stood motionless for a moment, then glanced back at the distant tree-line and the fields beyond. He frowned, shook his head, and stepped forward.

His legs were only a half-step from my snout. It was a difficult angle to hit his chest, but I pointed my stunner upwards anyway. I'd need to shoot and scurry. Pray I didn't get crushed along the way.

"I know something's here," the soldier said, touching his nose. "I can sense it." He poked his gun at the bush to my left. "Now, what is it?"

I should have run. Let the soldier become distracted by Stradds' blood, then take him out somehow.

The man's eyes widened. "Hey! What's this?" He bent over and studied a narrow branch to my right, his left. He dabbed at it, then brought his fingers up near his eyes. "Looks like blood." He turned and waved at the others. "Hey, fellows! Come over here!"

I pressed the stunner switch.

Nothing happened.

I gave the stunner a firm shake and tried again. Still nothing.

Why me? Why always me?

Two soldiers headed my direction.

I was stuck.

I could smell more soldiers in the surrounding forest. Hear more. I still heard stunner clicks too, but all seemed distant. Too far to help.

Stradds grunted beneath me.

The nearest soldier turned back. "What was that?"

Great.

CHAPTER 30

Despite doom staring me in the face, foremost on my mind was the safety of the *Granum*. How were the others doing? Had any umans broken through our wall of resistance?

And what about the mission? Were we even close to our goal? Was it worth the risk to try? If an uman saw us, saw the ship, and returned to his people—what then? They might join forces against us. Thousands of men from however many armies headed toward this woods with guns blazing.

How long would the ship's shields hold against a hard matter onslaught? Given the reliability of our technology, I'd guess not long enough. The Teril Massacre would seem insignificant compared to "The Granum Slaughter." Ours would be the new cautionary tale. An intergalactic missive against ever setting down on primitive soil.

Three uman soldiers approached me. All had swords drawn and were sweeping the brush in front of them. Trying to locate the source of the mysterious blood. The invisible grunt.

Scradds.

I startled as Scradds began to shift. I drew a little closer to him, in hopes of muffling any sounds he might make.

This was one time I could really use old stun-happy Krate. To have him blunder in, stunner on full, and save the day. But he wasn't near. I could've smelled him if he were.

I couldn't sense any mutos, in fact, aside from Scradds. Only a handful of smelly umans.

I looked at my stunner, frowned, and pointing it toward the nearest soldier, tried again.

Nothing.

Wait! Scradds had a stunner too. Where was his?

"I heard something over here," the first soldier said. "I know I did."

There was a half-hearted grunt. "You're shell-shocked, mate. Nervous like the rest of us. Jumping at shadows."

I felt around on the ground, first with my left paw, then with my right. I even used my tail, touching the forest floor on either side of my torso. Searching, desperately hoping...

And then, nearly out of reach on my right, I found it.

I snatched the stunner and focused on the nearest soldier. I caught him just as he turned away, and Emperor's bones, if he didn't fall into one of the others.

I sprung to my feet, darted a couple steps left, and shot the third soldier. He fell like a sack of cheese.

All that remained was the one who'd the first soldier had collapsed into and—

"Halt!"

The fourth soldier. The one who'd stayed with the stunned fifth.

"What's going on here?" He moved toward me, though he couldn't have known that.

Scradds groaned loudly. The soldier stopped, and turning Scradds direction, hurried toward him. A second later, he gasped, doubtless noticing the pool of floating blood.

I tapped my suit chest, bringing my shimmer to an end. "Hey!" I yelled.

The soldier wheeled around, sword raised.

"I'm Sedric," I said with a smile. "Glad to meet you."

He gasped again, but I shot him outright. He fell with confusion gripping his face.

The final soldier staggered to his feet. He was too confused to manage either gun or sword. Too surprised to even try.

I shot him without warning.

I reactivated my suit, and panting, surveyed the situation. Ten umans! We'd taken ten down on our own. How well had the rest of the crew done?

A few moments later, I saw the shimmer of a crew member hurry by. I hissed at him and waited for him to return. "This is the XO," I said. "I need some help." I indicated the soldier's bodies, along with Scradds. The latter was conscious, but he was moaning with pain. I wasn't sure of his condition, but it couldn't be good.

"Yes, sir."

The crew member saluted, and I realized then it was Cindel. Fortunate for me. "I'm organizing hovercarts," he said. "I have mutos on the way."

"I need one in a hurry," I said. "Scradds has been hit."

"I see that, sir." He held up a handheld com and shook it. "Let me make a call."

Handheld coms had never been my thing. Another device to mess with...or to mess up. Plus they had limited range in a situation like this. But here? Very useful.

Cindel talked into his com a few moments, then attached it to his belt. "Are you all right, sir?"

"I think so, yes." I checked on Scradds. The blood flow appeared to have stopped. One advantage of fur: quicker clotting. Didn't mean his internals weren't a mess.

Scradds eyes flickered, and he looked at me. "What hit me?" he asked.

"We'll discuss that later," I said. "For now, save your strength." I was tempted to move him on my own. Get him out of harm's way. "Do you think it's safe to take you back?"

He curled his snout. "I've been hurt worse."

I smiled and motioned to Cindel. "Let's get him as close as we can."

Nodding, Cindel helped me lift Scradds. There were some complaints and additional groans, but we finally managed it without too much trouble.

"How are we doing?" I asked Cindel after a few minutes' travel.

Cindel sidestepped a thicket of thorns. "No problem, sir," Cindel said. "Happy to help."

"No, I mean the conflict."

"Sorry, sir. Last count, about five hundred captures."

"Five...hundred...?"

"Yes, sir. We were productive."

What would we do with five hundred umans? And how would I keep that from the captain? There's no way I could.

Yet, I couldn't let them be killed either. Nor did I want them to wake up in the forest. Sure, they hadn't seen their attackers, but what would happen if they returned to their superiors with stories of fighting forest ghosts?

"Where are they now?" I asked.

"Scattered about the woods still," Cindel said. "Though some of them—sixty or seventy—have been taken to the ship."

There was no hiding them. A dozen or so, maybe. But not sixty. "We need to get them all collected," I said. "And quick. Have them taken to the ancillary bay. There's enough room there yet."

"Yes, sir," Cindel said. "I agree, sir."

Scradds coughed, then whispered. "Almost have yourself an army of your own."

My stomach tensed. "That's not what we came for." All I could think of was the mission. How we came to collect food but were instead collecting mouths to feed. "It's jeopardizing everything."

Scradds gurgled a laugh. "Nevertheless...that's what you've got."

I tightened my grip on Scradds and frowned. Cindel stepped over another downed tree and I carefully followed, paying special attention so as not to bump Scradds in the process.

I dreaded my next encounter with the captain. Especially after bringing hundreds aboard.

I needed to talk to Louis. And possibly Yentiss too. I needed a plan to get us out of this. To keep us safe. But I couldn't quite find it.

CHAPTER 31

Two hours later, Louis and Yentiss were with me on ancillary bay overlook. The former was dressed in a dark blue shirt and pants that were clearly constructed from material his wife had scavenged on-board. It had a glossy texture like no material I'd seen on his world. Oddly enough, it suited him. Made him look almost modern.

Louis leaned against the guardrail and studied the room below. "They're Prussians!" he said then.

"The new additions, you mean?" Yentiss asked.

"Yes. In the grey uniforms."

"Another army?" I said.

"Yes. From a country north of here."

The new captives were gathered—mostly seated or laying down—in the port aft corner. Unlike the bay's other corners, there were no privacy walls constructed there yet. So it was only a mass of grey-clad umans. Disoriented and doubtless confused. In relation to the other occupants, the Prussians were nearest the red-coated "British," but I saw no mingling between the groups.

"Who are they fighting for?" I asked.

"They're coalition soldiers," Louis said, pointing. "Aligned with the group in red there, see? They'll make good slaves. Hearty stock."

Yentiss wrinkled her snout. "From here they all look the same. Only the colors are different."

Louis smiled. "Yes, well, I suppose that's true." He pushed away from the railing. "But I'm concerned for my fellow Frenchmen. We're outnumbered now."

"So, you want us to capture more?" I asked.

"Would it matter if I did?" he asked.

"It might," I said. "You have good instincts."

The numbers were approximately even between the French and British—at about seventy-five each—not including the females.

Louis called all the females "Belgian," and thanks to our "scientific" studies, there were hundreds of them now too. They generally occupied the starboard corner nearest the front of the ship. They also had additional guards and a stun fence around them. Something Anne had suggested.

The bay's middle section was a corral of animals, which came with its own problems. Cleanup and maintenance being the biggest ones. I really wanted to release the animals. Or possibly gas the whole lot of them.

I was uneasy. We'd survived the Prussian onslaught, but we'd been lucky. Even now, more captured soldiers were being lead in. We'd only had a few hundred to repel this time. But what if thousands came?

I drifted down the overlook to a place where I could peer into the primary cargo bay. It was barely two-thirds full of cheese. In fact, it looked less full than the last time I'd checked.

"It's all going wrong," I said. "Our priorities are misdirected."

The others came up behind me. "You're worried about the food," Louis said.

"We don't have enough," I said. "I don't think we'll ever had enough."

Louis nodded. "And it needs to be full?" He waved a hand over the scene below.

"More if we can get it. Otherwise..." I shook my head. "The captain will kill himself or kill me."

"You need to leave soon?" he said.

"We need to leave *now*. Even if there were no soldiers outside, we have to make a delivery." I glanced at Yentiss. "And penalties if we miss."

"There's slop in the schedule," Yentiss said. "There always is."

"We can't count on it," I said. "Not this time."

"Still," she said. "If this war ended, we might—"

"Ended?" I shot them an incredulous look. "There are more soldiers every day."

Yentiss drew closer. "Maybe what you said before? About someone going to this Emperor and trying to—"

"As a red uman?" I said.

Yentiss shrugged. "It might work."

"I was joking, Yentiss."

Louis shook his head. "The red man legend has been around for decades. Many think him demonic." He looked at me. "A monster."

I waved my paws. "More monsters. Everything a monster." I checked on the food stores again. "We need to leave, but we can't."

Cindel entered the overlook from an entry between the bays. He walked part of the distance to us on all fours, before standing onto his back paws. He looked grim. Rigid.

What now?

Cindel saluted when he reached us.

I waved his salute away. We weren't a military vessel, though it was beginning to feel like it. "Status?" I said.

He bobbed his head. "Fifty more soldiers stopped, sir. They'll be delivered below soon. There's also a number of incapacitated non-combatants. Mostly female." He squinted. "Part of some experiment?"

I sighed. "Science. All the science."

"The females have been productive," Yentiss said. "More than the uman males, at this point."

"I'm more concerned about feeding them," I said. "Regardless of their sex."

"I talked to your stock manager," Louis said. "Five hundred people will burn through your reserves in a month."

And we had near twice that now. "We need to offload some mouths," I said. "This is costing too much."

My bumble-sore left paw ached so hard that my right paw hurt in sympathy. I frowned and wrung them together.

"There's more," Cindel said.

"More worse, or more better?" I could've used some better.

"Sorry, sir."

"Stop apologizing." I grimaced. "Now what is it?"

"Scouts say there are more troops on the way. Large numbers from every direction. Our deliveries have—"

"Stopped for the day," Louis said. "It was too big of a risk."

I nodded. "Yes, well, that's wise. A good call." I could feel my mind shutting down. We were in a tight spot, and there seemed no loosening it. I looked at the floor. Wrung my paws together harder. "How many this time?"

"Tens of thousands, sir."

"Tens of...?" I checked the storage bay again. Somehow, it looked emptier now than it had a few seconds ago. "Well, we can't stay for that."

Louis's face paled. "It's going to happen here," he said. "Or close by. Maybe Quatre Bras...yes, probably there." He shook his head slowly. "Tens of thousands. The Emperor won't survive."

I clenched my paw. "But we're going to. We have to." Could we relocate again? Doubtful. I gave Yentiss a worried look.

"What?" she asked.

"Go to the bridge and get ready to leave."

"Okay, Sed, but..." There was a strange look in her eyes. Doubt or indecision, I couldn't tell which. I had time for neither.

"I need to see the captain." I gave them all a parting glare. "Be ready to move!"

CHAPTER 32

We met in Captain Wendel's cabin, which—while twice the size of mine—always felt smaller. Nearly every space was filled with something: old accounting reports, stacks of government documents, boxes of trinkets he acquired along the way. Little of it was worth anything. But what it lacked in value, it made up for in volume.

The only spots free of junk were the captain's extra-wide sleep nook and half of his meeting table. Precisely half. Enough space for two to sit, but at an uncomfortably close distance. I always stood when I was in his cabin.

The captain sat at the table now, paws crossed with a pleased look on his face. There was half a round of orange cheese on the table in front of him, along with a bowl of something white.

A silver cheese knife protruded from the top of one cheese wedge, as if marking that one as his next victim. He already had a large wedge in his right paw, which he now raised. "This is excellent. Do you want some?"

I shook my head. The cheese's heady aroma was everywhere, and yes, it was amazing. The captain was known to
close-sniff his food, though. I wanted nothing that his snout
might have touched.

"Suit yourself," he said. "Fedwi brought me a sample of
our newest stock. I think our customers will be pleased." He
indicated the bowl. "Not sure about this. He called it 'chow
croute.' Said it was made from one of the local plants. Odd
taste, but it grows on you." He smiled. "Anyway, I'm glad
you're here. I wanted to see you."

Even the mention of the cook's name bothered me now.
A creature without limits. "You did?" I said.

The captain took a bite of cheese and chewed heartily.
"Yes! We have a translator the umans can use."

"Digestible, like ours?" I asked.

"No, but injectable and unobtrusive. The doctor found a
recipe in his files. Uzel cooked it up in the lab."

"Has it been tried?"

"It has." Another bite. "Bribed a few of the slaves with
extra food and lighter work."

I rubbed my bumble hand. I didn't like the idea of slaves—
even uman ones. But, in this case, the workforce had run into
our paws. Our every decision, every step, had followed directly
from situations we encountered. Unavoidable choices.

"And the translator works?"

He nibbled the cheese. "Does now. There were some
initial side-effects. Indigestion and bouts of mania, but—"

"Mania?"

He waved a paw. "Mild insanity! Passed in a few hours.
Easily contained."

I cocked my head, skeptically.

"Nothing long term. And perfect fidelity!"

"Well...that's good, then."

"It's remarkable! It will help the process tremendously.

Reduce our reliance on uman Louis too. Don't want him to know too much." The captain shoved the rest of the wedge into his mouth, chewed heavily, and tore the knife from the cheese. "Also, we can sleep them now!"

"Sleep who?

"The umans! Dontel modified our gas to work on them." He pointed the knife at me. "There were surprises, of course. Some faltering steps."

"Faltering steps..." I repeated.

He cocked his head. "Seems they take a higher dosage, the umans. If they don't get enough, they shamble around in a stupor. It's a little creepy." He stretched out his arms. "Walked with their paws up like this. Moaned a little."

I was glad I missed that research. I encountered a fiend dog pack on Diltus Seven once. They stalked me, ploddingly, for an hour before I finally escaped. "Why was Dontel testing sleep gas on the umans?" I asked.

The captain shrugged. "Byproduct of the translator test. Part of his physiology calibration."

I nodded slowly. That revelation might help with my idea. Might make it more palatable, given the slim chance of success.

I studied the stack of boxes in front of me. Servo tubes for a Preoun war horse? I hadn't seen a Preoun in decades. And a war horse? I had no idea what that was. But if it was made of metal and science, I never wanted to see one.

"I hope you're here to tell me we can leave?" the captain said. "That our bay is full?"

I sighed. "Well...the bay is full, sir, but—"

He stabbed a slice of cheese and held it up. "Straightens my tail to hear it, Sed! I've been tied in knots."

"I understand, sir."

"You're a fine XO. You've done this ship proud."

I added urgency to my voice. "We *need* to leave, sir. Right away. Tens of thousands of soldiers are nearby."

"Tens of thousands?" He dropped his cheese.

"Multiple armies, sir. We could be overrun at any moment."

"Lucky timing on our cargo then. Full and ready to go." He hopped to his feet. "Okay, let's get to the bridge and—"

I held up a paw. "There's more you should know."

He straightened his long shirt over his belly. "Not if we're in danger. Tens of thousands, you say?" He slid haltingly around the table, avoiding the stack of...slotted brackets...behind him. "Remember the massacre of—" He pushed past me on his way to the door.

"I have, sir. But—"

"None of that," he said. "The ship's in danger and our mission's complete. We need to leave." He turned to the in-wall communicator—which thankfully, was near the door—and with a few quick touches, hailed the bridge.

No answer.

He squinted at me. "What's going on with your crew?"

I shook my head. "Not sure. Yentiss should be there." I took a step his way. "She's doubtless tired. We all are." It wasn't like her to be away from her duties, though. She was the most dependable person aboard. "Maybe she's asleep at her desk? Try again."

The captain tried the bridge again. Still no response.

"We need to get up there."

CHAPTER 33

I was trapped in a whirlpool this time. Sleep gas was everywhere around me, swirling and pulling. Near the center, I was caught in its vortex, jerked downward. My feet, my legs, and then my tail—tugged, wrenched, and battered.

Finally, my whole body slipped downward. At the bottom, I didn't find death, though. Instead, a fresh burst of oxygen. A lightning strike straight up my snout and into my forehead.

My eyes snapped open. I saw shelving, a large office, and—directly in front of me—two hovering chairs, side-by-side. I blinked twice to see if they would coalesce into a single image. When that didn't happen, I slammed my eyes shut, willed my paws to my face, and rubbed hard.

"You're fine, Sedric."

I recognized the voice. The accountant who'd put me under. He had a hoverchair. His name was Tactin.

But why were there now two of him?

"See, the guilt?" My captain's voice, still nervous. Panicky. "It finally found where it belonged."

I opened my eyes again. The two hoverchairs were still there, but they weren't identical as I originally thought. One chair held the frail, blue Tactin, and the other—larger and more metallic model— contained a tan muto. This one was a hulking creature, with a bent snout. He appeared to be smiling.

Captain Wendel was in the chair next to me. Fidgeting and half-bristled.

"You're back again," Tactin said. "We're still in my office, but—" He motioned toward his companion. "My superior, Xedus, has joined us." He smiled. "I thought he could help."

The captain whimpered softly.

"Not to fear," Tactin said. "I've worked with Xedus for decades." He touched the other's chair railing. "He's a fair and balanced associate."

I nodded slowly, but even that was unsettling. How potent was the gas they used on me? "Pleasure to meet you, Xedus," I said.

"And you," Xedus said in a smooth baritone.

Tactin repositioned himself in his chair, breathing deeply. "In addition, Xedus is an expert on commerce and gaming. You mentioned gaming as a factor."

I felt a wave of nausea followed by extreme fatigue. How long had I been at this? "You mean because Captain Wendel likes to play? I don't think—"

The captain whimpered again.

"Yes," Tactin said. "Xedus has been briefed on all the particulars. Even from the beginning."

I gripped the edges of my chair and tried to stabilize myself. To stop the vortex from spinning. How long could someone head walk and remain healthy? I had no idea.

"Give him a moment," Tactin said. "It can be disorienting."

"I'm aware, Auditor Tactin." Xedus said. "I've done my share of these."

"Yes, of course. Of course, you have. My apologies."

"Accepted."

Tactin bowed his head, then looked at me. "Now, Sedric, I brought you out because it appears we've reached the purpose of our investigation. The umans. Your ship brought them off the primitive world. They were employed by your captain and his ship—"

"You saw how he tricked me," the captain said. "Failing to mention how many umans were aboard." He glared at me. "As if it were immaterial. As if it didn't matter."

"I hid nothing." I sighed and looked at Tactin. "You brought me out too soon. It was the exact wrong moment." I looked at my lap. "One of my worst times. She—"

"She? You mean, Yentiss?"

I nodded. "She was proficient at her job. Always measured. Yet she..." I glanced at the captain. "...did something rash."

"An excellent crew member," the captain said. "A fine doe too."

Xedus cupped his snout. "So, when you arrived at the bridge...?"

"I was concerned," I said, "of course. But we had bigger problems."

The captain snorted. "He's accurate on that, at least. Not twenty seconds later, our security head—"

"Cindel," Tactin said, consulting his screen.

"The same. He signaled that a huge contingent of umans was already in the forest. Thousands."

"We had to take off immediately." I glanced at the captain again.

"But she wasn't aboard," the captain added. "She'd deserted."

My stomach grumbled and I instinctively checked for the food cart. It was no longer in the room. How many hours since we'd last eaten? My stomach screamed, "Too many!"

"It wasn't a desertion, really," I said. "There was more to it."

"Were you surprised?" Xedus asked. "Surprised that she'd left?"

I shrugged. "Crew members do crazy things all the time. They come from all over galaxy. From lots of backgrounds. Rich, poor, strong or unsettled. There are always hidden undercurrents. Things that never come up until the most inopportune time."

"She lost a brother to the wars," the captain said. "She told a different story to most. But I did research later. He wasn't injured by a sea creature." The captain circled his right ear with his tail. "It was some sort of replacement in her head. The sea for the war. So when she said she hated the sea, she really—"

"She took one of those blasted shimmer suits," I snarled, "and—"

"Went to stop the war?" Xedus said.

"So she was mentally damaged," Tactin said.

"She wasn't!" I said. "She was only driven...and hurt." I massaged my knees, now sore from the seat. The uncomfortable posture of it. "It was a sad situation." My insides ached too, I realized. Even after all this time. Yentiss had been a friend and a possible mate.

Tactin puffed his cheeks and exhaled. "Well, that's not our concern here. We're here to determine your penalty. Clearly, you took umans from the planet. 'Over a thousand,' by your account. That act alone demands fines and penalties.

"It was the right thing to do," I said. "Under the circumstances."

"Aha!" the captain said. "Now, you understand. It wasn't me. It was him. So, can I go?" He stood, but a glare from Xedus made him sit back down again.

I grabbed the head walk mask. "Put me under again. I'll take you to the end of it."

"I'm not sure that's wise," Tactin said. "You've had four hours of recollection already. Beyond the recommended allotment."

I fit the mask to my snout. "This won't take long," I said. "Put me under."

Tactin gave his superior a questioning look. "Head accountant?"

Xedus shrugged. "He has the right of defense."

Tactin nodded and indicated the mask. "You remember what to do?" He rested his paws on the controls.

I gave an answering nod, slid the mask on, and held up a finger.

"Yes, Sedric?" he says.

"The next time I wake up..."

"Yes?"

"Could you have food?"

CHAPTER 34

The captain and I burst onto the bridge and found it empty. There was no sign of Yentiss, nor any of her trained replacements. The room had an eerie feel. Like an emergency airlock had failed, venting anyone that mattered into space. Even the *Granum*'s scent had shifted. It was now more sterile and sour.

"Where is she?" Captain Wendel asked.

I drifted toward her seat up front. "I told Cindel to check her quarters. See if she's there." I touched the back of her chair. "Not sure why she wouldn't be here. I thought this was where she was going."

Cindel appeared at the door, eyes wide, seemingly troubled.

"You didn't find her," I said.

Cindel looked between me and the captain. "I don't think she's on the ship, sir."

"Why would you think that?" the captain asked.

Cindel raised his com device. "I tracked her com, sir. It's outside."

"Did you contact her?" I said. "Ask her what she's doing?"

"She's not answering."

"She took her com, but she won't use it." I tapped the corner of her desk. "Seems about right for this ship." I glanced at the center screen, which still showed the view in front of the ship. At the moment, it looked peaceful. No explosions or signs of uman encroachment.

"She can't be far," I said. "I'll find her. I'll track her com."

Cindel nodded. "I'll gather a team to go with you, sir. It'll only take a—"

I waved a paw at him. "I'll go alone. We need all of security here. There are too many variables."

The captain slid into his command chair. "We have to leave, Sedric. You said troops were coming."

"From everywhere." I walked toward the door. "Another reason why I'm going alone." I looked at Cindel. "Get everyone on board and the ship buttoned up. I'll take a com with me, so you can find me."

"Yessir," Cindel said, saluting.

The captain gave me a worried look. "But if things are as bad as you said, if we're overrun, I may need to—"

"Do what you have to do, sir." I pointed at his console. "Make sure to check over all the systems first. You never know around here."

Ten minutes later, I was shimmer-suited and standing outside the ship.

Small groups of crewmembers were still transporting umans aboard. A hovercart being used for that purpose was at the bottom of the ramp. The escorting mutos guided it from either end, while inside—stacked one atop another as if they were felled trees—were eight unconscious soldiers. The crewmembers hadn't been careful in how they'd stacked them either. One uman had another's boots in his face, and vice versa.

I scowled, but I didn't have time to scold. I needed to find Yentiss.

I put my com in tracking mode, set it for Yentiss's signal, and entered the forest. My sense of urgency equaled what I'd felt a few hours earlier. I needed to find my errant com officer, and quick. Before we got left behind.

I had a fair idea what she was up to. She put it on her misguided self to save the ship by eliminating the threat. By stopping the war somehow.

On one level, I admired her instincts. Her dedication to the *Granum* might have superseded my own. But on another level, I was claw and teeth angry. I wanted to save her from herself, then bust her to kitchen duty. Let her work with that foul Fedwi for a couple shifts. See if she ever tried a stunt like this again.

I followed her signal as best I could, scurrying around trees and over bushes. She generally followed the game trails, but occasionally the signal would take me through thick terrain.

Unfortunately, I seemed to have grabbed the tight-fitting suit again. So, my scurrying wasn't near as fast as I might have liked. In fact, I caught the garment a few times along the way too. One time was particularly bad—a thorny growth managed to wrap my left leg and arm. It took many heavy twists and tugs to get free, and in the end, there were two small tears in my suit. They didn't seem to affect the suit's ability, but I could feel the late morning air through them.

The continual tightness was distressing too. My tail never felt comfortable.

I made steady gains, though. Yentiss had a head start, but she didn't appear to be running. She didn't have the urgency I had.

As I neared the end of the woods, my device showed her location right ahead of me somewhere, not more than a few meters.

I got down on all fours and surveyed the open field ahead. Clusters of blue-clad soldiers were scattered across it. There was little cover aside from a couple stands of trees.

Where was Yentiss? She was suited, sure, invisible to the umans, but where *was* she?

I risked whispering her name. No response.

Over and over I called, stooping into every hollow and checking behind every bush. In the process, my suit ripped a little more.

Nothing could be done for it, though. I was too far from the ship. And Yentiss too close.

Finally, I reached a spot where her signal was so strong she had to be right beside me.

Except she wasn't. There were only trees, bushes, and a group of brown birds, chirping and hopping. I pressed to the ground—and removing my hood—took a deep whiff.

My nose supported the com's conclusion. She had been here. The scent seemed to be coming from a thicket near the forest's edge. I crawled to it and dug inside.

I pulled out her com unit. Still on. Still functioning perfectly.

She'd left it, and me, behind.

I rested against a large rock with a clear view of the field. I held Yentiss's com unit in one paw, and in the other paw, my own. Mine had a flashing red circle in the center to show that it had found the sister device it had been searching for. Yentiss's com showed weather information. Little of use.

Beyond the rock was a battlefield awaiting battles. The sky was overcast, and the ground was bright green. There were large swaths of blue-uniformed soldiers spread over much of it. Too many to count.

Men on horseback and on foot. Men minding carts and primitive munitions. All in the same army, possibly divided into divisions or under particular leaders. I had no idea, but there was structure to it. A sense of purpose.

The uniform color meant they were French—Louis's people—but from my perspective that made no difference. Every soldier was on one side, and I was on the other. Uman and muto. Advanced and primitive. At war and...simply trying to do my job. Wanting to get out of here.

I shook my head and studied Yentiss's com again. *Cool temperatures, wind from the northwest, and rain likely.* Not much help.

What should I do now? My search appeared hopeless. Probably I should return to the ship. Leave Yentiss to her fate.

But I didn't want to do that yet. Yentiss was one of the good ones. Not simply a fine crew member, but a good friend. At least, I thought of her as a friend. Maybe more. Wasn't sure what <u>she</u> thought because I hadn't had the chance to ask yet.

What plan was she following? Had she just walked up to a soldier and said, "Take me to your leader?" That didn't make sense. Not even doe sense.

My suspicions were confirmed, at least. She'd sought out the French, so my idea to go as the ugly red man must be her goal.

Maybe I should get Louis? See what he would do?

Yentiss was invisible to uman eyes. She could sneak as far as she wanted behind the French lines. Listen and learn. Find what she was looking for.

So could I if I followed. I was suited too, after all.

I shook my head. There was no point in it. I wouldn't know where to go. And out there, in that crowded field, there were too many dangers.

Could I sniff her out?

Not in my suit. And even if I could, it would be difficult with all the other scents around. Umans, horses and anything that crept or crawled.

Still, was it worth a try? For Yentiss?

As if to answer, it started to rain softly.

I felt a heavy sense of loss. I would miss Yentiss. Wasn't sure how I'd function, actually. The bridge wouldn't be the same. The *ship* wouldn't be the same. But my place was on the *Granum*. Taking care of it instead of a single crew member.

I heard something behind me, and turning, saw three umans—French soldiers—standing just inside the woods. They seemed frozen in place. As if they'd seen something completely unexpected.

I instinctively crouched down and was rewarded by the sound of my suit tearing. Next, I felt the morning chill on my belly and thighs.

I looked down to inspect the damage. My suit had split down the middle, exposing a good share of my stomach fur.

The soldiers exchanged looks and pointed their weapons my way. The lead one—fair skinned with a dark mustache—barked a warning and took a tentative step forward. I quickly stowed my com unit and took out my stunner. Given my suit's condition, I wasn't sure how much of that maneuver was visible, but since they hadn't fired, I guessed I did okay.

They looked unsettled, though. Who knows how I appeared to them? Probably like a mass of dark fur growing from a rock.

I raised the stunner and even allowed myself a smile. I'd take the lead soldier, and use the ensuing confusion to take the others, as well. Then I'd return to the ship.

I straightened my arm, aimed, and fired.

The stunner didn't respond. I grunted and gave it a little shake. It felt warm and seemed to vibrate a little.

I aimed again and pressed the trigger.

Emperor's bones: The cursed thing stunned *me*!

CHAPTER 35

As I regained consciousness, the events of the last few days transformed into small blue, red, and grey soldiers, all bare-knuckled fighting as one mass of humanity in the center of a green field. Spikes of yellow energy disrupted the battlefield, following a regular on and off pattern. As if my own heartbeat was creating the spikes. Brawling, angry umans with lightning strikes. That was my reality.

After a full minute, the chaos in my head began to clear. Only then did I realize my predicament. I was inside a covered wagon, one that banged, squeaked, and shuddered as it moved along. There were only a few openings in the covering where I could glimpse the world outside, and it was mostly green and grey. I couldn't tell where I was headed. Nor how far I'd gone. The forest and the ship it contained could be kilometers away, for all I knew.

I was positioned in the exact center of the wagon, with about a meter of empty wooden flooring around me. My arms and legs were bound together below the paws. My shimmer suit was in tatters—little more than frayed rags draped around my shoulders and hips. My stunner was missing, as was my com unit. All I could hear over the wagon's movements was an occasional shout, the crack of gunfire, and the distant boom of cannons.

I had no way to tell the time now, beyond the slices of sunlight that stole in through the wagon's covering. The wagon smelled of gunpowder and metal, so I had a fair idea what it had been used for before.

About twenty minutes of rocking and lurching travel, the wagon stopped, and I heard muted conversation. Next came footfalls and the cover at the rear of the wagon was drawn up.

A soldier—an officer, I presumed, given the heavily decorated uniform—peered in, squinting as he searched. When his eyes locked on mine, his face paled and he threw the cover closed again. There was more excited conversation, where I heard the words "Gévaudan," "immediately," and "his excellency" used. Then the crack of a whip and the wagon began to move again.

More time passed. My emotions oscillated between anger and fear. I was a prisoner of primitives. There was no way that could go well for me. Worse yet, I was most certainly their legendary creature, the "Beast of Gévaudan," now. It was known to prey on woman and children and had been blamed for the deaths of over a hundred umans during a few years' time. Many of its victims were found partly eaten.

According to Louis, the French government had dedicated a considerable amount of money and men to hunt the beast. They'd caught and killed several creatures before the attacks stopped. I suspected they weren't too picky about what qualified as the beast. Hairy and about the size of a uman were the primary descriptions. I was both, of course.

I couldn't help thinking about the *Granum*. I suspected that when I hadn't returned, they'd left the planet. We were up against our deadline now. In addition, the ship had been surrounded by soldiers. We had hundreds of umans in our hold already. The captain would've left. He should have left, for the good of the crew and ship. That was all that mattered. At least, it was all that had mattered for me.

Hopelessness threatened to consume me. I tested my bonds, then searched the wagon around me. I contemplated shouting. Screaming until the umans heard. How would they respond if they knew I could speak? Would they still think me a beast? Or would they think me something worse?

I decided to remain silent. At least, for now.

Eventually, the light outside the wagon began to dim. Evening must be approaching. Where was I now? How far had I gone?

The wagon slowed and I heard the sounds of umans outside. As if we were passing through a large contingent. Crowds like those found in a city. All the worse, then. I was surrounded by umans that would want to blame me for past ills. For feasting on their brethren...or capturing children!

Why couldn't they have captured Fedwi? He liked the idea of eating umans! It would be just deserts for him to be blamed.

But no, they got me. The one who stuck up for them. Who tried to keep them alive.

Is this how Louis's creator god answered prayers? Letting me save the ship and the crew in battle, only to sacrifice myself without cause? The irony.

The wagon came to a complete stop and the back covering was lifted a couple more times, each time to let another declorated soldier gawk at me. There were more hushed conversations. The words "hideous" and "filthy" were used. I heard the phrase "Royal Majesty" more than once too. Was that who they were taking me to? One of their leaders?

I hated that idea, of course. In the case of the Teril Massacre, one of the crewmembers had been taken to a leader. He'd ended up shaved, skinned, and ritually slaughtered.

I strained at the ropes that bound me, but that only made my wrists hurt. My bonds didn't slip or loosen at all.

The area around the wagon got quiet. So much so that I wondered if the soldiers had abandoned me.

Or were they planning on shooting me with a cannon from a kilometer away?

Then I heard something unexpected: "Sedric? Is that you? Are you okay?"

There was no mistaking the voice, but I had a hard time believing it real. That it wasn't simply a figment of a strained and hopeless mind.

"Yentiss?" I whispered. "Where are you?"

"Out here," she said. "Behind the wagon."

I lurched ahead, hoping to get to my back paws, but managed only a few centimeters for the effort. I was stuck on my posterior, with all four limbs in front of me. Not an enviable position.

"What are you doing out there?" I asked.

"I'm...not sure now," she said. "I mean, about the why. I had a plan, but I think it is doomed. I was going to—"

"Go to their Emperor and get him to end the war," I said.

"Right," she said. Then: "Hold on. Someone's coming."

There was silence for half a minute, then the rear cover flap moved. Were they coming for me now? Was it time for their primitive sacrifice? I braced myself.

The flap moved aside, but I saw nothing except the grey sky beyond it. I could smell something, though. The missing part of the *Granum*'s scent.

Yentiss.

There were a couple squeaks and the wagon shifted slightly. The flap on the back closed and my surroundings dimmed. Better than it would've been for a uman, though. Rhats have excellent night vision.

I sensed a presence in the wagon with me. There was a flicker of light—a shimmer suit being shut off—and I saw Yentiss kneeling in front of me.

She looked ill-at-ease. Almost embarrassed. "Sorry, sir," she said and gave me a nervous smile.

"And you should be," I said. "Do you know why I'm here?"

Her smile broadened so that I could see teeth. "Following me?"

I lurched forward. "Of course. Why did you—?"

"I was trying to help," she said. "The ship was in trouble and—"

"And now look at me!" I said.

"I know. I'll help you. I'll get you free." She leaned close and started to pull at my bonds. She fumbled for a few seconds, then pulled away. "They're really tight."

"I've noticed!" I grunted, then nodded toward the opening. "Can you get a knife? There has to be one out there somewhere." I remembered the souvenir I'd taken when we rescued Louis. "A metal sword would work."

"Maybe," she said, glancing at the end flap. "Yes, I could probably find something." She rubbed at her snout nervously. "I'm sorry, Sed. I don't know what I was thinking. I lost my com unit somewhere. Didn't notice that until I was out in the battlefield. Then, worst of all, I realized I didn't even know how to make my plan work. I mean, I had a suit, but—"

I felt compassion for her now. Unexpected twists were part of my everyday life. Like the stunner that got me. Could I expect more from her?

"The suit," she said. "I didn't know how to make it go red. I know how to turn it on and off, but..."

I chuckled. Despite my bonds and the hard floor, I laughed.

"What?" Yentiss said.

"Science," I said. "Just when you think you have it figured out, it shoots a hole in the hull." I laughed again.

"This isn't funny, Sed. You're stuck. We're both stuck."

I shook my head. "I know. I know. For me, it went red for no reason at all. But making it happen on purpose? Impossible to predict. Maybe slapping the tail or beating the chest? Maybe nothing. That's science!"

Yentiss's eyes narrowed and her whiskers straightened. "You're delirious. I need to get you out of here." She touched her chest and disappeared again.

"Hey," I said. "Don't be mad."

"I'm not mad," she said. "I'm going to find something to cut those ropes with." With that, the exit flap opened, and she was gone.

A minute later, I heard uman voices.

CHAPTER 36

Two uman males were locked in conversation. One seemed rushed, nearly to the point of anger. The second had a calmer tone and cadence. As if he were trying to sooth or reassure the first. The voices got louder and more distinct, such that I knew they were approaching the wagon. Finally, I was able to hear their words clearly.

"We are in the middle of a battle, general. There's no time for such distractions."

"I believe you'll find this important, sir."

"One shouldn't presume."

"It's a sign. An omen for our armies' success over the invaders."

"Omen? Where is this omen?"

"Here. In this very wagon."

"In a wagon? Why is it covered?"

"We didn't want to risk alarming the men, sir."

"You would rather distress me, your Emperor?"

Emperor? The fur on the back of my neck stood. Louis's

emperor was here? Right outside the wagon? Should I feel honored or anxious?

And where had Yentiss gone?

I strained at my bonds, then tried to pick at them with my tail. All for naught.

"Let's see this omen then, shall we?"

The end of the wagon was uncovered, and I saw two umans beyond. Both wore dark, two-cornered hats and blue uniforms. The hat of the leftmost uman was decorated with a feather and ribbons, but the other was plain. The decorated uman also held a lit torch. I did not like the looks of that.

"There you are, sir," the man with the decorated hat said. "What do you think?"

The plain-hatted man looked puzzled. "What have you brought me?" He sniffed the air. "It smells horrible."

"Hey—" I said.

Their eyes widened. "Did you hear that?" the plain-hatted one said. "It sounded like speech."

"I don't know, my Emperor. I'm not sure." That man seemed nervous now. Uncertain. "It's one of the Beasts. Bound and secured."

"From Gévaudan? I thought they'd all been slain." The uman with the plain hat climbed inside. He stood up, though the wagon's overhead covering caused him to have to stoop slightly. "I always wanted to see such a creature." He turned toward the opening. "Hand me your light."

The torch changed hands and the Emperor, Napoleon, held it out toward me. "Mon Dieu," he whispered. "I expected a wolf or a dog. But it looks like neither." He squinted. "And what is that about its loins? Is it clothing?" He looked at the rear opening again. "Was it clothed?"

I could find no reason to remain silent. "Yes, I had clothes. A nice blue suit. But your soldiers must've taken it off."

Napoleon's eyes widened and he said something that didn't

translate. I suspected it was a profanity. "You can talk. How did you learn to talk?"

I snorted. "How did *you* learn to talk, Emperor?"

He drew back, then shook his head. "An incredible thing. A talking beast. Like Balaam's donkey."

"Where's Balaam?" I asked. "It is near this Gévaudan place?"

The Emperor chuckled. "Listen to it! Incredible."

"I can show you lots of incredible." I raised my front paws. "Let me go first."

The Emperor slapped his knee. "And now it asks to be let go. General, you have brought me the highest treasure! I only wish that we were not in the middle of a campaign. I would—"

"You shouldn't be." Yentiss's voice, coming from outside somewhere.

The Emperor swung his torch left and right, then glanced behind him. "What was that? It sounded like a woman."

A few seconds passed, then I heard movement behind me, near the front the wagon. I recognized Yentiss's scent. She was close behind me. "You're mistaken," she said, this time with a deeper tone.

I looked at the voice but saw nothing. She was still invisible. I hoped she didn't show herself. That would only complicate matters.

"Who's here?" the Emperor said. "General, do you—"

I heard a flurry of thumps and what sounded like a hiss of anger. Then the interior of the wagon lit up in red.

"Mon Dieu," Napoleon said again. "The man of destiny. Is it you?"

"Yes, it is I." Yentiss raised her arms. She was an ugly, red man now. Round face, smashed nose, and tiny ears. Amazing. "You need to release this beast. It is with me."

Napoleon glanced at me. "But why? It's dangerous. It has—"

"It's innocent," Yentiss said. "You must release it, or your campaign will suffer."

Napoleon stooped until he was almost bowing. "You sound different, spirit. When we talked at Fontainebleau you—"

"I appear as I choose. Sound as I choose. What is that to you?"

Napoleon bowed his head. "I apologize. Of course. You do as you wish."

Yentiss nodded. "Now, will you obey me?"

"Of course. I will let the creature go." Napoleon knelt near my paws, then returned to the opening. "General, give me your saber."

A second later, Napoleon had a knife in his hand. With red man Yentiss looking on, he pressed the blade to my ropes. "How do I know that it won't attack me, spirit?" he said.

"I will protect you," she said.

Napoleon bobbed his head and started to saw on my bonds. A couple minutes later I was free. I rubbed the places the ropes had been, hissing slightly when I rubbed my bumble-addled left hand.

The Emperor startled and stepped back. "Will it attack?"

I raised my front paws. "We're fine. Everything is fine."

"Now!" Yentiss said. "Let him leave!"

I glanced back at her. She waved a hand at me and nodded.

I frowned but stood and made my way for the back opening. The Emperor, and his General outside, stood aside to let me by. The wagon was located at the edge of a large encampment. Rows of white tents formed concentric half circles for hundreds of meters beyond it. I could smell umans everywhere. Torches gleamed from a hundred spots.

I had the darkness as a friend now, though. I crept away from the wagon toward a large stand of trees. I figured I'd wait there for Yentiss to exit the wagon, and then we'd go together.

I wasn't sure *where* we'd go, since I had no idea where

Bossu woods was from my position, or if the ship were still present. But we'd figure that out somehow, Yentiss and I. If nothing else, we would be together on a planet with lots of open space and lots of cheese. We could hide out somewhere. Maybe find a way to contact another ship and get away.

I reached the stand of trees, turned, and crouched down with my eyes on the uman camp. It was an orderly design. A stark contrast to the chaos of battle I'd seen in the past, even in subtle ways.

I heard a twig snap behind me, and my heart stopped.

Not another run-in with soldiers. Not already.

I got on all fours, slunk up next to the nearest tree, and slowly peered around it. In the clearing on the other side I was surprised to see Krate and Cindel. They wore shimmer suits, but for some reason had them turned off. They were both examining something in Cindel's paws.

I almost laughed aloud. I hurried around the tree toward them.

"Hey, mutos!" I said. "Am I glad to—"

My voice startled them. They whipped around...

And Krate shot me.

CHAPTER 37

I was mildly disoriented when I awoke. I saw an image of the clearing in Bossu Wood that had been our home. An overhead view as if we were taking off. The clearing drew smaller and the panorama beyond it consumed more of my vision.

Soldiers dotted the landscape in all directions. Groups of uniforms surged and shifted. There were flashes of light as cannons were lit, hurtling dark projectiles into the air. Smaller flashes echoed. Gunfire from a thousand rifles.

So many flashes.

I opened my eyes and found I was back in my *Granum* cabin. Nestled deep into my nook with a pile of covers on top of me. Someone was seated at my desk, but the angle was such that I couldn't tell who. Yentiss? Cindel?

I groaned and pushed the covers away.

The seated muto shifted and bent forward, peering in at me. "Ah, you're up! You had me concerned." Captain Wendel, wearing a bright smile and a yellow longshirt. "Everything is fine now, then."

I sat up on the edge of my nook slowly. The motion made my head feel full of rocks. With both paws, I attempted to massage the feeling away. "The ship?"

"Safely away," he said. "Headed to our destination."

I nodded. "Krate stunned me."

He leaned back in his chair. "Yes, he did. A good shot, that one."

"He shouldn't have a weapon." The heaviness eased, so I dropped my paws into my lap.

"He feels terrible about it. Said you scared him."

"I probably did. Still shouldn't be armed. He's too impulsive."

I heard the sound of repetitive movement and looked at the captain. He had his snout up and was scratching hard at the nape of his neck. "That world dried me out," he said. "Always scratching now."

I suddenly felt nostalgic. I wanted to return, not just to my home world Trix—but strangely—to Earth. I would've liked to have seen our departure. The colors of the primitive world playing out below us. Blue, green, brown, and white. It wasn't such a bad place. Not that different than many worlds in the Empire.

"I've seen a lot of that lately," I said. "The scratching."

He paused and looked at me. "Where?"

"On the crew, sir. I wonder if—"

He snorted. "Good we're away then." He smiled. "We did it, Sed. Got what we came for, and got away in one piece."

"Did we?" Again, the heaviness hit me. Cursed Krate and his quick trigger finger. I had questions but wasn't able to verbalize them. It felt like too much work.

Then I remembered the state of our cargo bay and felt ill. "I don't think we have enough, sir."

"Have enough what?"

"Cargo." I rubbed my head again. "Food stores. There isn't enough."

His snout wrinkled. "But you said we had a full bay! Coaxed me into leaving and then abandoned the ship. I had to send people after you in a shuttle. Good thing they found a com signal, or you would've been left."

"No, sir, I went to get..." I shook my head. "That wasn't how it was at all. Wait...our shuttles work now?"

The captain leapt from his seat and waved both paws in the air. "What do we do now?" He moaned. "If our cargo is short, we're dead. You realize that?" He dropped into his seat again. "We can go anywhere, but it won't matter. They'll find us. They never forgive a shortage." He cupped his snout with his hands and rocked back and forth.

"*Who* never gives up?" I asked.

"The Naaklik, of course!"

"The Naaklik?"

Not a crime syndicate then. Instead, a race of predatory and poisonous arthropods that resembled a flawed attempt at crossing an uman and a centipede. "How are they involved?"

The captain waved his paws again. "A tale of trickery and gaming tables."

I squinted at him. "Is that what happened at Lutis Five? You were tricked?"

"Yes, but I thought I'd won. That fool Captain Bry wagered an Imperial job that paid double the going rate. The only requirement was a ship with cooled storage. So, I thought, 'Great! The *Granum* meets the requirement. I'll settle our debts with the proceeds!' All I needed to do was win. And I did. Or so I thought."

"Because it was for the Naaklik."

"Precisely," he hissed. "I was tricked. And now we're stuck. Caught between the Emperor's contract and bugs that will hunt us if we fail." He looked at the floor and shook his head. "Guess I lost my lucky snout."

So there it was. Not only were we in danger of imprisonment, loss, and death, but Captain Wendel's unique skill was on the line. His profit snout. No wonder he'd been so secretive.

Our situation was worse than I'd thought.

I felt another wave of nostalgic longing, this time for the company of Louis and Anne. Not that they could necessarily help. But they were reasonable umans. Surprisingly consistent in all this, despite their imprisonment.

I shook my head. "We might've been able to come up with a solution," I said. "If the umans were still with us. We have months of travel left—"

"Of course they're with us!" The captain tossed his paws in the air. "Why wouldn't they be with us?"

I straightened in my nook. "The umans are still here? On the ship?"

He glared at me. "We were out of time, Sed. We had to leave. I wasted all our extra time finding you."

"You didn't drop them off, though? I thought we agreed, promised them, that—"

He stood. "We'll have time later," he said, waving dismissively. "After everything is done."

"To go back to Earth?"

"No, not there. Of course not there. I deleted the coordinates."

"Deleted!"

"Foul, itchy place." He walked past the desk toward the door. "There are lots of uman planets. We'll just find a good one and release them to the wild."

"I can't believe you kept the umans aboard. The resources they'll consume—"

He pointed his tail at me. "We can sleep them though, remember. They'll consume very little."

I climbed free of my nook. The change in posture, the solidity of the floor, seemed to help my head. I grabbed the top of the chair the captain had been sitting in and took a step toward it. "They won't be happy, sir."

He scowled. "I don't care about uman happiness. We have a contract to fulfill." He checked his look in my wall mirror. Adjusted his shirt. "We need to find a way to do that, Sed. You need to think of something."

I shook my head slowly. "I don't know...maybe the umans could help somehow..."

He smiled. "See there! You're thinking now!" Walking back, he a paw on my shoulder. "That's why you're here. Why I sent people out to find you. We're a team, you and I." He patted his chest. "I find the jobs. You make sure they get done."

We all had goals, our own purposes. The captain's place was to sniff out whatever work a lucky snout could find. Mine was to keep the ship and crew alive. Functioning.

I gave him a worried look. He returned a confident smile.

"Okay," I said. "I'll talk to the umans. Tell them the risks. Try to work something out."

He squeezed my shoulder again. "Perfect. Promise them a world if you have to."

"A world?"

"Sure. Has to be one available."

I snorted. "I'll work out something. Maybe Yentiss has an idea. She's good with them. You should've seen—"

The captain released my shoulder and turned away. "About Yentiss, Sed. I'm sorry for how it turned out." His tail was wrapped close to his longshirt. Almost hidden.

I took a step his direction. "How *what* turned out?"

He looked at me again.

My neck fur shot up. "You got her, didn't you? You brought her back to the ship."

His paws were together. Twisting and turning. "We didn't know where she was! Cindel was lucky to find you!"

I hissed slowly. "She was right behind me. There was a wagon. She was inside with a couple umans. She would've been along any second. All Cindel and Krate had to do was—"

"Wait?" The captain shook his head. "I told you. We couldn't wait any longer. For anyone." He pointed a finger at me. "Figure this out, Sed. Figure it out, or everything is lost."

CHAPTER 38

With the ship underway, our system of extended travel preparation began. Rotating skeleton crews were determined, non-essential systems were shut down or reduced, and the process of ship-wide hibernation enacted. In a few days, nearly everyone would be asleep.

To the uninitiated, it might seem strange to worry about leaving "on time" when there were months of travel ahead. What difference would a day or two make over such vast distances?

The travel duration was a known quantity, though. Something we couldn't fudge or step around. A hundred and seven travel days with a slim two-day window on the other end.

Our destination? An arid planet in the woolly south of the Orion spur named Nesa Three. It wasn't under the direct control of any government, though the Naaklik Overwatch was the nearest enforcement service. It was a far reach from the Muto Empire or anywhere else we might call home. And our customers? They would make us look scrupulous in comparison—uman slaves and all.

There was a lot to do. A lot to worry about. I should have been verifying everything before the big sleep—top level systems, the scientists, the medical personnel, the umans—everything. Even the captain's itch was a source of concern. Anything could become a larger issue on the *Granum*.

What I most wanted to do, though, was turn the ship around and find Yentiss. She'd rescued me, and how had she been rewarded? Abandonment on a planet where she'd be constantly in danger.

I was angry with the decision. Disappointed in Cindel and Krate. But those big decisions were the captain's to make. Usually he was right. Usually his snout took us where we needed to go.

So, why did I feel so unsettled? And hadn't he deleted the coordinates, leaving us no way back? No way to rescue Yentiss. No way to return the umans either.

My job required moving ahead. Moving past any loss. But this time, it was difficult.

The cell Louis shared with his wife was considered their cabin now. When given the option to move into the uman "camp" on the storage level, they'd chosen to remain apart. To retain their private space.

I couldn't blame them. There were a lot of smelly creatures in the ancillary bay now. Lots of noises. Plus, the couple deserved a reward for their help. We wouldn't have been as well off without them.

Did that make them traitors to their kind? I didn't know or care. I had a mission.

Someone had repainted the hallway outside their room.

Much of it was abstract. A bright blending of colors that swirled from wall to ceiling to wall again.

I initially suspected our shipboard graffiti artist—the one that frequently used Deck Two as his easel. But the scene immediately across from Louis and Anne's door changed my mind.

The image was of a landscape with a central hill. Atop the hill were three wooden crosses—the center being the largest and straightest of the three. Much of the sky above the hill was a dark purple, but the horizon had a sliver of orange and red. A coming dawn. It was a strange image—haunting and cheerful at the same time.

Was it a view from Louis and Anne's home on Earth? I didn't remember seeing anything like that. There were many uman customs I didn't understand, though. And Earth umans were a breed apart.

Regardless, the scene was better than the standard graffiti. I might just let it stay.

I knocked on their door, called Louis's name, and was invited in.

The interior had changed since the last time I saw it. There were no traces of the original yellow and green colorations. Everything was beige and orange now. The sleep nook was stuffed with comfortable looking blankets and pillows. The corner waste and wash appliance had a light blue curtain hung around it. There were pictures on the walls. One was a shot of our crew that included Yentiss.

Where had Anne found all that stuff?

I couldn't help but smile.

Louis sat on the nook's edge, left of the door. Anne was seated at the table to my right. She wore a blue dress, but no bonnet. Her hair, dark and long, draped her face. Both had furrowed brows and piercing eyes—indications of uman concern.

"What's happening, Sedric?" Louis asked.

Anne grabbed her hair, pulled it behind her head, and started to manipulate it into an artificial head-tail. "We were sent to our cabin," she said. "After that, we heard sirens and movement."

"Has the ship been discovered?" Louis asked.

I shook my head. "No. We moved."

They glanced at each other. "Left the woods?" Louis said.

I took a deep breath. "Yes...and your country."

"We left France!"

"We have family there," Anne said. "Friends. People we should've told."

Louis's eyes narrowed. "You promised we'd be freed if we helped."

My gaze found the floor—which was also beige. "I never said for certain," I said. "Only what I hoped to make happen." I glanced at their faces. "But there were other factors in play. Unforeseen circumstances."

"Where are we going?" Louis asked. "To another country? Or—"

Anne's eyes went wide. "Are we in the heavens!" she said. "Beyond the Earth's sphere?"

I nodded slowly. "Yes. Beyond your system, in fact."

"Our system!" Louis stood suddenly.

I raised a finger and loosely circled it with my other paw. "You're aware of how your planet travels around its star? There are other planets too and they—"

"We know about the solar system," Louis said. "We aren't as backwards as you might think."

"Right." I rubbed my left paw. "Sorry." It was hard not to emphasize, having recently taken a covered wagon ride I hadn't planned.

They exchanged looks again, but neither spoke. Their

faces were lighter in color. Did that mean shock, anger, or sickness? I couldn't remember.

"So, to be clear," I said. "We *left* your solar system."

Louis shook his head slowly. "That was never discussed, Sedric. I was curious about space, but didn't expect..." He looked at the wall to his left. "We don't even have windows. We can't see anything."

"This is a containment cell," I said. "It isn't made for sight-seeing."

"Well, it should be!" Louis shook his head again. "The other umans won't like this. I can barely keep them from fighting as it is."

"It's kidnapping!" Anne said. "Even more than—"

"Wasn't my decision," I growled. "But it's where we are now." I made a calming motion with my tail. "I want to keep everyone alive. Umans included."

Anne placed her hands flat on the desk. "We were to be dropped off," she said. "We hoped in America. Or one of the islands."

"The captain might have left you in the polar region," I said. "Without coats." I shrugged, attempting to reason with myself. "Probably better this way. Better he did nothing."

A lock of Anne's hair fell in front of her face. "I thought he was beginning to like us," she said. "I tried to be cordial."

"He's afraid. There are dangers. Ones I didn't know about." I glanced at the picture of the crew. Yentiss was smiling in it. "I'm fighting emotions myself."

Anne nodded. "I've noticed that about...um...mutos. Much fear."

"When we first met," I said, "you were about to jump from an airlock."

She blew at the wayward hair. "I'm terribly fearful at times too, of course." She gestured at me. "But, can you blame me? You looked like a—"

"Beast?"

"I was going to say, 'large rat.'" She frowned. "But beast will do."

I snorted. "You look odd to us too. Like worms with legs."

They glanced at each other, then laughed. I didn't mind uman laughter. It was strange, but not displeasing. Not like their yelling.

Louis sat on the nook edge again. "What are your plans for us?" he asked. "Can we return to Earth later?"

I chuckled nervously. "This is where it gets uncomfortable." I leaned back against the door. "This room needs more seats." I frowned. "Actually, it needs more room. We could probably find you a larger—"

"You go on tangents when you're nervous," Anne said.

I scratched at my chin. "Yeah, I probably do." I shifted on the door. "Listen, my job is problem solving. My waking time spent hopping from one problem to another. Problems with personnel, problems with the ship, problems with the captain. It's never-ending."

I raised a finger. "Some might see it as a job filled with random events. Or not a real job at all. But there's purpose in the madness for me." I glanced at the crew image again. "I keep the ship safe, the captain safe, and the crew safe. Typically in that order." I felt a touch of guilt but smiled anyway. "Now that we have umans aboard, I have more to look out for."

Anne nodded. "Oh you poor thing."

"Pardon?"

"You must be at your wit's end. I couldn't imagine having so much responsibility."

I frowned. "Yeah, that's what it is. *Responsibility*." I leaned forward. "I mean, technically, the *Granum* is the captain's thing. It and everything in it. But things rarely go by the book around here." I felt an itch on my spine and rubbed the door against it. "I'm at a spot where I'm not sure how to proceed. Or even what to tell you. Part of me wants to...eh...give you only what you need."

"Deceive us?" Louis crossed his arms. "Haven't you done that already?"

"Not intentionally, no." I raised a shoulder. "Circumstances sort of slipped from my paws."

"Follow your better instincts," Anne said. "In whatever you say."

I wrinkled my snout. "Better instincts...yeah. Not sure rhats have those, exactly, but..." I gazed at the ceiling, still conflicted. How would umans react to all that was going on? This was their first time off the planet!

"We have to meet some dangerous creatures," I said finally. "Some very bad 'beasts.'"

"And you're bringing them a shipment of cheese," Louis said.

Anne nodded. "The stuff we've been gathering, yes?"

"Yes, but we didn't get enough. And even if we had a full bay, we'd have to use some to feed you all."

"Which is why you were going to drop us off," Anne said.

I pointed a finger at my head. "The captain is a simple thinker. Always wants a clear path." I shrugged. "I try to give him that. Sometimes, I fail."

Louis nodded. "So you're stuck now. Not enough food to make your quota."

"Right. And if we don't make our delivery...well, things will get ugly. Not only will we not get paid, we may..." I resisted telling them about the Naaklik propensity for eating those that cheat them. "...have to fight."

"You want us to help fight?" Louis asked.

"Is that possible?"

"The men aren't of the same army." Louis shook his

head slowly. "They...don't get along." He narrowed his eyes. "And why *should* they fight? You kidnapped them!"

"I agree," I said, nodding. "That could be a problem."

"A problem? It's a riot!"

I sighed. "Could we trick them into it?"

"Trick!" Anne said.

"Did I mention our customers are ugly?" I described the Naaklik in full detail, including their armor and weapons. That only made Anne seem more frightened—and Louis —angrier.

"I'm not their leader!" Louis said. "The French listen to me because I was an officer. But the others?" He searched the wall again as if still trying to find a window. "I can't help you."

"More than half of the people are women," Anne said. "Not trained to fight."

I crossed my arms. "Yeah, we'll have to sleep everyone. I don't have time for more problems."

"Sleep 'em?"

I scratched my neck. "We hibernate between stops. There's over three months of travel ahead."

They exchanged looks. "Humans don't hibernate."

"Our scientists say you can." I waved a paw. "There's gas involved. It's painless." I studied the wall-mounted crew image again. "Doesn't solve my problem on the other side, though. Only complicates it."

"Could we return to Earth after your delivery?" Anne asked.

I took a deep breath. Should I mention that the captain had removed all chances of a return trip? That without coordinates, even I couldn't go back? Regardless of how much I wanted to? "The captain has suggested compensation..."

"Compensation?" Louis said. "We should be taken home. That was the—"

"Did I mention the Naaklik will eat us if this goes bad?" I said.

"Eat us!" Anne exclaimed.

"Yeah, they're rude that way."

Louis rocked on the nook's edge. "Well, if the choices are fight or be eaten..."

I frowned, remembering the last time I'd seen a Naaklik. It was twice my size and heavily armored—both naturally and artificially. Then there were the weapons it carried. Heavy particle rifles. Fusion grenades. Light-based throwing stars.

And that was a male of the species. The females were larger and fiercer—or so I'd heard.

"Never mind," I said. "I shouldn't have involved you."

"What about being eaten?" Louis said.

Anne leaned back and drew her hands into her lap. "This is a most distressing conversation."

I pushed away from the door with my tail. "My fault. Sometimes the ideas collapse in on themselves." I shook my head. "I wish Yentiss was here. She might have something."

"Yes, I like her." Anne said. "She's wonderfully creative. Where is she?"

"Got left behind." I pointed my thumb over my shoulder. "Back on Earth."

"What?" Anne said. "How did—?"

I clicked my teeth together nervously. Shook my head. "Sorry. I shouldn't have bothered you." I turned and opened the door. "I need to get back and think this through." I pointed my tail at them. "Be ready for some extended sleep. Probably want to tell the other umans too. Make sure they eat well and make use of the wash and wastes." I stepped into the hall.

"Where are you going?" Louis asked.

"I don't know exactly." I studied the hillside scene. There was a lot of darkness in it. A lot of emotion. Maybe I should have it painted over.

I felt a hand on my shoulder. "I'm sorry," Louis said. "We didn't know."

I snarled and the hand retreated. I didn't need emotional distraction now. I only needed solutions.

"Mister Sedric, sir." Anne's voice.

The couple stood just outside their room now. There was a loop of reds and oranges on the wall outlining their door. Outlining them. "Yes?"

"We can help," she said. "The women, I mean. If we could only—"

I cut her off with a scowl. "We <u>can't</u> go back."

Anne retreated and her eyes grew moist.

I softened my tone. "We have to play the situation as it is now, is all. Respond to it."

She raised both palms. "I wasn't asking for Earth." She glanced at Louis. "But if we really have months yet, then we should be able to make what you need."

I shook my head. "We can't have everyone up and roaming around."

"Only a small group," she said. "We could work in rotating teams."

I straightened an ear. "You really think that's possible?"

"Just give us space to work in and let us go."

I frowned. An on board cheese factory? Could that work?

Anne smiled and brought her hands together. "We'll fill the bay, Sedric. I promise."

I was skeptical, but I found myself nodding anyway. "We'll try that then."

What else could we do?

CHAPTER 39

The downside of travels within the Five Galaxies are the periods in between. The years and months it takes to reach one location from another. Even with the occasional gift of a jump portal—we would use two in our journey to Nesa Three—there was too much time spent waiting.

Prior to the gift of hibernation gas, space travel often turned disastrous. Ships journeyed into the big dark, healthy, and functioning normally, only to be lost forever. Some of the losses were doubtless due to malfunctions, but there were many legends. Ships found with no bodies aboard. Ships found with *only* bodies. Pieces of wreckage appearing in strange places.

All such mysteries shared the same diagnosis: travel death. The result of long distances, confined spaces, and the vast emptiness in between.

For that reason, I took my first sleep cycle early. I didn't want to stew over Yentiss's loss or worry about our coming rendezvous. I wanted only the oblivion of sleep and the forgetfulness of time. Three weeks passed while I occupied the nook in my cabin. Countless parsecs were crossed.

There were still images, though. The rat in the uman's garbage. Anne on the verge of leaping from the *Granum*. The artwork of Deck Two—both the satirical graffiti and the three crosses the uman couple had painted. Yentiss's image was present too. Poor smiling Yentiss.

My mind wrestled with itself, attempting to find solutions to problems past and present. But none were found. I awoke with a dull ache in my skull, and cramps in my legs and tail.

I squinted at the room's green and silver coloring. I briefly pondered whether I was in the right cabin still. Hadn't I had the cabin painted before the gas?

No. It was the umans who'd changed their cabin color. Not me.

Everything was as it had always been.

Except it wasn't. I wasn't. The ship, crew, and captain *weren't* out of danger. We were barreling straight for it.

I spent three weeks in command while the captain slept. My time at the bridge was torturous. I avoided looking at Yentiss's chair. Tried to forget that we'd left her on a primitive world, alone. The only muto for hundreds of light years.

Was she still even alive?

The captain seemed ambivalent to her loss, concerned only for how her absence affected the ship. But after being assured that there were crewmembers who could be trained to replace her, he mentioned her no more.

My reaction should have been similar, but it wasn't. It couldn't be. Yentiss was meaningful. She was useful. She was good.

Away from the bridge, I drifted down empty corridors, amusing myself with solitary games and written legends. I spent hours in the cargo bay overlooks, silently counting the boxes of cheese and wine, before checking the progress in the tertiary bay.

At a quarter of the size of the other bays, it was typically used for storage. But now it housed the cheese production facility—long rows of tables filled with tubes, vats, and canisters, rivaling the science lab in complexity.

On one end, raw milk was coagulated using enzymes and organisms. From there it was cut, stirred, cooked, drained, milled, salted, and poured into round molds. These completed rounds were then pressed and placed on racks to ripen.

Dontel and Uzel had assisted in the facility setup—always a source of concern—but so far, everything appeared to function. A couple dozen women had produced a considerable amount of cheese.

Would it be enough?

It had to be. It was the only chance we had.

At the end of three weeks, I returned to sleep. The on-and-off cycle continued until we were a week from Nesa Three. Then the ship-wide wake-up cycle began. Over the course of a few days the entire crew was returned to consciousness.

I looked forward to the normalcy of a restored crew. There were maintenance jobs to catch up on, along with additional chores created by the uman's presence. Plus, having a hundred or so blaster-capable rhats available was a bonus. I wasn't certain how our encounter with the Naaklik would play out. I thought we were ready, but I'd been surprised before.

One day into the wake-up, Cindel messaged me to meet him at the tertiary bay overlook. He didn't elaborate, but I assumed it had something to do with the bay's clean out. Cheese-wise we had what we needed. I'd checked the primary hold repeatedly. Counted and recounted. The uman females somehow managed to reach our quota. Now the third bay could return to being a large, grey room.

Cindel was waiting in the overlook when I arrived. Below were nearly a hundred uman males, dressed in the blue uniforms of French soldiers and arranged in a rectangular formation. They also appeared to be armed, which caused my neck fur to stand on end.

"What's going on here?" I said, pointing below. "They shouldn't be awake."

There were three mutos with the umans, dressed in the black longshirts of security. No armor. Only three weapons between them.

Louis hurried onto the overlook. "Have you told him yet?" he asked Cindel.

"Told me what?"

Cindel wrinkled his snout. "Good news and bad news, sir."

I glanced at the soldiers. "Give me the good news, please."

Cindel nodded. "The translators are helping," he said. "The uman's overall morale has improved and—"

"Morale isn't a concern now," I said. "They shouldn't be awake at all. Who said to wake them?"

Cindel nodded at Louis. "Louis and I discussed it, sir. It seemed like a reasonable move given what we're up against."

"Up against?" I snarled and looked between them. "You mean the Naaklik?"

Cindel gripped the overlook's guardrail. "Have you talked with the doctor?"

"Not for a while, no. Why?"

Cindel shrugged, nervously. "Well, he'd know more. Have all the statistics and numbers for you."

I looked at Louis. "What is he talking about?"

"It's the bad news, sir," Cindel said. "I'm running short on personnel."

"Short?" I hissed. "I thought everyone was awake?"

"They are, yes, but the uman parasite is everywhere. The doctor has a way to remove them once discovered, but—"

"I thought the suits were modified!" I said. "Made to kill the bugs so the crew couldn't get infected."

"I don't know anything about that." Cindel pointed below. "All I know is that I have a handful to work with."

One of the guards pawed at the top of his leg. Clearly scratching. Was he infected too? "No one tells me anything," I said.

"Nearly sixty percent infected." Cindel said. "Might be better to put everyone to sleep again. Quarantine until medical can make the rounds."

"Except we can't for the recovery time," I said. "And the extra food required."

The soldiers packed tightly together now, with those in the outer rows aiming from their knees and the inner rows standing. A defensive position or an offensive one? I had no idea.

"I'm only looking for a solution, sir. Fedwi is stretching the resources now. Rationing—"

"Which is its own concern," I said. "Who knows where he'll look for food if pressed." I drew closer to the overlook railing. "Hopefully not the umans."

Cindel got a worried look. "I'll have someone watch him, sir."

"One of your healthy few, you mean?" I sighed and indicated the scene below. "Are those soldiers armed?"

Louis joined me at the rail. "Only props from your science group."

"They can't be armed." I looked at Louis. "The captain wouldn't allow it."

"There's still a level of fear to overcome," Louis said. "A level of trust to build on both sides. I understand. I just thought—"

I shook my head. "It's a bad idea. Arming umans. Too many things could happen."

Louis pointed below. "They were simple soldiers in a

known cause, Sedric. Now everything is different. Their perceptions shattered. They've been forced to accept the presence of other planets and other life. Strange life." He turned and leaned against the rail. "I have problems with it all myself."

I scowled. "Sounds like more bad news to me."

"Maybe not."

I raised an eyebrow. "No?"

"Many of them are young and faced uncertain futures on Earth. Offering them a purpose, even wrapped in the unknown..." He shrugged. "It could mean something." He looked toward the interior of the ship. "It did for me, anyway. I wasn't more than an errand boy before. But now...?"

"Is it a purpose worth fighting for?" I asked.

"Maybe." He glanced at Cindel and pushed away from the rail. "Probably."

There were barked orders from below, followed by the movement of men. It wasn't a unified procession, though. Some raised their fake guns. Others stepped forward. Others turned to the right.

I shook my head. "What was that?"

"There's a saying on my home world," Cindel said. "'Even in certain defeat, still play the game.'"

"Eh?"

"We won't know how it will play out until we're there. Anything could happen."

More orders were given. The group of men charged from one side of the room to the other, yelling. It was loud and haphazard.

"See there," Cindel said. "They can almost swarm."

I let out a long breath. "I have more faith in their ability to scatter." I thought of the Naaklik again. Aside from standard arms and legs, they had multiple, poison-bearing appendages—called "forcipules"—in the vicinity of there "neck." If they had necks, that is. The width of a Naaklik above the shoulders stayed roughly the same all the way to the top of its "head."

Forcipules could hold and manipulate ranged weapons too. It made a single Naaklik a small army all by itself. How many were we meeting?

I shook my head. "All the more hopeless."

"Sir?" Cindel said.

"Never mind." I waved at the scene below. "We can't do this. It just won't work. I'm sorry."

"Yes, sir." Cindel's snout wrinkled with disappointment, but he saluted anyway.

I turned to leave, but Louis raised a hand and stepped closer. "I know I'm new to this, Sedric. I can't begin to imagine what the universe is really like." He snorted. "I thought there was only one galaxy. Five times that seems...unbelievable."

"There's more, actually," I said. "Thousands more."

His eyes widened. "Have you been to them all?"

I shook my head and looked toward the exit. "I need to go, Louis. Need to check on the bridge." I couldn't escape the ache in my gut. Or the way my bumble hand throbbed. Even with a full hold of food, I had a bad feeling about what was ahead. Too much could go wrong.

Louis nodded. "I'll let you leave, Sedric. Sorry."

I took a step, then curiosity caused me to pause. "The picture outside your room, Louis. What is it?"

He looked surprised again. "You mean Anne's Golgotha?"

I flicked the air with my tail. "The one with the crosses," I said. "And the sunrise."

He glanced at Cindel. "That would take a bit to explain."

"Is it near where you lived?"

"Not at all." He smiled. "It's a historical scene. The site of Jesus's crucifixion. He was the, um—"

I held up a paw. "Give it to me in a word or two, Louis. What does it mean?"

He thought for a moment. "*Hope*, Sedric," he said. "If I had to use one word, I'd say 'hope.'"

CHAPTER 40

Mutos were children of a darkened sun. Forced to survive in even the harshest of circumstances. We didn't expect a better life. We eked out whatever we could with what we found. Or stole.

Hope was an alien concept. It belonged to species like umans and the Briddarri. Fur-less beings with bright, yellow stars. Relentless travelers and wide-eyed adventurers.

Any hope I'd had, any wish for something better, got left on Earth. All I had now was devotion to my job, along with a simmering, deep-seated dread.

Cindel, Louis, and Anne joined Captain Wendel and I on the bridge. The two umans sat near the captain, while Cindel and I occupied the front consoles. All watched the central screen in silence. The view was of Nesa Three. It was a vibrant, seemingly unoccupied planet. Naaklik, like the centipedes they resembled, were good at hiding.

"It's beautiful, this world," Anne said. "Is that what Earth looks like?"

"Similar," I said. "Yes."

The captain grunted. "Don't let the pretty face fool you. If the large bugs are there, it might as well be a desert."

A few minutes later, we received a signal from the Naaklik. A warning to maintain our current position. It was a terse audio message, and though my internal translator handled the translation fine, the source—the originating Naaklik's tongue sounded like two dry bones being banged together.

The captain nodded slowly. "Tell them we'll wait here."

I fumbled through crafting a message and sending it. I was at Yentiss's control desk, after all. Doing *her* job.

"Gunship inbound," was the response.

Twenty minutes later, our sensors acknowledged an approaching ship. A few minutes after that the glimmer of a vessel appeared on the central screen. It was moving toward us from Nesa's eastern hemisphere. Larger and larger it grew. More and more oppressive it seemed.

It was a Naaklik gunship, and as such, outmatched the *Granum* by a factor of ten. Its shape was slightly rectangular, but only if one were looking down from above. The exterior was infused with complication. Two sections on the ship's top—one on either side—had repeating sloped structures, giving the impression that large centipedes perched there. There were four small and delicate-seeming wings along the ship's top near the back, and similar wings on each side. A line of script on the nearest side translated to "the Hardened Claw."

Most apparent, though, were the two forward-facing berserker-class phase guns. A single volley from one of those would tear our ship in half.

We couldn't run or outfight it. Even with our guns and engines at full strength.

The Naaklik ship—the *Claw*—requesting a video connection. I glanced at Captain Wendel. "They want to talk," I said.

He nodded. "Let's see them then."

I accepted the connection and the central screen flickered before resolving into the image of an umber-colored Naaklik face. A squiggly blue line was tattooed across his forehead, just below two curling antenna and above a row of seven eyes. All four of the smaller, poison-laden limbs near his mouth wore gold bands.

Anne gasped.

I muted the connection and I glanced at her. She and Louis were transfixed by the central screen. Neither looked comfortable.

"You all right to continue?" I said.

Louis reached for Anne's hand. "We'll be fine." He patted her clasped hand with his free one.

"Perhaps I should go to our room," she said. "I don't like bugs." She wriggled her fingers in the air. "Always crawling everywhere."

The captain hiccupped a laugh. "This will do nothing to change that opinion." He tipped his snout. "Let's talk to him, Sed."

I restored the audio connection.

The Naaklik's mandibles flared, and his antennas went erect. Never a good sign. "You have the code word?" he asked.

Code word? I glanced at the captain.

He looked confident. Relaxed. "Of course," he said. "Lair Ree Law Rence."

The words translated to nothing. Were they meaningful to the Naaklik?

The Naaklik spokesman was silent for a moment, then nodded slowly. "Late, rhats," he said. "You're very late.

The captain raised a paw. "We are well within the agreed upon—"

The spokesman waved a large, black pistol. "No chitchat! We must get to business. The ceremony's in two days."

"What ceremony might that be?" the captain asked. "I wasn't told."

More mandible flares. "A Fle' Te ceremony for the regent's niece. A potency celebration."

Captain Wendel's seat creaked. "A potency what?"

The spokesman did his best impression of an icy seven-eye stare. "Those not of the Overwatch wouldn't understand." He shook his pistol. "We must begin the transfer."

"Certainly,' the captain said. "Is there a place we can dock, or—"

"Your ship must not touch ours! It is forbidden!"

"That will make it difficult to—"

"Do you have shuttles?"

"Yes," the captain said, nodding. "We have two."

"Load them and send them across."

"They'll have to touch your ship to unload," the captain said.

"We will purify them."

"How exactly does that work?" The captain wrinkled his snout. "There will be a pilot on board."

The Naaklik's mandibles lifted slightly. Was that a look of surprise?

"Your pilot must be of the knowledge class," he said. "Surely you know this."

"Knowledge class?"

"I think he means a scientist, sir," I whispered.

The captain gave me a stern eye before addressing the screen again. "Give us a moment to arrange your delivery. Are there any more requirements?"

"Only that you hurry." The Naaklik pointed the pistol our way. "You have an hour."

The connection dropped and the screen went black. There was silence on the bridge for a few moments, all of us pinned in place by the weight of the conversation. The Naaklik's presence, even though they were many kilometers away, felt tangible and oppressive.

"Intelligent bugs like that..." Anne winced and shuddered. "All part of God's creation?" She placed a hand to her temple. "Hurts my mind to ponder it."

"They aren't the only insects." I looked at her and Louis. "Though they're doubtless the ugliest."

"What have we been brought out to?" Louis shook his head. "We should be on Earth. Not here."

"I know," I said. "I'm sor—"

"We can't sit here blubbering," the captain said. "We have shuttles to load." He stood, then tail-pointed at me and Cindel. "Get a team together. Get the food loaded. As much as both shuttles will hold."

Cindel gave me a desperate look. "Much of the crew is incapacitated, sir."

"Incapacitated?"

"Affected by the uman louse. It's everywhere. The doctor—"

The captain's fur bristled. "We can't worry about the itch! We have shuttles to fill. Wake more umans if you have to."

"Control is a problem, sir," Cindel said.

Louis stood now too. "You shouldn't push the soldiers into service," he said. "Most of them haven't adapted to...um...their new circumstances. It may not go well."

The captain hissed. "All of that...fine nostalgia for their home world, will be meaningless if we're blown from the sky." He glanced at me. "Or captured."

I exited the console. "Sir..."

"We have what they want, correct?" the captain said. "A bay full of cheese and wine?"

"Yes," I said.

"All we need do is deliver it then! No stalling now!"

Cindel joined me as I moved toward the door. "We'll get it loaded," I said. "Right away."

Anne stood and placed a hand on Louis's elbow. "What was that about the knowledge class?" she asked.

"The Naaklik have a collection of rules they follow," I said.

"Impossible to keep track of them all." The captain patted the back of his chair. "They don't interact with other species much." He squinted at me. "They want our scientists, did you say?"

I nodded. "They hold those that work with knowledge in high regard. Consider them a special breed." They'd never met our scientist, of course. Uzel and Dontel might upset the whole Naaklik hierarchy. "*Escorts of certainty*, or something."

The captain cradled his snout. "They won't eat them, will they?"

"I don't think so."

He slapped the back of his seat. "Get our scientists on the shuttles, then." He paused and held up a finger. "They can fly the shuttles, can't they?"

I nodded. "I believe so, yes. We could always send them over on auto if need be. Fly them from here."

He slapped the seat again. "Good to go then. We have an hour. Get those shuttles ready!"

CHAPTER 41

The loading process went better than I expected. In just under an hour we had the first shuttle loaded and ready for delivery. Cindel, the captain, and I gathered in the bridge again to watch the process. Louis and Anne chose to stay with their kind.

A yellow, wire-frame version of the *Granum* appeared on my console. On it, a portion of the rear, representing the shuttle bay doors, flashed red. Next came a textual confirmation that the doors were fully ajar followed by a wire-frame version of the shuttle leaving the ship. A flattened tube with wings.

"First shuttle away, sir." There was a feeling of relief as I said it. The expectation that this task was one step closer to being complete. That soon we'd have an empty primary bay and could disembark, leaving the giant bugs in the past.

"Get the Naaklik on screen," Captain Wendel said. "Make sure they know it's coming."

"Sure..." I stared at the console, trying to remember the

exact sequence of swipes and presses to raise the other ship. I gave it my best guess.

A second later, Uzel's profile appeared on the central screen. He was dressed in a white science shirt, paws wrapped around the slender shuttle control stick. He glanced our way, looking surprised.

"Oh, hello!" he said. "Doing fine here. Got everything under control. Glad the captain had us do that maintenance, Sed. Operating at max efficiency."

"Sedric," the captain bellowed.

"Sorry, sir." Scowling, I took another guess at the proper swipe-press sequence.

"Hello to you too, captain!" Uzel said. "Interesting how the Naaklik value science, isn't it? Seems like—"

Uzel disappeared. I pressed two disparate portions of the console and reconnected with the Naaklik *Claw*. The representative with the forehead tattoo reappeared. A wisp of white smoke trailed from his right antenna. A pleasure drug of some kind?

"You have the code?" he asked.

"We gave it to you last time," I said. "Remember?"

"You must present it again."

I resisted scowling.

The captain repeated the "Lair Ree" code phrase and the Naaklik nodded. "We are tracking your shuttle," he said. "It's piloted by the knowledge class?"

"Yes," the captain replied. "One of our scientists. Lots of knowledge."

I suppressed a groan.

The Naaklik's mandibles widened. "It will be purified when it arrives. A painless process."

I was happy I wasn't Uzel. The fact that the Naaklik had mentioned pain suggested their purification process might not be for the shuttle only.

My console reverted to an exterior view of the *Granum*, with the shuttle making its way peacefully toward the Naaklik ship. Below it, the colors of Nesa Three played out over a winding coastline. Blue, green, brown, and white. Nesa wasn't that different than many of the worlds I'd visited. It reminded me of my home world, Trix, except Trix had a little more orange and black in the mix.

The bottom left corner of my screen flashed red, and the image shifted to the *Granum* wire-frame view. This time one of the forward guns was outlined in red.

"What's it showing me?" I said.

"I see it too," Cindel said. "Some sort of power surge in the port forward gun."

My heart fell into my gut. "What's it doing?" I manipulated the console again, attempting to steer my way to the armaments section. Trying to find out what the warning indicated. Why it would—

"Oh no," Cindel said.

The scene switched to the exterior view again with the shuttle now farther away. Closer to the waiting Naaklik ship. A bolt of blue light escaped our gun's barrel, arced across the panorama of Nesa Three, and struck the shuttle dead on.

I swore.

I couldn't manipulate my console fast enough. Couldn't reach all the information I needed to reach. I managed to terminate our connection with the Naaklik, though. Thankfully.

"What was that?" Captain Wendel asked. "What happened?"

Cindel glanced at me. I bobbed my head, giving him the go ahead to answer. "One of our guns fired," he said.

"What?" The captain's seat creaked as he stood. "Who fired it?"

I located the gun logistics. From there, it was a simple task to check the firing history for the gun. I shook my head. "Wasn't fired by anyone," I said. "It was some sort of test protocol." I scrolled until I found the maintenance list for the suspect gun. It was as I feared. "It's the same gun." I groaned. "The one they had in the lab when this all began."

"Look at me!" The captain said. "What did you say?"

I turned toward the command chair. The captain was less than a meter away. Hovering over me.

"One of our guns misfired and shot the shuttle," I said.

The captain's fur bristled. "Was the shuttle destroyed?"

I'd forgotten to check! I switched the central screen to an exterior view. Most evident was the looming *Hardened Claw* and the planetary expanse below it.

The shuttle was nowhere to be seen.

"No sign of debris," Cindel said, studying his console screen. "Can't seem to locate the shuttle either, though."

I navigated my console to the com systems and tried to raise the shuttle. No response. I wasn't sure if that was because the shuttle was destroyed, or because I was doing it wrong. I could really use Yentiss's skills.

The Naaklik signaled. Strongly.

I let the captain know.

"I guess you have to put them on." The captain returned to his command chair. "What else can we do with them just staring at us like that."

A second later, the Naaklik spokesman appeared. His antennas were upright, his mandibles were flared, and his eyes—all seven of them—were huge. "What have you done!" he clattered. "You've endangered our ship!"

"We've had a malfunction," the captain said. "Give us a moment—"

"The *Claw*'s guns are locked on us," Cindel whispered.

"You will taste our wrath," the Naaklik said.

"Hold on a second!" The captain's chair squeaked again. "We had no ill intent toward you. We're here to deliver cargo. Not start a war."

The Naaklik's forcipules flared out and back in succession, creating a loud flapping sound. This seemingly uncontrolled emotion continued for a full five seconds. "I doubt your Empire would fight for you," he said then.

Were the forcipule flares Naaklik laughter? I had no idea.

"It was a figure of speech," Captain Wendel said. "I'm sorry our malfunction frightened you. We can't locate our shuttle. We may have lost one of our—"

"It entered Nesa's atmosphere," the Naaklik said. "Headed for the sea. Along with our delicacies."

The captain exhaled strongly. "Thank you. We'll send our other shuttle down to—"

"You will do no such thing."

"We want to look for our lost shuttle. Recover the pilot and possibly the—"

"You've cheated the Overwatch," the Naaklik said. "Our deal is forfeit. Reparations must be made."

"We still have food aboard," I said. "We'll give you what we have."

"Is it enough to fulfill our agreement?"

"Probably not," I said. "But—"

"Then it will be insufficient." His mandibles and forcipules came together slowly, causing the fur on my neck to stand. "We too have a contract to fulfill."

"What would you like us to do?" the captain asked.

The Naaklik tipped his head forward. "I'm sending you coordinates on Nesa. You will land there, and we will follow."

The captain gave a confident snort. "I can't see how that will help our situation. I regret we are short on our contract.

Such things happen in the Five Galaxies. Losses and shortfalls are a part of—'

"Do you have the coordinates?"

Planetary positioning information appeared on my console screen. "Yes," I said, nodding.

The Naakik brought its appendages together again. "We will meet you there."

CHAPTER 42

Again we were left staring at a black screen. This time it might as well have been the rotting core of our collapsed sun for the finality of it. It was as if we were circling darkness, being drawn slowly toward a crushing, hopeless and terrible end.

"What now?" Cindel said finally.

He and I focused on the captain, who now sat slumped in his chair, snout cupped in one paw.

"Sir?" I said.

Captain Wendel raised his free paw. "It's been a good run, gentlemutos. Thousands of light years, hundreds of planets, dozens of good days."

"Could we outrun them?" Cindel asked. "The *Granum* is smaller, more maneuverable. We could take to space and—"

"We won't outmaneuver those guns," the captain said. "They have too much range. Too much power."

"If we waited until after our descent," Cindel said, "we could find a place on Nesa to slip into. A ravine or canyon. Maybe even a large cave."

"Those bugs have the best scanning technology in the quadrant," the captain said. "They'll find us."

Cindel gripped the back of his chair. "Then we fight, sir."

"The bulk of the crew is quarantined."

"Only with the louse. They could still fight."

Captain Wendel snorted. "How well will they aim while scratching?"

"Well enough," Cindel said. "Their lives would depend on it."

The captain studied his right armrest, then shook his head. "You have the coordinates, Sedric?"

I nodded. "It's a spot on one of the smaller continents north of the equator." I turned toward the console, and with a few presses, entered the coordinates from the Naaklik message into the ship's mapping system. A second later a view of the rendezvous point appeared on my screen, which I shared with the central screen.

It looked inviting. A quarter kilometer clearing surrounded by forests and ponds. "I was expecting worse," I said.

The captain cackled. "To them, that's as bad as it gets."

I glanced his way. "I thought they liked temperate climates?"

"They do." He indicated the screen. "But Nesa Three will have been stripped of any life larger than my foot." He scratched and smoothed the back of his neck. "That's the kind of hunters they are. Kill any rival, fill their stomachs, and move on."

Cindel gave me a worried look. "They've killed <u>everything</u> here?"

The captain shook his head. "Not everything, no. Just the big stuff. Anything that's easily eaten." He pointed his tail at the screen. "That beauty you see? Those trees and flowers? Means nothing to the Naaklik. Once they've gotten the meat of it, they're done."

"Looks can be deceiving," Cindel said.

"Aye," the captain squinted. "And usually are." He shifted in his seat. Sighed. "Still, it's not a bad place to die. Better than in orbit. The cold of space."

My instinct was to find an escape path. Some way to fly out safely. Or hide until we could. But the captain was right in his assessment. We didn't have a lot of options.

My console signaled another message from the Naaklik. A textual warning that we had ten minutes to begin our descent.

"What's that?" the captain asked.

"A reminder."

Captain Wendel nodded. "I'll lay in a course. Signal the department heads about what we—"

"Sir?" I instinctively looked Cindel's direction. His neck hair was puffed, and his eyes were wide, staring at his console. "I've got a screen full of warnings here," he said. "Shipboard warnings." His paws danced across the console, then stopped. "Lost contact with deck two and the storage deck."

"What?"

Cindel manipulated the console again. "I'll try to contact someone in a nearby deck. See if I can get a read on what's going on."

I looked at the seats Louis and Anne had occupied earlier. I'd invited them to join us again, but they'd wanted to be on the lower decks *with their people.*

Something about that didn't feel right. Why would they want to be down there? Louis seemed to love the *Granum* almost as much as I did. Always asking question. Delighting in every new thing he encountered.

Cindel opened a com line to our science deck. He muttered a bit, then with a gesture, put a captured image on the central screen. It showed dozens of umans moving through the hallway. Every color of uniform. Long rifles in their hands.

"What's this?" the captain asked. "What's going on there? Some kind of training?"

It felt like I was trapped in that uman wagon again. Angry and scared at the same time. "I don't think so, sir," I said.

"No? Then what is it?"

"It's a riot."

"A riot! We don't have time for a riot."

I needed to find Louis and Anne. See if they could talk sense into whoever was leading the umans. Unless, of course, *they* were the ones leading the umans. Then I wasn't sure what to do.

"How are they all awake?" Cindel asked. "There shouldn't be that many. Not enough to overwhelm our guards."

We helped create the situation, of course. "Umans helped load the shuttles."

Cindel curled his snout. "Not that many. Not as many as we just saw. And they were to go right back to—"

I thought of Louis and Anne again. "Doesn't matter. We have a situation to deal with." I glanced at the central screen, still showing an image of the rendezvous point. "Two situations, actually." I stood. "I should go down there. See if I can talk some sense—"

"You can't go anywhere now," the captain said. "We need to land!"

I couldn't keep my anger from showing. "You don't need me here for that. You left Earth without my help. I'm sure you can handle a landing."

The bridge lights flickered and went out for a full second before returning again. I looked at Cindel, whose eyes were still locked on his console screen. "Where are they now?" I asked.

"I've checked other decks. I see umans on many of them. Medical, Engineering—"

I remembered the many tours I'd given Louis during his time aboard. All the many questions he'd asked. Had I created a monster? My own rampaging Beast.

Cindel got up and cut in front of me. "Security is my department. I should take care of this. I'll find who I can. Get stunners and get this back in order."

I wrinkled my snout. Cindel was capable, but this was—

The ship pitched such that I fell into one of the consoles beyond the captain's chair. Cindel dropped to all fours and the captain screamed: "We've been hit!"

I righted myself, found a seat at the nearest rearward console, and searched for the ship's status. I sighed when I saw the external schematics. There were some anomalies—as always—but structurally, we were fine. "Not hit, captain," I said. "I think the Naaklik sent a warning shot."

The captain gripped his piloting controls, his tongue peeked out the side of his mouth, and the *Granum* began to move.

The central screen shifted to an external view of the ship. The perspective was such that the curve of the planet was visible. A few seconds later, Nesa Three filled the entire screen. He was taking us in.

I heard the bridge door wheeze as Cindel exited. I rose to follow but checked the captain again. Could I trust him to be alone? He already seemed defeated. Where might panic take him? If he thought the Naaklik would use us to make up for the lost food, or thought the rioters would take over the ship, what then? His "profit snout" had long since forsaken him.

Anything was possible.

It was the worst situation I'd ever been in. One where every second reduced our chances of survival while adding more variables.

"You know where we're headed, captain?"

He hissed with annoyance. "Of course, I do. You gave me the coordinates."

"And you won't do anything rash?"

Another hiss followed by a glance my direction. "Rash? What do you take me for? This is my ship." He tail-pointed at the central screen. "I'm going to land safely, and we'll talk to the Naaklik. Work out a deal."

I nodded slowly. "Maybe if we give them the rest of the food stores...maybe that will be enough." I moved toward the front consoles. "Or we could offer them free future deliveries." I took the seat at Yentiss's station.

The captain shrugged. "Maybe. It's worth a try."

I wasn't feeling better. "But about the umans, sir. The riot—"

He waved a paw. "Cindel will handle it. It will be fine. We have weapons."

I didn't mention that the umans appeared to have weapons. Their weapons. I'd glimpsed uman rifles in their hands. Those might not kill as efficiently as blasters, but they'd still kill us just fine. Fur or no fur.

I sat quietly for a moment, attempting to think of a way out of this all. But the answer wouldn't come. I was still mourning the loss of Yentss, whether I admitted it or not. I wanted everything back the way it was before the scientists scorched our original load. Before Earth, France, and the uman Emperor. But there was no route to that from here. None.

I was alerted to another incoming message, this time from the shuttle bay. I opened the connection and was greeted by Dontel's face. He had a manic, disheveled look. More so than usual. Leaning close, I reduced the volume. "Yes?"

"There are umans here," he said. "They're demanding that I fly them off the ship."

"There are over a thousand umans on board," I said. "You couldn't possibly take them all."

Dontel looked nervously to his left. "It's a group calling themselves the 'Emperor's Lost,'" he said. "I believe you know some of them?"

Louis stepped into view. "Sed?" he said. "Everyone is awake now. British, Prussians, French, everyone."

I checked on the captain. He seemed intent on his piloting. Tongue hanging from his mouth. Eyes on his console.

"Did you do it?" I whispered. "Set everyone free?"

Louis shook his head. "Let us go, Sed. That's what you promised. I have most of the women here with me. And the French soldiers." He glanced to his left. "The others, I can't control them. But that planet down there. I think we could live there."

"It's a wasteland!" I said. "Picked clean by—"

"I saw it," he said. "It didn't look dead. It looked green and—"

"Well, we're headed there now!" I said. "Just stay put for a couple minutes!"

"To meet the bug people?" He frowned and shook his head. "I can't expose Anne to that."

I understood that point perfectly. I didn't want to be exposed to the Naaklik either. "Are you asking for permission?" I said. "You've overrun the ship already." I tipped my snout. "And you have a pilot."

Louis brought Dontel into view. "According to him, you need to open the door."

Well now, here was one thing I actually had control over. It wasn't much—I couldn't see how it would affect the ship's safety in any way. But the shuttle leaving certainly wouldn't make our situation worse.

For Louis and his people, though, it might be the difference between life and death. For a period of time, anyway.

Did I owe them that?

I glanced at the captain again, then unlocked the shuttle bay door. "There you are," I said. "Be gone with you."

Louis eyes widened. "God bless you, Sedric," he said, nodding.

I returned the nod. "Good luck to you both."

CHAPTER 43

The ship bucked and shivered as we entered the atmosphere of Nesa Three. The *Granum*'s scent shifted too, taking on a pungent hint that reminded me of cleaning fluids. Was it possible that some of the planet's ozone had leaked onto the bridge somehow? I wouldn't have been surprised.

A few minutes later, I received a textual confirmation from the Naaklik, along with a vocal "Proceed to coordinates, humble muto."

The captain snorted loudly. "'Humble' means 'crushed,' in their tongue." He leaned forward and rubbed his hands together. "Shows where we stand, eh?"

"Sir...?"

He fanned a paw at me. "Tell them we're almost there." His gaze returned to his controls. "Let's get this over with."

I nodded and sent the Naaklik a confirmation. Nothing about this felt right. The state of our ship was unknown. The crew unaccounted for. Everything I felt responsible for was endangered.

The rendezvous point was a quarter kilometer clearing surrounded by forests and ponds. The clearing's perimeter was marked by four dark brown buildings. They shared a round-but-segmented architecture reminiscent of the beings that had built them. They looked like giant insect carcasses to me. A horrific thought.

I brought the largest building into focus on the central screen. Over a hundred Naaklik were gathered near it. Among them were a half-dozen workers outfitted in bio-mechanical loading suits. Doubtless to aid with transferring our cargo.

"How much of their order do you think we have left?" the captain asked.

"No way of knowing now, sir."

He nodded once and looked at the console Cindel had used. "Haven't heard from our security officer in a while."

"We haven't," I said. "No." I thought about Louis and Anne. The captain hadn't said a word when their shuttle departed. Had he even noticed?

There was distance in his gaze. Utter defeat and loss.

"Less than a kilometer out now," he said. "Their gunship is right on our tail. Guess they want to make sure they'll get everything they came for. One way or the other."

As we dropped those last few meters, our view of the Naaklik became more distinct. Black armor and sophisticated weaponry. Orange exoskeletons complete with mandibles and poison-bearing forcipules. A formidable and dangerous-looking group. Doubtless hungry too. They were always hungry.

I attempted to contact Cindel on his personal com. It took three tries before he finally answered. His facial fur was matted, and his eyes were blood shot. "The umans hold three decks, sir," he said. "Security is mostly on deck four with me. I'm short, remember. Could only reach a paw-full. The rest are either dead or infected." He frowned. "Even some of those with me are suffering. Rubbed raw from all the scratching."

"What about the rest of the crew?" I asked.

"Some are hostages," he said. "Though some are back asleep."

It was like searching for Uzel inside the access tunnel again. Following his distant and haunting voice through a tangle of wires and cables. Except this time the cables were alive and wrapped around my body. Slowly drawing tighter.

"Gather whoever you can," I said. "Get to whatever weapons you can find."

"The umans have demands, sir," Cindel said. "They want to be returned to Earth, where they will be released—"

"Perfectly reasonable," I said with a snort. "We'll get to that right away." I shook my head. "Do they have any idea what we're up against now?"

"Brace yourself!" the captain said. "Setting down in ten, nine, eight,..."

There was a slight lurch as the ship touched ground. I took a deep breath, then checked on the scene outside. It was early evening, the sky a light purple. The Naaklik preferred evenings, I knew. Dusk was one of three prime hunting times.

The forest beyond the buildings reminded me of Bossu Wood, the trees lush and inviting. Easy to hide in, should the need arise. My bumble paw ached at the notion. Running and fighting for survival.

The bridge shook as the Naaklik <u>Claw</u> approached and landed. A quick scan of our sensors showed that they'd taken a spot next to us, turned so that their storage bay aligned with ours. Perfect for transferring cargo...or prisoners.

The bridge lights flickered again. Was it due to the rioters or another scientific oversight? I had no idea. Both scientists were gone now, though...

There was pleasure in that notion.

The bridge lights failed completely, and the captain laughed. "Good thing we can see in the dark, eh?" His seat creaked as he stood. "Come on, Sed. We'll head out the nearest airlock. Meet our hosts."

I scowled. "I hate this, sir. The ship overrun. We can't just leave it!"

He pointed his tail at the central screen. "What choice do we have?"

"But, I—'

He hissed softly. "You know I like the games, Sed. One thing I never quite learned, though, was when to walk away." He waved a paw over the bridge. "This time...where we're at now...I think it's my walk away." He smiled. "Come on. Let's do this as friends."

I shook my head but stood to follow.

The nearest airlock was just beyond the bridge exit. It was a small, emergency affair, with a tiny room and a narrow ramp. The airlock's external sensors showed that Nesa's atmosphere rivaled Imperial standard. Not that different than Earth, excepting a slightly higher oxygen content and a bit more ash. The latter was doubtless due to Nesa being younger and more volcanically active. Neither deviation would cause us harm. The extra oxygen might even help if we had to flee.

We exited the airlock to a force of twenty Naakliks formed into a loose semicircle. In height, they ranged from two and a half meters to over three—nearly twice my size. Three of them were in loaders and so were taller still. I doubted they'd fit through the airlock's doors.

As we reached the ground, an especially tall and slender specimen stepped forward cradling a silver rifle between his primary arms. His umber-colored carapace banded smaller limbs, and that blue squiggle of forehead ornamentation marked him as the same Naaklik we'd communicated with in orbit. Possibly their leader.

"How's everyone today?" the captain asked.

The leader's mandibles flared. "Open the rear boarding ramps, rhat. We will have our cargo."

The captain made a calming motion. "Now, about that—"

The entire Naaklik contingent straightened, becoming more imposing. Like a latticework of steel. A pair of lighter-colored Naaklik took positions on either side of the leader. Enforcers, I guessed.

"You will fulfill your contract, rhat," blue line Naaklik said.

"That's our intent," the captain said. "But, as you know, there have been complications. It's a complicated galaxy."

The leftmost enforcer sprung, grabbed the captain by the longshirt, and lifted him to eye level. "No complications," he said. "You will open your ship now."

Every Naaklik gun pointed our way. Forcipules retracted too, as if preparing to strike. Could they hurl poison through the air? I had no idea. Even the proximity of poisonous limbs made me shiver.

Of all the creatures in the galaxy to have an issue with, why did it have to be armored, poisonous, giants?

Fighting to keep my eyes from the forest, I focused on the bug-like buildings instead. There was an intricate arrangement of antenna on every exterior. Most were spiraled and crisscrossed, though some were more upright in nature. Doubtless communication and security sensors. More eyes than the Naaklik's own.

I'd never make it to the forest without being seen. I should've grabbed a shimmer suit. What was I thinking? I was hopeless and dim.

"You were to bring solid milk proteins of exquisite tastes and textures," the tattooed leader said. "In the absence of those, other animal proteins will suffice."

Captain Wendel's captor drew the captain closer and clicked his mandibles together. "Muto protein is a delicacy on my world. Saved for the highest occasions."

"Like Fle' Te!" one of those wearing a loader said. What followed was a chorus of unnatural clicks and titters that sounded like bones shaking inside a metal can. It curled my neck fur.

The captain glanced at me. "Maybe we should show them what we have?"

Open the primary doors? Who knew what that would bring. "I'm not sure that's a good—"

"Sedric," the captain implored.

"Right," I said. "Of course!" I pointed at the airlock. "I'll just go back inside and—"

"You'll stay with us, rhat," the leader said.

I made what I hoped was a soothing motion with my right paw. "No problem. Let's just all walk back toward the middle of the ship together, okay?" I lifted my personal com device. "I'll try to get someone to open it for us."

CHAPTER 44

I had no idea who to call. Cindel? Krate? Who was in a position to open the bay doors? Another situation that would've been easier had Yentiss still been with us. If she were safe on the bridge, awaiting my call.

I took a couple hesitant steps toward the back of the ship. The Naaklik ship loomed large to my left, dwarfing the *Granum* in any measurement that mattered. The *Granum* radiated versatility and utility, sure, but the *Hardened Claw*—with its sharp edges and triangular lines—simply looked dangerous. Ready for a fight.

I tried Cindel's com. No response. I took a few more steps, striding as confidently as I could. I noted the *Granum*'s circular mid-ship sensor array, its rectangular venting ports, and the solitary band of red that served as its only exterior decoration. For all its quirks, it was a fine ship. A good ship.

I lamented our current condition: Infestation and revolution within. Predatory bugs without.

The Naaklik group shadowed my every move. And

Captain Wendel—still held by the Naaklik enforcer—dangled above the ground as they came. The tension was pervasive. Inescapable.

I tried Cindel again. When that didn't work, I tried Krate. That got me nothing either. Were they all captives of the umans now?

"Muto!" the Naaklik leader screamed. "Open the ship!"

I pointed at my com, then lifted a finger. I was trying. Was it my fault there was a riot in progress?

I tried the medical bay and the kitchen. No response from either place. Was anyone even alive in there? I turned toward the Naaklik with both paws up. "I don't know what's going on," I said. "We've had a lot of technical difficulties lately." I pointed toward the forward airlock. "If you let me go back in, I'll get it all straightened out."

The leader sprung at me. I dodged left, but he still managed to snag my tail. With a jerk, he hoisted me into the air too. I was high enough that I could—with a little arching—glimpse the buildings again. The crisscross of antennas.

"I will feast on you here," the leader said. "Then we will board your ship and take all that—"

There was a heavy "clunk" followed by a repetitive grinding sound. I fanned the air, spinning myself toward the ship again.

The main loading doors were opening.

"Well, there you go," I said.

The leader walked toward the ship, taking me with him.

The pain at the base of my tail was excruciating. I fanned again to keep it from twisting more. But oh, the hurt.

A minute later, the doors were open, and the loading ramp began to extend. There was no sign of anyone inside. No lights, nor any movement aside from the ramp. The bay was a dark emptiness. Even for muto eyes.

The leader lifted me to where my face was next to his. It

was a horrific vista, full of wiggling appendages and teeth. The stench of his breath made me gasp for air.

"What's this?" he asked, pointing his rifle at the loading ramp.

"I have no idea," I said, using as little oxygen as possible. "But it's an open ship now." I attempted a smile. "Go unload it."

The leader made an indeterminate clicking sound, then dropped me to the ground and waved at one of the loader-wearing Naaklik's. There was a repetitive *clunk-clunk-clunk* as the metal-clad underling made his way to the ramp and began to climb it. The loader had small lights in front to illuminate its path. Their beams shifted with every step.

The loader reached the top of the ramp and stomped into the gloom. Its footfalls got quieter and quieter as it disappeared from view, then stopped completely.

A full minute went by.

The leader's mandibles clicked nervously together. He looked at me. "Where is he?"

I shrugged. How would I know? "Never used a loader before," I said.

His mandibles flared and his forcipules rippled out and back. He shouted a Naaklik name that sounded like "Wick we flit!".

There was an answering twitter and the sound of the loader in motion again. Soon its lights appeared at the top of the ramp. It *clunk-clunked* down the ramp to about the halfway mark, then pitched sideways, landing on the ramp's edge. It seesawed there an anxious moment before gravity pulled it completely off. It hit the ground with the sound of a glacier calving.

I scrambled around the ramp to investigate. The operator was clenched into a tight ball, with every limb pulled together his midsection. I detected no movement at all. No life in its eyes.

Most telling, though, was the length of metal that protruded from the center of its carcass. An English sword.

The Naaklik was dead.

The leader roared up behind me. "Is this your—?"

There was a chorus of uman voices. Next, a cluster of soldiers, arrayed in a formation resembling a square, charged down the ramp. They wore red uniforms and brandished the archaic rifles they'd used on Earth. A few carried our pistols too.

"I guess they found the armory," I said.

The soldiers began to fire. Smoke filled the air as volley after volley exploded from their barrels, striking ship and Naaklik alike. One shot buzzed by my head. Another struck a loader-operator standing just behind me. I slipped past him as he fell.

Other bugs were hit, including the one holding the captain. Muto and Naaklik fell in a muddle of fur, armor, and limbs.

The Naaklik swung into action, shifting, and regrouping in a way that somehow trapped the captain within their midst. They began to return fire, creating a crisscross of light bolts and metal shrapnel. Like being in a storm of hail and lightning.

Captain Wendel and I dropped to all fours and tried to stay alive. I searched for the forest but couldn't see it for all the surrounding bugs.

The captain crept close to me. "The umans don't care if they hit us!"

I shook my head. "Probably not, sir, no."

He snorted. "And after all we did for them!"

I wrinkled my snout. There were losses on both sides, but it appeared the umans were getting the worst of it. Projectile rifles couldn't equal blasters. Cloth uniforms were no match for armored exoskeletons.

The umans maintained their fighting square about ten meters past the bottom of the ramp. Dead bodies—soldier and

Naaklik alike—formed a mound all around them. In some places the mounds were large enough for the umans to shield behind. A small comfort, doubtless adding only a few minutes to an otherwise hopeless stand. The Naaklik rarely missed.

There was another wave of uman shouts. A second square of soldiers—dressed in blue and grey—appeared at the top of the ramp. Prussians, I assumed. They took a more methodical approach to their incursion—shooting and reloading as they descended.

The Naaklik twittered louder and shot more. A half dozen Prussians fell.

The *Granum*'s external lights snapped on. The bugs around us screeched and recoiled. Then came more smoke as umans in both groups fired.

We needed to get away. The Naaklik were distracted by the conflict. Unaware that the captain and I even existed for their blood lust.

I tugged the captain's longshirt and pointed in the direction of the outlying buildings. "Come on," I said. "While they're busy."

CHAPTER 45

More Naaklik exited the surrounding buildings and rushed into the fray. In their fury, they shot past Captain Wendel and I, their antennas and eyes locked only on the umans. Hind legs propelling them across the clearing to the ships.

I felt better about our chances of survival. I began to hope.

Other mutos were clustered near the front of the *Granum*, having escaped, presumably, through the airlocks. I recognized the nurse, Krate, and a couple of the kitchen staff. I waved and pointed toward the forests. They seemed to understand.

If we could keep enough of the crew alive, if the ship remained intact and flight-worthy, we might be able to regroup later and leave. After whatever happened here was over.

I was most worried about the guns from the Naaklik ship. Those, and any other armaments that might be lurking nearby. Nesa wasn't one of the Naaklik prime worlds. Its population might not be more than a few hundred. But they would still have defenses. Mobile armaments or—

There was an ear-shattering concussion, enough that

everyone near us ducked and covered their heads. At first, I thought the Naaklik had sent a pulse grenade into the *Granum*'s engine core. I was afraid to look yet couldn't keep my eyes from tracing the red stripe down the ship's side. Searching for any sign of vaporization or structural damage.

The explosion hadn't come from our ship, though.

Both sides of the Naaklik ship, specifically those sections directly above the main guns, had taken a hit. There were now gaping, smoking wounds there. The guns' barrels sagged like broken limbs.

"What was that?" the captain asked.

I shook my head. I couldn't make sense of it. We hadn't taken any of the uman's canons with us. Nothing in our arsenal would've caused the sort of damage I was seeing. Even at close range. It was like the Naaklik's ship had caught the *Granum*'s tendency for disaster simply by being so close.

The air erupted with Naaklik chatter, a pervasive chorus of clicks and buzzes that bounced between structures, ships, and forest. A nightmare symphony.

The sanctity of the *Hardened Claw* had been broken, exposed by creatures they thought beneath them.

There would be no mercy now. No bargaining. The Naaklik swarmed like the insects they were. The umans wouldn't survive.

Barely perceptible over the clamor came another uman charge. With it, a third wave of umans exited the *Granum*. From our position, I could just make out their uniform colors: grey and red. That suggested a mixture of troops, now fighting together against a common threat. Something even Louis couldn't manage.

It was too little too late, though. The infuriated Naaklik would overwhelm them.

There was no retreat or surrender. No time for another plan.

I felt regret for what we'd done. Imprisoning the umans. Wresting them from their home, only to die on an alien world. There was nothing we could do, though. Nothing I could do.

The forest was less that twenty paces away. We needed to escape and regroup. That was our only chance.

Three Naaklik darted in front us. These were taller and broader than those we'd encountered earlier. There were subtle differences in their apparel too, both in the colors and where the armor was placed. Sure signs this group was female.

"Where are you going, rhat!" one of them asked. Another looped an arm around the captain's neck, securing him in place.

I checked to see if other mutos were close by. No such luck.

The largest female grabbed my shoulders and pulled me closer. "Are you the captain of that vessel?" she asked. "The one who betrayed us?"

"No, I..." I glanced at the captain. Would lying keep him alive? Could I succeed in that one small way?

The female tightened her grip such that I could feel her claws through my fur. One of her forcipules extended until it was only a few centimeters from my face. "Answer me!" she screamed

"I'm hungry," the one holding the captain said. "Let's eat."

I noticed the antennas on the building behind her. Ironically, there were three, standing upright, with a single crossbar through the center near the top. It reminded me of Anne's Golgotha in the detention area hallway. Three crosses on a hill.

All the image needed was a sunrise. All it required was a little hope.

"I'm the one you want," I said. "Let him go."

My captor cackled. "We'll have you both," she said. "We'll skin you and—" She grew rigid, and her eyes rolled back into her head. She released me and fell away. The other two retched and convulsed, and dropped to the ground too.

Captain Wendel and I stood dumbfounded for a few seconds. Then other Naaklik started to perform the same exercise: retching, convulsing, and falling.

What was going on?

Next came gunfire and smoke. The shots didn't come from the ships, though. Instead, the shots seemed to come from the forest's edge and the hidden areas between buildings. From every shadowed nook and cranny.

The Naaklik started to fall in large numbers, either pitching forward from gunshots, or convulsing and retching like those near us had. They went trapped within the mandibles of ubiquitous uman weaponry.

Pandemonium reigned and I had no clue what had started it. What was going on?

There was a flicker of light to my left, and in that formerly empty space, Louis appeared. He was cloaked in a blue shimmer suit. One of *our* shimmer suits.

"How does that fit you?" I asked.

Louis chuckled. "It's a little snug, but it works." He handed me a stunner. "Aren't you tired of watching?"

"You have another one?" the captain asked.

Another flicker, this time to the captain's right. The scientist, Uzel, appeared.

"You survived?" I said.

Uzel bobbed his snout. "Yes. And these fine umans found me and picked me up." He handed the captain a stunner. "Here you are, sir."

I looked at Louis, then at the fallen Naaklik. I felt a wave of emotion. A surge of hope. "We owe you, Louis," I said. "I don't know how we'll—"

"Business later." Louis smiled and indicated the battlefield. "Let's finish this first."

I raised the stunner. For the first time in months, my bumble hand felt fine. Completely right and strong.

And inside, a sunrise of hope.

CHAPTER 46

I was buffeted about. Flung this way and that. As if the female Naaklik had captured me and was now swinging me around. Smashing me against some Nesa-native tree.

The painful grip relented, and I floated midair. My extremities felt larger, inflated like balloons. They drew me into a cloud of air. Air mixed with sleep gas. Larger and larger my paws grew. Lighter and lighter I felt, until finally, a release.

I smelled cheese. Wondrous, rich cheese. Delectable and dark.

I opened my eyes and saw the shelves of Tactin's office. There were three hovering chairs now. One for Tactin, one for his superior Xedus, and another for a young red-furred muto. The latter was perfectly trimmed and shiny. There were gold rings on his fingers.

Most imposing, though, was the food-filled tray to my left. Cheeses and breads of all varieties. Fruited drinks and dark deserts. A smorgasbord that made my stomach howl with desire.

"Welcome back, Sedric," Tactin said, still gripping the head walk mask. "We have everything we need from you now." His eyes looked wider than I remembered. Like someone crimped his tail.

I couldn't see the captain, but I heard him, moaning from somewhere beyond Tactin's chair. Near the door again.

Tactin sighed and shook his head. "Your captain has taken ill. He blames our food." He nodded toward the tray. "Perhaps you should be careful."

I snatched a cut of white cheese and pushed it into my mouth. "No time for that," I said. "I'm famished."

Tactin nodded. "I must congratulate you. Seems you've set a record for head walks. How do you feel?"

"Better than ever," I said, and meant it. "Like a load has been lifted."

Tactin nodded, and turning his chair slightly, indicated the red muto to his left. "This is Xedus's superior, Erchus. We wanted him here for the final deliberation. He's an expert on extra-imperial relations, including the Naaklik Overwatch. He has knowledge of dark funding, silent operations, and the purview of the inquisitor's—"

The captain moaned. I resisted looking his way.

"You've seen it all," I said. "All that I can show you."

Xedus tapped the edge of his chair arm nervously. "The shuttle, the one that started this investigation...?"

I palmed a paw-full of pickled cheese squares. A rare delicacy. "Must've been the one that crashed," I said. "We took the other with us." I nibbled a cheese square. "We visited Nesa later, even worked with the umans on occasion, but the wrecked shuttle..." I raised a shoulder. "I don't think we ever looked. Our scientists—"

"Were abominable," Tactin said. "Disgraces to their profession."

I smiled broadly. "We left them on Nesa too."

"You left them both?" Xedus said.

"Part of the deal with Louis. And the scientists didn't mind. Said they 'felt appreciated' there." I glanced the captain's direction. "More losses we've forgotten."

Xedus snorted. "And the Naaklik?"

"Hundreds died in that fight." I tapped my chest. "The few survivors lost something inside, I think. Their bug pride, or whatever. They surrendered the planet, boarded their ship, and never returned."

Erchus's eyes narrowed. "That seems peculiar for the Naaklik. To simply give up."

"They were done with Nesa. Or maybe just wanted to forget about it." I reached for a cup of drink. It smelled of dashenberry. Rich and tart with sedative qualities. "Maybe they forced themselves to."

"Your story is filled with losses and questionable decisions," Tactin said.

I shrugged. "My conscience is clear. I did my best."

Tactic puffed his cheeks. "But you've put us in an uncomfortable position." He searched the faces of his superiors.

Xedus wrinkled his snout. "Ask him about the mystery phrases," he said.

"Ah, of course..." Squinting, Tactin leaned closer to his screen. "One of the uman raiders, one of the thieves, said they were 'Representatives of the Duchy of Brunswick.'" He jiggled the mask. "Are those Earth terms? 'Duchy' and 'Brunswick?'"

"Those are Earth words," the captain said. "See how they twist the tongue? Nearly steal the breath?"

I sipped my drink and gazed at the ceiling. A forested scene was painted up there. It reminded me of Bossu Wood, and in a small way, of Yentiss. "Duchy sounds like something Louis would say," I said. "Sure."

Erchus shook a finger at me. "I believe this one. I think he did the best with what he had." He smoothed the side of his head. "Might be considered admirable, his decisions."

"Perhaps," Xedus said. "But fraud of this magnitude carries heavy penalties. Harsh—"

The captain whimpered.

Tactin shook his head. "Disciplining these two won't affect the results of their actions."

Xedus frowned. "These Brunswickers are formidable, though. Who knows what further damage they will—"

Erchus hissed. "But *their* actions—" He nodded at me. "Might have saved the entire Empire."

The euphoria of my head walks lingered, causing me to doubt my senses. "Did you say 'saved?'"

Tactin shifted in his seat. "What do we do now, gentlemutos?"

Captain Wendel popped up behind their chairs. "I heard that," he said. "'Saved the Empire!'"

Tactin exhaled slowly. "Do we wish for them to know?"

Erchus laced his front paws over his midsection. Shrugged. "I see no reason they shouldn't."

Xedus pointed at me. "Harsh penalties will come should either of you—'

"We won't talk," Captain Wendel said. "We hate to talk."

Erchus looked at the captain, then snorted. "The job you won was an unsanctioned accounting operation. The food you started with had been laced. Poisoned. Would've killed any creature that consumed it."

The fur on the back of my neck bristled. The *Granum* had a number of close calls over the years, but nothing as significant as that.

"We were going to kill Naaklik royalty?" the captain said. "And we messed that up?"

"And doubtless prevented a war in the process," Erchus

said, nodding. "The operation was ill-conceived. No one in governance knew what happened. But since no one died, it was struck from the books. Written off."

"You've solved more than one mystery today," Tactin said. "But we still have a raid to account for. You've created a new danger that—"

Erchus waved a paw. "They created the Duchy, yes. But you might also say that <u>we</u> created it." He waved a paw over the room. "Imperial Accounting."

I raised my cup. "If I might make a suggestion?"

The accountants looked at me. "Yes, Sedric?" Tactin said.

"Wipe your books."

"Wipe our...?" Tactin coughed and began to wheeze heavily.

Xedus patted the elder muto's back until the wheezing subsided.

I shrugged and indicated the shelves behind them. "Make up a cover story for the raid. Paint the Brunswickers as cultists who worship Terran technology. Or a splinter group of early colonizers. It doesn't matter. The Empire has the resources to make it stick. Or, at least, make it palatable."

"A notable plan," Xedus said and glanced at the others. "Not impossible."

Erchus nodded. "But what should we do with these two?"

"Release us!" I grabbed another triangle of cheese. "We aren't to blame for the Duchy's success. They did that on their own." I pointed my cheese at the shelves. "First rule of trade: Winners deserve their spoils."

"Can we count on your silence?" Tactin asked. "You'll repeat none of this?"

"We hid the umans for decades," Captain Wendel said, still poised behind the chairs.

"I'm thinking about retiring," I said. "I hear Candis has lots of forest. Think I might like a little green again."

Erchus looked at the captain. "And you, captain?"

"I'm no trouble." The captain nodded his snout at me. "You heard him. Sed looks out for me."

Tactin shook his head, Xedus sighed, and Erchus nodded.

Tactin hummed as he poked at his screen. "It's decided. Your ledger is clear, and secrecy must be maintained."

I grabbed a half-loaf of bread. "Didn't want to talk about it this time," I said, smiling. "So, we can leave?"

"On pain of death," Xedus said. "But, yes."

I rose from my seat, then pointed at the mask. "Can I have that?"

His eyes moved from mask to tubing, then to the shelf above. "Our synaptic reviewer?" He looked puzzled. "I don't think—"

"Nah." I covered the end of my snout. "Just the mask part. As a souvenir."

Nodding slowly, Tactin detached the mask and handed it to me.

I tucked it into my belt and bowed my head. "Enjoyed the time, gentlemutos." I raised my paw-full of food and smiled. "You're good hosts."

CHAPTER 47

Neither Captain Wendel nor I spoke during our return to the *Granum*. Led by the same two "assistants," we passed through gilded arches and beneath sculpted domes in silence.

I was largely oblivious to everything, anyway. Bite by delectable bite, the food I'd pilfered from the accountant's office made its way inside me. Renewing me, in a way. Filling the voids left by my journey through a complicated past. It was the most satisfying meal I'd ever eaten.

Food was a form of hope for rhats, I realized. We ate, gaining fuel for the hours ahead. Preparing for whatever future the day would bring. A slice of that sunrise on the hill.

I wondered about Louis and Anne. When we last saw them, they'd been the de facto leaders of the umans. Were they still? Had the raids been their idea? It didn't seem like something they would do, but time has a way of changing sentients. Umans and mutos alike.

They'd done more than survive. They'd prospered. Taking a shuttle to the stars? It hardly seemed possible.

We reached the landing platform where the *Granum* waited—a solitary bay that hung out over a portion of the city's lower levels.

It was nighttime. Surrounding us in all directions was a dark brown cityscape, brightly lit. There was the hint of petrol in the air, along with the hearty musk that clung to every rhat city.

The assistants left us without ceremony. That was fine too, as they had little appeal to me now. They were part of a machine that I couldn't wait to escape. A system that agonized over details, yet missed the creation of a new civilization. Louis's "duchy."

Captain Wendel watched the assistants until they entered the nearest building—a circular structure with connections to the city's tramway. He took a deep breath and slowly let it out again. Turning toward me, he smiled and clapped a paw on my shoulder. "Well, that played out perfectly!"

I raised an eyebrow. "You don't think we...overdid it a little?"

He straightened as if shocked. "What do you mean?"

"Pounding on the door...the moaning...the time you—"

He smiled broadly. "All part of my plan! They needed to focus on you, because you're where the answers live, Sed. Always have been." He tapped his chest. "I'm the idea rhat." He tail-pointed at me. "You're the one that gets things done."

I cocked my head. "Our version of the swarm and scatter?"

Another shoulder clap. "Exactly!" He groaned and massaged his hip. "Though being on that floor..." He scowled. "...wasn't as easy as I'd hoped."

I shoved the last bite of cheese into my mouth. "Those walks are draining."

"Your perspective was best."

I nodded slowly. "Wouldn't want to risk your lucky snout."

He touched his nose. "That's right. This is what keeps us flying."

I glanced at the circular structure. "That meeting...it made me a little..." I circled the air with my tail tip. "Sad, I guess. Missing what we lost."

He squeezed my shoulder. "I had no idea, Sedric. About Yentiss, I mean. You should've said something. We could've found a way back."

I shook my head. "Don't think I realized it myself." I glanced at the ground. A zigzag pattern dominated the entire platform. "Yentiss is someone I'll always wonder about."

He chuckled. "Well, she doesn't need to be. Not anymore."

"But Earth is—"

He snorted. "Oh, I forgot! You were away while they were talking."

"While who was talking?"

He indicated the circular building. "The bean counters. They said our former communications officer was found."

"Found?"

He wrinkled his snout. "There was a lot of squinting at screens. Talk of trade routes and communications lines." He shook his head. "I didn't get it all. They muttered a lot."

He raised a finger. "But! I caught the meaty part. Someone with the name 'Yentiss' was recovered from a primitive planet two years ago. A chance encounter with a salvage team." He fluttered a paw. "What matters is where she is now: Rhotaris Two!" He pointed to the sky. A cross of blue stars. "Isn't far at all now, is it? Right over that way."

The warmth in my stomach shifted to my chest, then to my face. "Yentiss is on Two? Really?"

There was a loud "clack" and the ship's forward airlock ramp began to extend. Captain Wendel took a step toward it and waved. "Come on, Sed. Let's go see what she's been up to all these years."

"Do you think she stopped the war?"

"Knowing her, she probably did." He snorted. "Probably started a few too."

What would she think of us—of me—for having left her behind? "I don't know, sir. It's been so long. So much has—"

"What was that stuff back there? The thing about the paintings."

"The hope, you mean? The picture Anne drew?"

"It's still down there, isn't it? That painting."

"Yes, but—"

He clapped his hands together. "Because it means something. Something maybe even you didn't know."

I took a hesitant step forward. Then another.

"That's an order, Sedric!"

I realized the floor pattern wasn't zigzags at all. They were crosses.

THE END

ABOUT THE AUTHOR

Kerry Nietz is an award-winning science fiction author. He has over a half dozen speculative novels in print, along with a novella, a couple short stories, and a non-fiction book, *Fox-Tales*.

Kerry's novel *A Star Curiously Singing* won the Readers Favorite Gold Medal Award for Christian Science Fiction and is notable for its dystopian, cyberpunk vibe in a world under sharia law. It is often mentioned on "Best of" lists.

Among his writings, Kerry's most talked about is the genre-bending *Amish Vampires in Space*. AViS was mentioned on the Tonight Show and in the Washington Post, Library Journal, and Publishers Weekly. Newsweek called it "a welcome departure from the typical Amish fare."

Kerry is a refugee of the software industry. He spent more than a decade of his life flipping bits, first as one of the principal developers for the now mythical Fox Software, and then as one of Bill Gates's minions at Microsoft. He is a husband, a father, a technophile and a movie buff.

TAKAMO UNIVERSE BOOKS

Empire's Rift
Steve Rzasa 2016

Strife's Cost
(Empire's Rift sequel)
Steve Rzasa 2019

Aphelion
(Anthology)
AR DeClerck 2017

An Enduring Sun
(Aeon Project Book One)
AR DeClerck 2016

Dark Star
(Aeon Project Book Two)
AR DeClerck 2018

Decaying Orbit
(Aeon Project Book Three)
AR DeClerck 2019

Resonance Factor
(Aeon Project Book Four)
AR DeClerck 2020

Escape Velocity
(Aeon Project Book Five)
AR DeClerck 2021

Rhats!
(The Muto Chronicles Book One)
Kerry Nietz 2017

Rhats Too!
(The Muto Chronicles Book Two)
Kerry Nietz 2018

Rhataloo
(The Muto Chronicles Book Three)
Kerry Nietz 2021

For God and Mars
(Anthology)
Shona Husk 2017

Last Run of the Ice Duchess
Shona Husk 2019

The Ice Cold Heart
KS Augustin 2017

Degara's Mark
(The Omiata Chronicles Book One)
Amber Draeger 2019